HAPPILY EVER HERS

SINGLETREE, BOOK TWO

DELANCEY STEWART

Get early releases, sneak peeks and freebies from Delancey Stewart!

Join my mailing list here and get a free story!

And join Delancey's Fancies on Facebook for fun, frivolity and the latest news!

Don't miss new releases, book bundles and flash deals in my shop!

CONTENTS

PROLOGUE - TWO YEARS EARLIER

JULIET

"Tess," I was excited, but I forced myself to speak slowly, to stay calm. I guided my car into the covered parking spot outside my apartment building, keeping the engine on so I didn't drop the call.

"Hey sis, what's up?"

"I just talked to my agent. *Memories of You*—remember that movie?"

"Was that the one last year where you were a waitress?" My sister saw all my movies.

"Yes, yes." My excitement was making me impatient. "It's nominated for an Oscar, Tess! *I'm* nominated!"

There was a brief pause on Tess's end, and for a moment I thought maybe I'd lost her. But the call was still active.

"Tess?"

"Jules, that's great." There was a long pause, and then she said. "I'm proud of you."

There was something awkward on the line between us, and I wished for a moment that we were closer, that we had the kind of sisterly relationship I read about in books, or saw in movies, or even the kind I'd portrayed in films myself. But I'd left years ago. And though I still talked to my sister a few times a month, sometimes I felt like I was acting in our relationship just as much as I did on film. Acting like there wasn't a strange distance there. Acting like we were best friends.

"It's amazing, Jules. Wait till I tell Gran."

"I hope she doesn't say something awful."

"Fifty-fifty chance. But no matter what she says, you know she'll be proud too. You deserve it." Tess's voice had grown warm again, like it had just taken her a moment to actually be happy for me.

"Thanks, Tess."

"Miss you, Jules."

"You too." I hung up, feeling a little space inside me where my family sat, wishing the connection I had with them was just a little fuller, a little rounder somehow. But I turned my focus from that emptiness and to the prospect of the ultimate career achievement. An Oscar!

I got out of the car and climbed the stairs to my apartment to find a guy waiting for me on the landing. He was dressed like a Fedex delivery driver, so I didn't think anything about heading up to the front door and greeting him with a smile.

I was still floating, the unreality of the announcement in the front of my mind and my thoughts reeling through ridiculous things like red carpets and getting a dress for the event. And that's why I thought at first I'd misheard the man who stood waiting for me to get far enough up the stairs to speak to me.

"You stupid whore," he hissed, which was not the usual way the delivery drivers I'd met had greeted me before. I was more used to things like, "sign for this?" or "here."

"Excuse me?" I figured I'd misheard him.

"Why did you take your clothes off for him? You knew he couldn't love you right." Spittle flew from the man's lips and he took a menacing step toward me, his face reddening under a scruff of scraggly beard.

At this point alarm bells were sounding in my head, and I had stopped three steps from the landing. I began backing down, getting ready to run back to my car.

"Where are you going, Juliet?" The guy went from angry to hurt in a heartbeat, his eyes widening in surprise and his mouth turning into a frown.

Crazy, crazy, crazy — my alarms were ringing for real now.

"I'll take care of you, baby," he started to come down the stairs, reaching for me, trying to catch me, and I turned and jumped down the last three steps. The door of the unit below mine had just swung open, and I barreled in, pushing it shut and locking it behind me.

"And hello to you too," Marina said, laughing as I threw myself into her arms.

"I'm sorry," I said to my neighbor and friend, my voice nearly a shriek. "Call the police. And lock the door. Did you lock the door?" I was shaking, terrified.

"You locked the door. What's going on?" Marina held me out, looking me over. "Why do you look so freaked?"

"There was a guy. Upstairs, in front of my door." Tears were streaming down my face now, and I thought I might hyperventilate. I gripped Marina's hand.

"What guy?" Marina went to the peephole in her door. "I see a Fedex guy standing around."

Oh God, he was still there. What if he had a gun? "Yes! Call the police."

"On Fedex? Damaged package?"

I pulled Marina away from the door, into her bedroom where I locked the flimsy doorknob as she stared at me. "Call the police," I said again, nearly hysterical.

I explained what the man had said as Marina dialed, and she calmly related everything to the police, putting the phone down once they'd assured us they were on the way.

"Well, I guess that's it then," she said, crossing her arms in front of her chest, her pointed chin lowering in a knowing nod.

"What do you mean?"

"This and the Oscar nom." She winked at me and smiled, much calmer than I was, considering there was a potentially armed stalkery type guy outside. "Congrats, by the way. You're officially a movie star. Not just an actress. Now you have to make some changes."

I shook my head. Marina was an actress too. We'd been on auditions together, had commiserated about missed roles, lost opportunities. "What?" My mind reeled.

"Stalker equals stardom equals private security." She nodded and pursed her glossy lips.

The police showed up then, and we spent then next thirty minutes talking with them as they took Mr. Fedex into custody. The guy had been dumb enough to hang out, waiting for me to come back outside. Relief flooded me as they pushed him into the back of a cruiser and I dodged behind one of the bigger cops where the man couldn't see me from where he sat.

"Miss Manchester," one of the policemen had said after the cruiser departed. "I recommend you look into a bodyguard. We'll leave a squad car outside for the next week or so, but once a person reaches a certain level of notoriety, there's only so much we can do."

I nodded numbly and spent the next two nights at Marina's, afraid to be alone. After that, my manager had made arrangements with a security firm he trusted.

JACE

"KEEP YOUR HEADS DOWN, assholes, unless you want to lose them!"

The skipper's voice was loud, even over the sound of the explosions ricocheting through the demolished city to our right. I did as I was told, running as fast as I could with my unit toward the cover of a low bluff. With all my gear on, and the M4 in my hands, it was hard to move quickly, but the force of the adrenaline pumping through my body and the sound of the V-22 lifting off overhead added the motivation I needed.

I wasn't planning on dying over here. My preferred method of departure would be mid-orgasm if I got to choose. Or potentially partway through a pint of ice cream. That would be okay too. But getting shot, exploded, or generally maimed in Afghanistan? No.

My unit dove behind the low hill where mortars were already set up, joining the unit already firing on the targets out ahead of us.

I'd just begun to catch my breath when a jet came in low above us—one of ours—and dropped its payload just ahead of our location. I glanced over the guns to see the forward air controller lift his arms and hoot, probably not the smartest move, considering we were under fire. But I couldn't blame him. Every Marine was a rifleman, and while the rest of us grunts were corporals on our first and second tours of duty, the FACs were officers, and usually pilots themselves. The guy on the radio calling in the airstrikes was probably used to being the guy in the jet, not the guy on the ground, and the guy flying overhead was likely his buddy.

"Get in over there," our CO ordered. "We're laying in some indirect fire to help support the guys up front. If it moves, you hit it!"

I was at the end of my second tour, and after almost eight years as a Marine, I wasn't particularly impressed by much of what I'd seen. At least geographically. On a human level, the

Marines I served with were some of the most loyal, intelligent, and steadfast fuckers I'd ever come across, and as much as I was glad to get the hell out of the Middle East, I was going to miss them.

I'd had my fill of Osprey and helicopter rides, mortar fire, and dust. I was heading back to our forward operating base. This was my last firefight. Home was on the horizon.

* * *

"THAT WAS GOOD TIMES, RIGHT THERE," one of my fellow grunts said a week later, sitting next to me in the Humvee that was giving us transport back to the base from which we were headed home.

"Got that check in the box," I said. "But I'm going to have some strong words with my travel agent about the accommodations on this so-called tour, man."

"The food was shit, too," he laughed, and we relaxed more minute by minute as we moved farther from the action and closer to home. "I've got some thoughts about the nightly fireworks show too."

When we were finally seated side by side in first class on a commercial jet from Germany to DC, we were practically regular guys.

"Nice of those folks to give up their fancy seats," my friend commented, tapping his champagne flute to mine.

"It was." Since Marines didn't travel in uniform on commercial flights, it was rare that folks would even realize the guy sitting next to them might have been in a war zone the day before. But the passenger who'd approached us on the terminal had been a Marine himself, and whether it was the close crop of our hair or the just-avoided-certain-death set of our eyes, he knew the look.

"You guys want an upgrade?" he'd asked us, after saluting and offering an "ooh-rah." He and his wife were insistent that we take their seats, and though we'd said no several times, they finally got their way and I wasn't unhappy about it.

Thanks to that man, I found myself sitting in a restaurant next to America's most famous movie star a year later, wondering how things could have changed so much. The woman beside me was gorgeous and sweet, bright blue eyes and honey-blond hair complementing what felt like a genuinely kind personality. Juliet Manchester had me a little bit star struck, but mostly I was happy to have found a job. I was a world away from the war zone where I'd spent a big part of my life and maybe left a little piece of myself—thankfully nothing I couldn't live without.

The star's manager was there, and so was the rest of her security detail. I'd just been brought on board, and I couldn't pretend it was an everyday thing for me. Security was new. It was the job that had been offered when I'd followed up with the former Marine who'd given up his seat to me. It was his firm.

Since I hadn't finished my degree yet, I was interested. I could work as a bodyguard while I focused on my education.

Make some money while I got myself right.

I just didn't expect any of what happened next.

CHAPTER ONE
JULIET

"I hate these guys," Zac had always said about my ever-present security detail from the moment we began dating. But Zac Stephens, the man I was dumb enough to marry, probably hated pretty much everything about me. Maybe he only pretended to love me. I knew he loved what I could give him.

When filming wrapped early for the day and I got home earlier than usual, hoping to surprise Zac with a quiet dinner at home. I nodded at the security guards stationed at the driveway as I parked, and made my way to the kitchen door, fumbling my phone and car keys as I pushed the door open.

I walked into my familiar kitchen with its stark white tile and gleaming marble counters, and it took a few minutes for the scene before me to make sense. My husband was bent over, face-first in something our personal chef Maribella was offering him. Something that had definitely not been on any of the menus she'd shared with me.

Our personal chef was on her back on the huge marble island, her legs spread wide as Zac's head bobbed between her thighs, and her throaty moans turned quickly to high-pitched shrieks of alarm when she spotted me staring at them from the doorway.

"Seriously? On my kitchen island?" I yelled, as if the location of the act made it any more awful than the act itself.

My furious shouts brought Jace and Jack inside immediately, and I watched, open-mouthed, as they hauled both Zac and Maribella outside and left them there. Jace swiped their discarded clothing off the floor and counter and tossed it out before following them out. Jack stayed with them, evidently supervising their efforts at dressing themselves in the driveway, and Jace came back inside to see if I was all right.

I wasn't. I definitely wasn't.

He found me where I'd sunk to the kitchen floor, crying pitifully with my head in my hands.

"Hey." His quiet deep voice broke through my humiliation and misery. I looked up to find deep concerned chocolate brown eyes watching me thoughtfully.

Jace reached a hand down to me and I took it. The firm solidity of his big hand was reassuring, and I realized numbly that if Zac had walked in and found me crying on the kitchen floor at any point in our marriage, he would have told me to get up before asking what was wrong or reaching out a hand to me.

I had been so stupid.

"You okay?" Jace asked once I was on my feet again. He stayed close enough to make sure I was steady, but took a step back, clearly not wanting to crowd my space. He was handsome, strong, and he projected an air of quiet confidence.

I shook my head. "No. I'm not okay. I'm an idiot." I dropped both hands onto the counter before realizing with horror that was the very surface on which I'd just caught my husband with the chef. I whipped them away, crossing my arms over myself instead. "God, I'm so stupid."

"Hey." Jace caught my attention again with a low patient voice. "You're not. He's the asshole here."

I blew out a breath. "I don't think it's the first time."

Jace lifted a shoulder.

I squinted up at him. "Do you know? Has he done this before?" I would hate to think of the security team knowing my husband was cheating on me, knowing I didn't know. I would feel like even more of a fool than I already did.

He shrugged. "Not that I know of. But he's an asshole, so I wouldn't put it past him."

"Thanks a lot." I rolled my eyes, wiping at the angry tears that had collected on my cheeks. "You could have told me."

He smiled, wide full lips parting to reveal teeth that were perfect except for one chip at the corner of the top front. "Tell you that your husband is a choad? Not part of the job description, Miss Manchester."

"God, call me Juliet. You've known me at least a year now." I sat down heavily on one of the stools, motioning to the other and feeling happier by a fraction when Jace sat down beside me. I felt like such an idiot. I wanted to make sure I'd never be this clueless again. "Make me a deal?"

"What's that?"

"For one, tell me what a choad is."

A dark flush crept over Jace's handsome face. The light skin at his jaw, covered with a scruff of beard, twitched with a hidden smile. "I think you'd better check Urban Dictionary for that. I'm not really comfortable using those words with a lady."

I sank my elbows to my defiled counter. "Oh for fuck's sake."

He didn't tell me, but he did pull out his phone and swipe until he found the definition on Urban Dictionary.

"Oh. I see. Okay, yes. Zac is a choad." I stifled a giggle. This was not the time for giggles.

"What else?" Jace asked, shoving his phone back in his pocket.

"What?" The definition I'd just read had me forgetting whatever I'd been about to say.

"The deal."

"Oh. Promise me you won't keep things from me again. You see more than I do. You know what's going on when I don't. Can you be my second set of eyes, Jace?" I knew it was more than I was supposed to ask of my security team. But I didn't have anyone else. I didn't have family here, wasn't close with the family I did have. And now I didn't have a husband either.

He shifted on the stool and I got the sense he was uncomfortable.

"I'll pay you more," I said quickly. Was he worried I was asking him to do more work?

"No," he said. "It's not that. It's just ..."

"I need someone I can trust." I dropped my head into my hands. "It's like I don't even know what's real anymore. Does that make sense?"

He didn't say anything for a long second, and I swiveled my head so I could see his face. I'd had lots of bodyguards since that first incident, most of them kept their distance and didn't say much. They opened doors, they lent a hand when needed. But they were like shadows. For some reason, since the day Jace was assigned to me just over a year ago, I'd felt something different from him. I was more comfortable in his presence, more at ease.

And I couldn't pretend I hadn't entertained a fantasy or two about those muscled biceps, that hard wide torso. He was like a statue in a dark T-shirt, and something about him looked fierce and dangerous. But at the same time, he was always quick with a gentle smile, a kind word. The other guys didn't speak to me most of the time, but Jace always said hello. I'd come to think of him differently.

It was possible I had a little crush on him. And the thrill of having him alone here with me, in my kitchen, even in the face of having just discovered my asshole husband face down in our chef, was intriguing, even through my misery.

"You can always trust me, Miss Manchester," he said, his rich dark voice earnest and sincere.

"Please call me Juliet."

"Juliet."

I smiled at him then. My heart was ripped to shreds and I

felt lonelier than I ever had, despite being more successful professionally than I'd ever dreamed I could be. But there was a little glimmer of something inside me when Jace smiled back.

CHAPTER TWO
JACE

I'd never been the kind of guy who went after the most popular girl. I knew who I was—and that was just a regular guy from a small town. Not a celebrity, not even a fan. But there was something about Juliet Manchester that made me rethink everything.

In the weeks after Zac made his spectacular exit, the firm decided to station one guard inside Juliet's house based on the fact her on-again, off-again stalker had been spotted in the neighborhood. We'd always held posts outside—two of us taking quarters in the two-bedroom guest house off the drive-way. But in light of Juliet's changed circumstances, I'd been assigned to move into the main house.

"Hey, Jace?" A light knock came at my door one night after I'd seen Juliet off to her room and turned in for the night. Things had been polite and a little tense between us. We were both getting used to the change. I liked being closer to her, and I told myself it was only because I could do my job better if I kept her in sight. But when her quiet knock came at my door in the stillness of the night, the twisting want stirring inside me had little to do with work. I knew there was nothing urgently wrong—her voice was too soft, too calm for that.

"Juliet?" I pulled open the bedroom door, realizing a beat too late that I hadn't managed to pull my shirt back on before answering. "Oh, sorry, I was just ..." I moved across the room, pulling a loose USMC T-shirt over my head quickly. She didn't say anything until I faced her again, and it was hard to read the expression on her face. "Everything okay?"

"Yeah, I uh ... listen, I'm sorry, I shouldn't have bothered you." She began to pull the door shut again, looking so sad and defeated I nearly pulled her into my arms as my pulse raced.

"Hey," I said, stepping to block the swing of the door. "What's up?"

Those blue eyes met mine then, her little chin tilting up to meet my gaze. She stared at me a second, and then her expression shifted and fell before she gathered herself again. "It's silly really, I just ... I didn't feel like going to sleep and I kind of wanted some company." She looked around the dark hallway at her back. "It's hard to admit this, but I guess I don't really have a lot of friends. And Elvis is out for the night. Sometimes it's lonely, that's all." She didn't meet my eye again.

The part about the dog was no surprise. Elvis, Juliet's narcoleptic pug, was often "out." I didn't see the appeal of this particular dog, but Juliet seemed to love him, so I took on the additional responsibility of scooping him up whenever he went to sleep in the midst of a run or out in town. But the idea of Juliet being lonely made me think for a second. She was arguably the most beloved star in America—how could she be lonely? The idea made me sad.

Juliet was watching me consider, and my heart squeezed at the pleading look in her eyes as I thought. I wanted to keep her company. She had no idea how much. But this was a job for me—one I'd been given on the back of an honorable discharge from the Marine Corps, and it would definitely be something less than honorable for me to forget that Juliet was a client. Not a friend. Definitely nothing more.

Still, those liquid eyes and the defeated slump of her shoulders told me maybe my job was about more than just physical safety. At least right now.

"I play a mean game of Uno," I told her, not sure quite where the words came from.

"You do, huh?" She smiled at me. "My sister and my Gran used to play that with me."

"Yeah?" I imagined a little white-haired lady patiently playing cards with two little girls. I was sure Juliet came from a picture-perfect background.

"Yeah, until they got tired of losing." She practically sneered this last part, and a spike of amusement and surprise whipped through me. I hadn't seen this side of Juliet before.

"Is that right?" I chuckled. "Well, bring it on."

"I've got Mastermind, too," she said over her shoulder as we stepped out toward the stairs.

"Well, now you're talking."

We settled ourselves on the floor in her living room in

front of a gas fire that made the space seem cozy, despite it being bigger than most people's homes. Juliet insisted on bringing a bottle of red wine in and pouring for us both.

"I'm on duty," I reminded her.

"Jace, it's after ten o'clock. You're off."

"As long as I'm with you, I'm on." Technically, she was right—I wasn't on the clock. But that didn't mean I was about to let down my guard. If anything happened to her on my watch, I'd never forgive myself.

She lifted her wine glass and gave me a pointed look, daring me not to drink mine. I lifted it and we sipped. At two-hundred and twenty pounds, it would take more than a glass of wine to muddy my senses.

"Wanna start with Mastermind? I probably intimidated you telling you about defeating all my enemies at Uno back in the day," she said. There was a playful glint in her eyes that I loved, and I relaxed a bit, enjoying myself.

"Sure," I said, lifting the lid off the box.

"You have played before, I take it?"

"I loved this game when I was a kid." I smiled at her as I turned the code maker side toward me and put up the little shield so she couldn't see what I was doing.

"Did you play with brothers? Sisters?" She huffed out a little breath. "I'm sorry. I'm just realizing I know nothing about you. And I'm being nosey."

"No worries," I told her. I didn't share with many people, preferring to listen instead of talk most of the time. "I played with some of my cousins when I was a kid. I have a brother, but that's it."

"But it sounds like you had a big family. That's nice."

It was the combination of the wine, the fire, and Juliet's easy posture across from me as she leaned against the armchair and tried to break my code as we began to play. It made me want to talk.

"My mom came from a big family. But I didn't know most of them well. She married a guy they didn't approve of, and we didn't get invited around a lot."

Juliet's head snapped up and her eyes met mine, full of sympathy. "That's awful," she said.

I tried to shrug it off, the old hurt of being unwanted, not good enough, was like a roughened scar that only ached a little if I bumped it. "I grew up in the south and Mom fell in love with a guy who had the wrong family and not a lot of money."

Her eyes held mine and warmth bloomed inside me. It was actually nice to share—I knew a little bit about Juliet Manchester. Now she would know something about me.

"They let us come around now and then. Her parents wanted to know my brother and me. But we weren't exactly first on the list for family gatherings. The older we got, the more we understood how it was. Her family had money, ours didn't, and Dad's family was part of a social caste that just didn't mix with Mom's. For a while, her family treated us like their own personal charity case. When we were little and cute, it was fine. But it got harder as we got older and started to understand. When we weren't cute little boys anymore, they treated us like we didn't fit, didn't belong. It was hard not to resent it. For Mom too, I think. And for Dad."

"That had to be difficult," she said. "I'm from the south too. Kind of."

"Yeah?" I didn't know where Juliet was from. She hadn't talked about family before.

Juliet had still not cracked my code, though her guesses were getting close. She was only two colors off.

"Maryland," she said. "South of the Mason-Dixon line, but not exactly the deep south."

"Y'all were on the wrong side in the war, weren't you?"

She laughed at my twang, something easy for me to pull back on when I wanted to. "I think you're right. I'm not exactly a history buff. You'd have to talk to my sister Tessy for that."

"I'd rather talk to you." It slipped out before I could help it. I forgot my place, crossed a line. Something my family history should have made easy enough to remember. "I'm sorry, Juliet. That was inappropriate."

"Was it?" She leaned slightly toward me, finishing another guess at my code. "Or maybe you're just being honest."

I lifted the shield over my code to show her that she'd gotten it.

"Yes!" She did a little fist pump and there was something so charming and real in the motion. If we'd been other people, in another situation, I'd have leaned across the board and kissed her right then. Maybe she felt it too, because there was a lingering moment when her gaze tangled with mine and something shuddered and shivered around us.

I dropped her eyes, took a big swallow of wine. "Again?"

"Yes." She busied herself setting up the board, and I sensed that she was relieved, that we'd dodged a bullet.

As the night stilled outside and the level in the wine bottle decreased, we laughed and played childish games, and it felt more and more like we were two friends. Or something more.

"Juliet?" I asked as we packed up the games. I felt like we'd built a bridge of sorts, like maybe now it was okay to pry a little bit. And I found that I cared about Juliet. More than I should. And I understood she was lonely, but I thought there might be something else going on. She'd looked upset when she'd come to my door.

"Yeah?"

"Was there something going on tonight? Earlier, when you came to my door. Is everything okay?"

She squeezed her eyes shut a long second, her hands stilling over the game box. Then she blew out a controlled breath. "Zac is making some accusations."

Indignation swept through me. That asshole. I'd watched him treat her like shit for a full year before she'd walked in on him. I hated the guy and had been glad to see him go, though I knew it had hurt Juliet. "Against you?" The words came out like a honed steel blade.

"He says I cheated on him. He's suing me for a huge amount of my estate." She paused, cringed. "And there's a tape."

I felt my eyebrows shoot up. It was hard to imagine Juliet in the kind of tape I figured she meant. "A tape?"

"You understand," she said, blushing and dropping her eyes. "When we were first together. We made a tape."

"Shit." I forced myself not to think about how much I might like to see such a tape. Even if it meant seeing her with Zac. I swallowed hard.

"Yeah. Pretty much."

"So he's blackmailing you," I said, anger sending every cell in my body into violent overdrive. I shot to my feet, unable to help it.

"There's nothing you can do. My lawyers and manager are handling it. They'll give him a settlement to make him stop."

"You sure?" I thought about how I'd like to settle things with Zac Stephens.

"I hope so."

Hope was rarely an effective offense. I knew that from my time in the Corps, but I wasn't going to overstep the bounds of my engagement here by inserting myself. She was handling it. I took a few steadying breaths in an effort to calm down.

"Thanks for hanging out with me," she said, switching off the gas fire and picking up the bottle. She turned to head to the dark kitchen, but I stepped close, taking the empty bottle from her hand.

"I'll take care of this. You go on up. I'm just going to do a quick perimeter check. Make sure everything's secure before I turn in."

She sighed and the little line of worry on her forehead eased. "Thanks, Jace." She took a couple steps toward the stairs and turned back. "If I haven't said it, it's really nice having you here. Thank you."

I watched her slim form head up the stairs, and forced my mind to shift back to where it had lived before we'd sat on the rug drinking wine and laughing together. No matter how much I liked her, Juliet Manchester was not my friend. And I was absolutely the boy from the wrong side of the tracks where she was concerned.

Besides, it didn't matter how I might feel. Even if I wasn't her employee, she'd never consider dating a guy like me.

CHAPTER THREE
JULIET

I listened as Jace made his rounds downstairs after I'd told him goodnight, satisfaction warming me when I finally heard him come up the stairs and close the door to his bedroom, just down the hall from mine.

My hand rested on the door, my forehead leaned against the cool wood. I wanted to go to him again, but he would think I was some crazy desperate woman. And what would I say? Just one more round of Uno?

It was hard, having him just down the hall, all that warm, comforting muscle. That careful smile of his.

I didn't want it to be true—lord knew I didn't need the complication—but since Jace had moved in, my crush had begun to grow. And I was having trouble sorting through the list of actions I was considering taking as a result of my attraction to him. I was pretty sure most of those actions were completely inappropriate. Tonight I'd been desperate for company. I told myself that was it, that it was less about him and more about me. I was probably lying to myself, but I had needed a friend—even if it was one I was paying to be here.

I glanced over at Elvis, who'd actually made it to his little white satin bejeweled dog bed before disappearing into sleep, where he spent a lot of his time. His little side was moving up and down as he snored softly, and now and then his paws twitched in a pug dream. Probably about figs. Elvis was the only dog in the world who adored figs. Good thing we lived in California.

Elvis was a companion, when he wasn't asleep. But he wasn't exactly a friend.

A year ago I would have called Marina, even late at night, but my marriage to Zac had created some serious distance between my best friend and me. I hadn't been able to close it since Zac had made it clear she wasn't welcome at our house. Maybe he felt threatened because she'd never liked him and had told him so. I should have listened.

I thought about reaching out, offering an olive branch. Marina had been a good friend. She'd seen clearly things that I hadn't been able to. It just felt like it might be too late.

But Jace. He was so close, and so tempting. What was I going to do?

I had decided playing children's games would be safe and not something I'd selected out of a complete misunderstanding of the situation between us.

Other options on the list I'd considered had included things like:

- Asking him to remove all my clothes, douse me in chocolate sauce and lick every inch of me clean (probably inappropriate)
- Letting me snuggle in his lap and investigate the actual size of his massive biceps. And maybe some other parts of his anatomy (also most likely not okay). Or
- Just flinging open the door to his room and swan diving into his bed. (I'd never been great at diving. And there was the chance he'd turn me away. I'd had enough rejection lately.)

I just wanted to be close to him. The way he treated me, the way he talked to me like an actual person—it made me want to spend more time with him. He was different from the other people in my life.

The problem was that it was becoming harder and harder to sort through the kinds of things people said and did around me because of who I am supposed to be ... and not because of who I really was.

My life was built on acting. And it turned out that as my acting career made me more and more successful, it was becoming harder and harder to figure out what was real. I had a few friends, who I suspected were much closer to side actors, all participating in the Juliet Manchester show. I had a husband, and I knew now that he'd definitely been playing a role, working for a salary comprised of fame by association and a pretty impressive assortment of material goods.

The door to my bedroom, which I was leaning my head

against, was solid and real enough—I could trust it. But there wasn't much else in my life that felt trustworthy and real.

Except Jace.

I pushed off the door and went to the little table in the corner of the master suite, where a lamp glowed softly. I slid into the chair and spread the file on the table open again.

It was Jace's file, the one the company had sent me when he'd first started working for me. I was supposed to give it back, but I'd held onto it for some reason. Even back then, when I'd been married—happily, I'd thought—there'd been something in Jace's dark eyes, the steady confidence in his gaze, that had made me want to hold onto the pictures in his file. He was handsome and sure, and knowing he'd served two tours as a Marine impressed me. I stared at the service photo, Jace in his uniform, the soft olive green of the shirt beneath the camouflage setting off the dark eyes. He looked sure and capable. Just a little bit dangerous.

Here was a man who had done something real. The men I met in Hollywood tended to have done things like selling investment properties or attending law school and then never getting their licenses. People here were often constructions, flimsy and hastily built to look a certain way. Jace was real. And maybe that was why I liked him so much.

I tucked away the file, smiling as I thought of his kind mouth and the easy laugh he'd let slip as we'd played Mastermind.

It was probably the wrong thing to do.

But I already knew I wanted to get closer to Jace.

CHAPTER FOUR
JACE

The day after Juliet and I had played games together and polished off a bottle of wine was my day off. Since I lived in Juliet's house, that didn't mean a lot, except that my schedule that day was dictated more by my own life than hers. When I bumped into her in the kitchen, talking to Chad, who would be her in-house security in my absence, an irritating little wad of jealousy wedged itself into my gut. His blond hair—dyed, I suspected—stood straight up from his square forehead. He looked like an action figure, plastic and shiny.

"Good morning," Juliet said, sending a shy smile my way from where she sat at the kitchen counter, a coffee cup wrapped between her small hands.

"Good morning, Miss Manchester," I said. "Chad."

Chad gave me his cocky adventure-hero grin and wink combination, and I nearly gave Chad my signature throat punch.

But I restrained myself, filling my water bottle instead and reminding myself that he was a good bodyguard, a smart guy, and also had military training. Even if it was in the Air Force.

Elvis waddled in then, and I squatted down to give him a few pats around his thick little neck. He raised his lolling grin and google eyes my way and then gave an enormous yawn and toppled over, asleep.

"Elvis," Juliet sighed, her lips hooking up on one side.

"Miss Manchester, your dog is officially useless," Chad informed her. Jerk. If he wasn't so busy flirting with the client, he might have actually bothered helping her instead.

I scooped Elvis up and deposited him into the soft little bed in the corner. This one was black and had rhinestones all around the edges. "There you go, buddy," I said softly.

"What are you doing with your day off?" Juliet asked as I turned back around and returned to the counter to screw the lid on my water bottle tight.

Her eyes met mine and I felt that same pull I'd felt the night before, the same fire of recognition that something lay between us. I ducked my head. If Chad picked up on it, my job would be history. The firm had a strict no-fraternization policy, and I needed the job. My family needed me to keep it too.

I cleared my throat, reminded myself that most guys in this situation wouldn't feel a need to tell their client all the details of their day. "Just going for a quick run, then I'm going to take care of a few personal things."

"Getting your pubes waxed?" Chad muttered as he moved past me, too low for Juliet to hear.

"Some family stuff," I clarified, partially for jerkwad Chad.

"Hey, Chad, did that rash ever clear up, man?" I asked him as I moved toward the back door, sliding my sunglasses on and pushing my earbuds in.

I turned back to see Juliet looking concerned and Chad's face reddening. "Hey, man, that's not cool."

"Just wondered if it was like, you know, contagious or whatever." I kept my volume low for now so I could hear him.

"Dude!"

Juliet was on her feet now, moving toward the living room. "I'm going to get a workout too," she said, glancing between us. "Maybe you can just keep an eye on things down here?" she suggested to Chad.

"Of course, Miss Manchester. Also, ma'am, I do not have a rash." I heard this last part as I slipped out the door for my run.

The streets around Juliet's house were wide and clear, winding and tree-lined, and they lay between houses bigger than any I'd even known existed as a kid. Juliet and I had been running together weekly since I'd been working here, but we usually kept our own music going, me giving her space out of respect. Today I wished she were here, found myself longing for her company, even if it was silent. I let my mind wander, turning over the strange intimacy I'd felt the night before, even as I assured myself it was one-sided and that it was probably only natural to develop a crush on a movie star as beautiful as Juliet.

Only it hadn't felt one-sided.

I pushed my body harder, hoping to reconnect it to reality. My reality. This was a job, one I needed to pay for the degree that was just one course away at this point. And one I needed to keep to pay the rent on Mom's house. Once I'd gotten the degree, I could look at jobs that didn't rely completely on my physicality, positions that might require some intellect as well. I knew I wasn't a smart guy, but I still wanted a future that might support a family, a job that would let me be home at night to enjoy that family if I ever had it.

Being a bodyguard was temporary. But the pay was good, and for now it was all I had—all my mom had too.

After the run, I let myself back into the house, where Chad was seated at the kitchen counter reading a tabloid magazine. We had a lot of downtime. You learned a lot about the other guys by watching how they chose to spend it.

"Juliet's in here," he said, holding the magazine up.

"Don't let Miss Manchester see you with that," I told him. It wasn't our business to get involved in the rumors surrounding our clients unless those rumors affected their personal security. I thought about what Juliet had confided the night before about Zac. I hoped that wouldn't slip out any time soon.

He made a noise, sucking his teeth. "She's stayed in her room since your little rash comment. I should thank you—probably gonna be an easy day for me now."

"You're welcome," I told him, taking a protein bar out of my cabinet in the kitchen and heading for my own room to shower.

I could hear the fitness app Juliet used when she was at home through her door, and I did my best not to picture her lean fit form, glistening with sweat as she moved in the small studio attached to her bedroom. She didn't like working out at the gym, and once when Zac hadn't been home, she'd asked me for help getting a weight bench set up. Despite her small frame, Juliet was pretty strong, and her workout ethic was impressive. I was pretty sure she worked out six days a week.

I sighed, left Juliet's door, and returned to my own room.

An hour later, I was in the car, headed to Mom's.

Dad had been gone a long time now, but my mother and my brother shared a small house in Inglewood. They'd moved out here while I'd been serving, which was part of why I'd come west. The three of us usually hung out together for a few hours on Sundays.

I pulled up in front of the little house, noting that the lawn needed cutting and one of the shutters on the front windows was hanging askew. I tried to push down the anger that flared in my belly. I paid for this house now, and the only reason my brother Jarred was here was because he said he'd take care of things for Mom. We'd talked about the shutter the Sunday before, and he'd promised to do better. So much for that promise.

"Mom? Jarred? Hey guys, it's me." I let myself in with my key and stepped into the small dark entryway.

"Jace?" Mom's voice came from the kitchen, and I strode through the living room to find her, noticing the mess of dirty dishes and newspapers strewn around as I did.

"Hey Mom." She sat at the small round table, a cigarette in her hand and a mug of coffee in front of her. It was almost noon, but she still wore her robe and slippers, and her hair was a mess of tangles on her head. Mom looked tired, and she looked sick. But she wouldn't go to the doctor. I'd tried to take her for weeks, offering to pay, but she wouldn't let me and there was still some of the authority structure between us. She was my mom. I couldn't force her.

"There's my boy," she said, putting down the cigarette to stand, but as she pushed to her feet, she began coughing. The fit overtook her, and she leaned heavily into the table, hacking and wheezing until it passed.

"You still sick, Mom?" I was worried about my mother. And angry that my brother didn't care enough.

She stepped near, wrapped frail arms around my waist and looked up at me before pushing her cheek against my chest. "I'm fine, baby. How are you?"

I kissed her cheek and let her go, and then poured a cup of coffee and sat down, trying not to notice the mess on the counter, the overflowing trash. "Mom, where's Jarred?"

She sighed. "He's got a new girlfriend," she said. "He hasn't been home in a little while."

"A little while." Worry swirled inside me next to a new dread. I gave her a stern look. "Translate. Days? Weeks? He was here last Sunday."

"He left right after you did. So a week, I guess," she said. "But I understand. He's a grown man, he needs to live his own life—"

Mom had always made excuses for my little brother. He was her baby, and he could do no wrong. Except it seemed like a lot of what he did was exactly that. Wrong.

"If he's a grown man, he needs to get a damned job and

take responsibility for himself," I said, standing to begin the work of putting the house back together. "He should be keeping this place up, taking care of things. Of you."

I hated this. I hated that the best I could do for my mom was this rumble-down shack in a bad neighborhood. I hated that my brother was content to be a freeloader his entire life, catching whatever ride came his way and ignoring everything else. The obvious question rose in my chest and I thought about pushing it away, but I had to ask. "Is he still clean?" When Jarred was gone more than a couple days, it generally meant he was on a bender.

She sighed, coughed, didn't answer, and the ice forming in my gut made me feel sick.

"Shit," I muttered, washing dishes and stacking them in the drying rack. I glanced over my shoulder at Mom, who sat staring into the distance, smoking. "Mom, you need to quit smoking."

She narrowed her eyes at me. "I'm still your mother, Jace. You don't get to tell me what to do."

We'd been over this. Many times. Mom was sick and we all knew it. Smoking was killing her, but she refused to go get a diagnosis, preferring to wait and see how bad it got. I hated not knowing, but in a way I shared her hesitation. I couldn't stand the thought of losing my mom, and maybe denial was better than finding out she had something we couldn't afford to treat.

"You get your check this month?" I asked her. She collected disability, and it was about all that kept her eating. I paid for everything else. But there had been a month when

Jarred had intercepted the check. It was the first time I'd actually punched my little brother.

"I talked to the mail carrier," she said, ducking her chin like this was something to be ashamed of. "He puts the check in a different spot. For me."

I smiled at Mom. She might be sick and frail, she might have lost her desire to really live, but she was still sly and smart. "Nicely done."

"I'm worried about him, Jace." The defeat in her voice told me all the things I wished weren't true.

"I know, Mom. Me too."

"One day, I know he just won't come home."

I put the dishtowel over my shoulder, sank into the chair across from her again. "There's not much we can do, Mom. He's a grown man. He's making his own choices. He and I had the same opportunities—he went a different way."

Mom reached across the table for my hand, and I took her bony fingers into my palm, a sad little place inside me flooding with a feeling I couldn't let show. My mom, the woman who had cared for me my whole life, looked like she was dying. And there was nothing I could do.

"I thank the universe every day for you," she said. "And sometimes, when I'm not being so goddamn selfish, I wish you'd never been born."

"What?" I half-laughed in surprise. What did that mean?

"Because I have nothing to give a boy like you. So bright, so capable. I brought you into a family that didn't want us, a life with nothing to offer you." She paused, coughing and sputtering for a long minute before regaining herself. She looked back up at me, tears in her eyes. "But if it weren't for you, Jace, I'd be such a lonely sad old woman. I'm selfish, but I'm so happy you're here."

I felt the flood of sadness overflow as another little part of my heart broke. "No, Mom. You're not selfish. We're family. This is what we do for each other. I just wish I could do more." I cleared my throat and tried to gather myself. "I'm going to clean up a bit, do a little laundry, okay? How about you take a shower when you're ready, and I'll take you out to dinner?"

She shook her head. "No, you don't have to do that. Don't you have a girlfriend you'd rather take out?"

"Mom," I said, giving her a frank look. "The day I have a girlfriend, you'll be the first to know."

She smiled at me, and behind the drawn, wrinkled face, I saw a glimmer of my pretty mother, the woman I'd worshipped as a little boy. "Okay," she said. "I'll go get dressed."

"Give me a couple hours," I said. "I'm gonna cut the grass, too."

When Mom had slipped away to her bedroom, I pulled out my phone and texted my brother. As expected, there was no response. I put my phone back in my pocket and got to work as anger began to eat a little hole inside me.

Things couldn't go on this way.

By the time I slipped back into Juliet's house that night, I was exhausted. My days off usually went this way, filled with maintenance, cleaning, and worry.

I was just stepping out of the shower, a towel wrapped

around my waist, when I heard a gentle knock at my bedroom door and my stupid heart jolted in eager anticipation. It wasn't exactly professional to answer this way, but I wasn't really on duty either, not until the morning. Still, I pulled on a pair of shorts quickly before answering, keeping most of my bare chest behind the door as I opened it.

"Hey," I said, wishing everything inside me didn't feel immediately lighter at the sight of Juliet standing there in a soft pink sweater and jeans, her feet bare and her hair loose.

"Hey," she said, meeting my eyes and then dropping my gaze immediately. My stomach tightened.

"What's up?" I asked.

She laughed lightly, and shifted her weight. "Honestly? Nothing. I just wondered how your day was."

This was new.

My blood warmed at her interest, my heart picking up a quicker beat and a smile immediately coming to my face.

But this was dangerous. And I was pretty sure we both knew it.

CHAPTER FIVE
JULIET

I didn't really know what I was doing. I'd spent the day wishing Jace would return, and I hadn't left the house all day, staying mostly in my room to avoid Chad, who I wasn't fond of.

But I was beginning to realize I was very fond of Jace. And maybe it was more than fondness.

It was probably a terrible idea.

But I couldn't stop myself from going to his door. I just wanted to see those dark eyes light up once before I went to sleep.

When he answered the door shirtless, I lost my breath. Every muscle in his torso was defined and cut. He wasn't huge, but he was substantial, and I itched to run my hands over that body, to feel his big arms around me. He was inked, too. Not excessively so, but there was a tattoo on his left pec that intrigued me, an intricate symbol with a circle in the middle and three points. Celtic maybe?

I managed to ask how his day was, and I was sure I hadn't mistaken the sadness that passed through his eyes.

"It was okay," he said, his voice gruff, like he was covering some emotion. "Saw my mom. Took her to dinner."

"It must be nice to have her so close," I said. Jace didn't talk much about his family. I'd known they were local, but I didn't know much else. "You grew up in the south, you said. When did your mom move?"

"She moved out here after Dad died. When I got back, I got her a little house. My brother came out too."

"I'm sorry about your dad." I knew what it was to lose parents. It was like a door that opened inside that you thought should have led somewhere, but which just spilled out emptiness, an emptiness you couldn't fill. I'd been trying to shut my own door for years.

"Nah," Jace brushed it off. "He was sick. Got into some things he shouldn't have."

That didn't sound good. I wanted to know more—maybe everything, but I didn't ask. "I'm sorry."

We stood there a minute more, Jace using the door as a shield between us and the silence full of something more, something inviting, promising.

"Do you want to come in?" Jace asked, pulling the door wider.

I hesitated, the wiser side of my mind wondering what this invitation meant. But I trusted Jace, and I knew I was safe with him—he was being polite, that was all. I was curious, too. I'd been in this room, of course, but not since he'd moved in and made it his own.

"Sure, for a minute." I stepped in, looking around me. The bed was neatly made, a simple white duvet pulled up to navy pillows. A desk sat in one corner, a little lamp on its surface illuminating a pretty impressive collection of books, many of them open, and a laptop sat to one side. Jace was studying—he'd told me that, and I admired it.

The rest of the room was tidy, a set of dumbbells tucked under the armchair next to the window, another chair facing it in front of the gas fireplace.

Jace wasn't the type of guy to leave his clothes laying around, it seemed, and as I stepped in, he scooped up a towel and gave me an apologetic glance. "Make yourself comfortable. I'll just be a second."

He disappeared into the little hallway that I knew held a closet and led to the connected bathroom. When he re-emerged, he had a South Bay Sharks shirt pulled across that impressive chest, and I felt a wash of disappointment.

"I don't really have anything to offer you," he said, gesturing around the room. "A protein bar?" He smiled, his dark eyes framed by lashes I'd have to pay someone in a salon to get myself.

"I'm fine," I said, happy when he sat down in the chair facing mine, making it seem like he might relax, talk a little. "I'm sorry, I'm totally intruding ..." I was starting to realize how strange this was, how potentially inappropriate.

"No," he said quickly. "I mean. I'm happy for the company, actually."

A little flicker of happiness sprang to life in my chest. I settled back into the chair. "Okay, if you're sure."

He leaned his forearms on his knees and sighed, then looked up at me, a sadness in his eyes so profound that I wanted to fall to my knees in front of him, take him into my arms and comfort him. I had no idea what could make him look like that, but I thought I'd give anything to know.

"I am sure," he said. "It was kind of a rough day. It's nice to see you, actually."

"Is everything okay with your mom?" I asked, not sure how far I could intrude.

He looked away, straightening and glancing out his window into the darkness, and sighed again like a man looking at something terrible that he couldn't change. "Not really, but that's just kind of how things are."

His answer didn't invite me to ask any more questions, so I didn't. "That sounds so hard, Jace."

He met my eyes then, his head cocked slightly to one side, like he was trying to understand something. A sad smile crossed the full lips. "It just is," he said. "We can't fix everything."

Neither of us said anything for a minute, and I felt I owed him some kind of explanation, some reason I was pushing myself into his space like this. "I feel like I should apologize for last night. Or maybe for this," I began. "For asking you for more than I'm actually paying you for. I mean, your job isn't about hanging out with your client. I know that."

He was shaking his head slowly, but I couldn't stop talking now.

"I guess it's just that ... how sad is this? I'm lonely and you're here. Maybe that's all it is."

"Is that all it is?" His eyes were sharp on mine. Was his voice a little bit disappointed?

That was definitely not all this was. Not for me. It was a lot more than that. But it probably wasn't right. I didn't know if he could get fired if we ...

If we did what? What did I want, exactly? I didn't know. I took a breath, dropping his gaze. Should I tell him it was nothing to me? Could I lie? I was a pretty good actress, even if I hadn't won that Oscar I'd been nominated for. Jace deserved my honesty, and I found myself wanting to give it to him. Wanting to give him much more, if he'd take it. "No. That's not all it is. Not for me."

It was as if the entire room condensed around us then, narrowing to the next words that would fall between us, the next words that might determine what happened here.

"For me either." His voice was low and deep, these words rocky and jagged. I knew I could cut myself on their edges if I wasn't careful.

"So ..." I began. I wanted to ask what it was then, what we were. I wanted to find out if he was worried about his job, his family, if spending this kind of time with me was dangerous for him.

But then I realized.

Of course it was. And it didn't matter what I wanted. I wasn't the one here with everything to lose. I was being an entitled movie star, expecting everyone around me to cater to my whims. Here I was, in the room of one of my staff, expecting him to entertain me late at night, to let me feel like this crush wasn't completely ridiculous, to help me be less lonely. I was being entitled and selfish.

I squeezed my eyes shut and forced myself to stand. "Jace, I'm sorry. I shouldn't be in here. It's your day off, and I'm expecting you to spend it entertaining me just because I'm lonely, or confused, or—"

I was at the door of his room, had stepped almost out into the hallway, when his voice stopped me.

"Juliet." It was that dark-edged blade again, and I turned to face him. To see the pain and desire mingling in his deep brown eyes. "Don't go."

CHAPTER SIX
JACE

She paused in the doorway, the light from my room shining in her light hair, glancing off her smooth cheeks, tracing her upturned nose. Red hot desire flared inside me, and I knew this was a moment that would determine the next. And the one after, and maybe days and months after that.

I didn't know what this was, this connection I felt to a movie star so far out of my league it was a joke, but I knew it was real.

"Okay," she said softly, taking a step back toward me, not meeting my eyes.

I reached out and took her hand gently, and she let me, her soft fingers wrapping around and twining my own, and I felt myself exhale.

For me, that's what it was. When Juliet was close, it was like the vice that kept my feelings in check released a bit and I could breathe.

She stepped inside my room and I swung the door shut

slowly, the click of the mechanism sliding home signaling some kind of finality. A decision had been made, I just wasn't sure exactly what it was.

We stood for a moment, the air stilled between us, both of us frozen with our hands locked together. And then she looked up at me, those blue eyes framed by a thousand dark lashes, and it was like looking through a prism to some better future, something more perfect than anything that was real for me now.

I tugged her hand gently, and she was in my arms, her small frame pressed against my chest. My arms went around her, and an unfamiliar longing surged within me. I wanted to keep her there, keep her safe. Keep her forever.

Juliet's arms slid around my waist, her hands finding their way up the planes of my back, caressing and holding me in a way I didn't think I'd ever been held. And when she tilted her head back and looked up into my eyes again, any restraint I still possessed dissolved the heat of my want.

I raised a hand between us and traced her beautiful lips with a finger. Slowly, watching her intently the whole time, memorizing her exhale, the way she felt melting in my arms, the way her body pressed to mine. I couldn't help it then—I had to taste her.

With a finger still on her lip, I bent my head to hers and brushed my lips slowly across hers. She moaned lightly, and my reserve snapped. I dropped my hand to the back of her head, letting my fingers slide through all that thick soft hair, and angled my jaw to kiss her fully.

It wasn't a deep kiss—there was no tongue, no clenching

of hands on each other's bodies—but it was the most sensual kiss I'd ever shared with anyone. And it was long, soul-draining, and sweet. And when I moved my mouth away, needing to look at her again, she held my gaze and pressed herself hard against me.

"God, Jace," she whispered.

I let the smile that had filled my heart find its way to my face, and kissed her once again, lighter still, teasing us both. I could have kissed her for days. I could have thrown her on the bed and let myself go, let myself do all the things I saw racing through my mind in that moment. But I wasn't that guy, and Juliet was not that woman. She deserved my respect, and my patience. And she was the one who would have to ask for more.

I let her go, moving to settle myself in one of the chairs by the unlit fireplace before I gave in to the urge to carry her to the bed and keep her there for days.

"Are you? I mean ... don't you want ...?" Juliet stood where I'd released her, looking around uncertainly, her face flushed beneath darkened sapphire eyes.

Hell yes, I wanted. "There's no rush," I said.

She laughed lightly, shaking her head and moving to sit across from me. "Did I do something? Something wrong?"

"God, no." A shuddering release was moving through me, as if the soft kiss we'd shared had broken a lock I'd kept on feelings I had no use for, feelings I'd ignored for years. I was enjoying it, and I leaned forward, dropping my elbows to my knees.

"But, I guess I just thought ..." She looked so confused, and

I realized that most men probably didn't stop at a kiss when they had Juliet Manchester in their arms.

I knew I had no claims on her, but if I had a chance with Juliet, I didn't want to be like most men. "You thought right," I said. "I'd take you to bed in a heartbeat. God, I want to," I nearly growled the last part. Just thinking about it had me harder than steel. "But this is new. And this situation isn't exactly your run-of-the-mill Tinder or Mr. Match hookup. We can take it slow. See if it's what we really want."

Her eyes held mine, and I couldn't decipher what I saw moving in those sparkling depths. But she sat back into the chair opposite me, relaxing. "I'd like that," she said. "A lot."

CHAPTER SEVEN
JULIET

J ace kissed me.

And then he let me go.

I watched, my limbs shaky and my mind a tumult, as he moved to sit in one of the armchairs. I sank into the other as I realized something: I was in real trouble.

If Jace didn't want me for sex—or if that wasn't the bulk of it, at least—then this was potentially something more real than I'd experienced before. Even with Zac, who'd wasted no time taking me to bed as soon as he'd had a chance.

When the first sting of perceived rejection wore off, something else took its place. Something that felt a lot like security and peace of mind. Maybe even something close to happiness. Jace didn't just see me as an object.

"So," I said, unsure how to press down the sizzle of nerves firing through me as a result of Jace's kiss.

He smiled, his white teeth revealed by those full perfect lips curling up, and his dark eyes gleamed beneath the dimmed lights overhead. "So," he repeated.

Every cell in my body was flinging itself against the next, my entire body like an electrified fence. But Jace looked calm and relaxed, and completely focused on me. I took a breath. "Tell me something I don't know about you."

The smile dimmed a bit, and Jace dropped my gaze. At first I thought he wouldn't answer, and I worried I'd read everything wrong, but then he leaned forward and said, "What would you like to know?"

I glanced around his room, looking for a clue to his inner life, to the parts of the strong tough bodyguard I hadn't seen yet. "Those books. I know you're taking classes. What are you studying?"

"I'm close to finishing my degree." He looked shy as he said this, and I wasn't sure I should press, but I wanted to know what he spent his spare time reading, what filled his mind.

"What will your degree be in?" I asked. "When do you have time for class?"

The broad smile returned. "Physics," he said. "And I study at night. My classes are online."

"You don't sleep?"

"Not a lot, actually. I never really have. It used to drive my mom nuts, but I really only need four or five hours a night. Leaves me a lot of time for other things." He winked at me lazily, and there was something about the way he was sitting in that chair, his long limbs kicked easily in front of him, his arms draped over the armrests, that gave me a sense of peace for some reason. And knowing he was awake, studying, while I slept just a couple doors down—that made me feel safe too, in a way that even having Zac right next to me never really had.

"That must be nice. I'd get so much more done if I didn't need to sleep."

"And I think the complete opposite. Sometimes I think it'd be nice just to conk out for ten or twelve hours, to not have to focus, not care all the time." A cloud washed through the dark eyes, but he blinked and it was gone. "Your turn. What did you study?"

I felt my face heat and the sizzling discomfort in my cells returned. People assumed I had a degree for whatever reason. But I hadn't gone that route. I'd left high school and come to Los Angeles. "I don't have a degree," I told him. "I was young and stupid. I probably should have gotten one, had something to fall back on in case things didn't work out with acting." I dropped his gaze. I couldn't have explained exactly why, but I wanted Jace to think highly of me, to think of me as more than just some actress. But the truth was, there wasn't much more to me than that. Zac had seen it clearly enough. Maybe once he'd gotten enough of my body, my mind hadn't been enough to keep him around.

"Seems like things worked out pretty well though," Jace said, his tone pulling my eyes back to his face, where the gentle smile waited.

"Depends on your perspective, I guess."

Jace looked around. "We're having this conversation in your Bel Air mansion. Your latest feature is playing in every theater in America, and your face is on half the magazines in the grocery store."

"Right?" I said, wishing all of that felt more like happiness. "I can't complain, really."

"If you'd gone to college instead, what would you have studied?"

"Probably theater." A laugh escaped me when I told him this. "I'm not the brains in the family. And acting's all I've really ever wanted to do. But if I had a degree, at least I could teach if things didn't work out."

He shifted his weight, one of his shoulders rising as he said, "You could still get one."

I thought about that. Putting aside the fact that I couldn't even go to the grocery store without being photographed and mobbed, I had no real idea what it would be like to go to school. But I liked the thought. "Maybe someday. Maybe I could do it online like you do."

"You definitely could," he agreed, and the sheer belief those words carried made me feel it was true.

We were quiet a minute, and as my mind worked through what we'd just said, I realized I was intruding on his studying time. I began to stand. "I should let you study. I'm sorry, I didn't even think about what you might need to be doing."

"Sit, Juliet." His tone was calm but commanding. "I'd let you know if I was under the gun. I'd much rather spend this time with you."

A little thrill shot up my spine like a tongue of fire.

"Tell me about your family. You grew up in Maryland?"

I smiled because thinking of home—of Gran and Tess—always made me smile. I didn't fit in there, but I loved that place in a way a person can only love their home. "I did."

Jace smiled back, listening.

"I think I told you once before that I was raised mostly by my Gran. My parents died in a car accident when I was pretty young. My sister Tess and I went to live with Gran from then on, so she's kind of like Mom and Dad all rolled into one."

"What's she like? How old is she?"

My heart lifted a little, thinking of Gran. "She's not like any grandmother you've ever met, that's for sure." I laughed. "She's ... unique."

His brows lowered as he thought about that. "How?"

"Well, she tells dirty jokes in polite company, wears these matched sweatsuits like Beyonce, and refuses to quit smoking pot."

Jace let out a bark of laughter.

"She plays online games pretty much all the time—my sister has to drag her off the computer. And she's turning ninety in a little while. I'm supposed to go, actually."

"To celebrate her birthday in Maryland?" Jace asked.

"Yeah, but I don't think I can." I thought about the sheer complication of taking the trip. The airport, the cameras, the problems I'd be bringing to my sister's doorstep. She and I had never been as close as I'd like, and I thought part of the reason was my fame and everything that came with it.

He frowned. "Why not?"

The lightness and joy I'd felt in thinking about Gran fizzed out as darker thoughts about reality, about Zac, came back. "I need to lay low and let this mess die down. Pay Zac off to keep him quiet, and hope some other celebrity does something ridiculous to distract everyone soon."

Jace shook his head. "You can't miss your Gran's ninetieth birthday." His tone was adamant. "Is there going to be a party?"

Tess had emailed me, talking about a tent and a band. "Yeah, my sister's putting it together." I'd sent her money and my excuses about why I probably wouldn't come.

"Good. Talk to your agent. You should go."

I shot him a teasing smile. "Since when does my body-guard tell me what to do?" I kept my tone playful and light. It was actually really nice having him here, interested in my life.

"Since I can see how much you want to be there. Your whole face changes when you talk about Gran."

I felt myself smile again. "I miss her. My sister too."

"What's your sister like? I can't believe there are two Manchester sisters running around. Men of America, look out." Jace chuckled.

I raised an eyebrow. "We're different. Tess was always a tomboy." I thought about her as a kid, all scraped knees and wild hair. "She runs a water adventure business out there now."

"Water adventure. What does that mean?"

"There's water everywhere in Southern Maryland—bays and inlets, streams and runs. She takes people kayaking, teaches stand-up paddle board, takes people canoeing, jet skiing."

"Fun." Jace grinned like he was imagining himself on a jetski.

"Meh." I'd never been big on getting in the water. I liked looking at it.

Jace laughed. "I wish I could meet her. Does Tess look like you? I can only imagine what a force the two of you must have been in school."

I shook my head, remembering. "Tess never cared much what she looked like. She was into things besides boys and makeup. We were kind of opposites."

"You're older?"

"Yeah."

"You ever think maybe it was hard to compete with you so she went a totally different way?" His tone was soft, like he didn't want to say anything that might hurt.

I thought about that for a minute. "Tess has always been her own person. I don't think she ever meant to compete at all." Had she? "I don't know. I remember a few situations where she got angry, where she said things about being in my shadow, being the second sister. But I'd always figured that was just sibling stuff. I was older. I got to do things first."

Jace leaned forward, his elbows resting on his knees, listening intently. "I get that. My brother used to say the same things. Especially when I joined the Marines. He said he couldn't compete with a hero."

"It would be hard." I tried not to think about Jace in uniform, about the photo, but the sexiest images of him in camo came flittering into my mind, warming my blood all over again.

"I was no hero," he said, almost bitterly. "I was just another enlisted grunt trying not to get killed."

I shivered at the thought of Jace being in combat. "I'm

glad you didn't get killed," I said softly. "So what did he do instead?" I asked, curious about this brother.

"Drugs, mostly." The words came out dark, final.

"Oh." That was definitely not what I'd been expecting, and I felt a little ashamed for prying. I didn't know what to say, and Jace was staring at his hands now. "I didn't mean to pry. you can tell me to stop if you don't want to talk about it."

Jace shook his head.

"So is he ..." Is he what? I shouldn't make him continue talking about something that was clearly unhappy.

Jace sagged against the back of the chair. "He's no better. I was over there today, actually. With my mom. He hasn't been home in a while. That's not usually good news."

"Oh, Jace. I'm sorry." I thought for a minute. Maybe I could hire an investigator or something. "Should we try to find him? I could help." I couldn't really help. But I could pay for help.

Jace tilted his head to the side and squinted at me. "That's nice of you. But no." He sighed, stretching his arms over his head, and then standing up again.

I took that as a signal to leave, though I didn't want to go back to my quiet room, my night punctuated only by Elvis's snoring. I didn't want to be alone. I got to my feet slowly, and stood still, unsure what to do. "I guess I ..." I looked around. Darkness pressed thick against the windows and I knew it was very late. "I should ..." I trailed off again, turning to move toward the door.

Jace caught my hand, tugged me toward him. My feet followed gladly, and a second later I was pressed against his chest again, in the circle of those huge arms. "Get some sleep, pretty girl," he said. And then he leaned down and caught my lips with his, kissing me long and slow and soft. My body turned to flame, and then to liquid, as the kiss worked its way through me.

I didn't want to leave, but when Jace released me and then opened the door to his room, I knew it was time to go. I was just afraid I'd wake up in the morning to find this was all a dream.

CHAPTER EIGHT
JACE

We spent another week in the same rhythm, getting to know one another in the evenings, playing games, kissing sometimes. Things were moving slowly and we were both tentative, careful. But it felt good and I was in no rush. This one part of my life felt good and right—while the other parts, namely my family, were less right.

Juliet had been between movies for a while, so her days were spent mostly at the house, reading scripts for potential projects and fielding calls from her agent. That meant I had a lot of time to relax and study.

At least until Zac showed up again.

I was just coming downstairs, having showered after our Monday run, when there was a racket at the side door. I could hear Chad outside, in heated conversation with another male voice as the doorknob rattled.

I crossed the room and peeked out the window, surprised to see Zac standing on the step, red-faced and yelling at Chad.

Zac wasn't a big man, and I knew between Chad and I, we could subdue him easily if needed. What I didn't know was whether Zac had a weapon. I checked the blade I always wore to ensure it was strapped to my hip.

"What's going on?" I asked, pulling the door open.

"That bitch changed the locks on my house?" Zac screamed, turning to face me.

Zac had been gone for the last month, since the day Juliet had found him eating the personal chef's personal goods on the kitchen counter. The locks had been changed the next day at my direction.

I looked down at the man in front of me, trying not to think about the closeness he'd shared with Juliet at one time. I kept my tone professional. "No, Mr. Stevens. I changed the locks. The security company felt it was in our client's best interest."

"It's my house, you stupid piece of—"

"Ms. Manchester's name is on the deed." There was really no arguing this point, so watching this cretin get red-faced and angry was more entertaining than threatening. He wasn't reaching for anything in pockets or at his waist, so I was pretty sure he was armed only with his charming personality.

"Whatever. This is my house. Let me in."

Part of me thought Zac might be working himself into a heart attack, his face was so red. But at this point, my only obligation was to Juliet. Of course there'd be paperwork if he keeled over outside her house, so it was better to just keep things calm. "No sir," I told him. "As I'm sure Chad informed you, you're on our list of restricted visitors. I'll let Ms.

Manchester know you're here, and she can decide if she'd like to see you. Chad," I said, looking over Zac's furious head. "Does Mr. Stevens have an appointment?"

Chad made a show of looking over the clipboard he held again. "No, Jace, he does not." Chad grinned, unable to hide the fact he enjoyed having the upper hand now and then.

"Wait here please," I told Zac, closing the door in his face. His eyes bulged on the other side of the glass.

I turned to find Juliet hovering in the butler's pantry between the kitchen and the dining rooms. "Zac is here?" she said, her soft eyes wide and frightened.

My heart softened immediately, seeing her looking scared. I wanted to hold her, but of course I couldn't. "He would like to see you."

Her eyes became even wider, if that was possible, and they searched my face. "Why?"

I didn't want to let the guy in, but technically they were married. I probably owed it to Juliet to let her try to repair things with him if she wanted to. God, I hoped she didn't want to. I sighed. "Not sure. I guess you can let him tell you."

"I'm not taking him back, obviously. My lawyer's already working on the divorce papers." She sighed. "I mean, he's trying to blackmail me. Why would he show up here?"

I thought about that. No man in his right mind would leave Juliet. Maybe he realized what he'd lost. That idea only made me want to run him off the property even more. "If you want to talk to him, find out, I'll be right here."

Her eyes squeezed shut and her shoulders sagged, and if Chad and Zac hadn't been just a few feet away, I would have caught her in my arms and held her right then, she looked so vulnerable and sad.

"I can just send him away."

She shook her head. "No. I should be strong. Talk to him if I have to." Her big eyes found mine again as her hand pressed against my chest, sending warmth flooding me. "But you stay with me."

"Of course," I said. "I'll bring him in, okay?"

"We'll do it in the dining room." She turned and I watched her sit at the head of the table. I was glad she'd put herself there—it signaled that she was in charge. Elvis took that moment to totter into the room and jump into her lap. Despite the silly dog's affliction, he had a good radar for when Juliet needed support, and that made me love him. Even if he was kind of a mess. Elvis made a snarfing sound as if to signal that he too, was ready.

I escorted a sputtering Zac from the kitchen door and then stood at one end of the dining room with my arms crossed as he sat to Juliet's side. "Aren't you going to call off your fucking gorilla?" He shot a look my way.

"That's Jace. And he stays. I can trust him." She said this in a way that made it clear she saw a difference between people she couldn't trust and me.

"I see that silly excuse for a dog hasn't died yet." Zac glared at Elvis, tucked into Juliet's arms, and I swear the dog grinned at him.

Good boy, Elvis.

"What do you want, Zac? You're already suing me, making accusations, threatening me. My lawyer would tell me even letting you in was a mistake." Juliet sounded exhausted and my fingers itched to touch her, to soothe her.

"Can't we just talk, sweetheart?" He reached toward her and Juliet stiffened. I dropped my arms, took a step closer, and Zac let out a frustrated huff and leaned back in his chair. "Fine. We can do this your way."

Juliet waited, saying nothing.

"Is this the guy?" He threw a thumb my way. "Is this the guy you've been fucking?" It took every ounce of restraint I had not to dive at him, tackle him to the ground and pound those words back into his mouth.

Juliet's face went slack. "Excuse me?"

"While we were married? I should have known."

I realized he was just grasping at straws. For a minute I worried Juliet was about to cave, to sigh in defeat and walk away, but pride and a quiet respect flooded me when her shoulders stiffened and her eyes turned hard. "I find you face down in my personal chef and you have the nerve to come back here and accuse me of cheating? You have the nerve to ask if I was fucking my bodyguard while we were married, while you were busily sticking your dick in everything that moved? And you have the nerve to try to blackmail me for my money? My estate?"

Zac didn't even flinch. "This was joint property while we were together. Everything you earned while we were married is fair game."

"Listen to yourself," she said, her voice practically a hiss. "You're a snake."

"It was no picnic, being married to you," he said, clearly

trying to make her feel sorry for him. "You were never home, always on location, with movie stars like that last guy, that Ryan whatever. I was supposed to believe you weren't fucking them while you were away for months at a time? Leaving me here with this bag of narcoleptic slobber?" He jerked a thumb at Elvis, who made a snarfling noise in response.

Juliet passed a hand over her face, as if this conversation was testing her last nerve. "Zac," she said quietly. "I didn't have sex with any of my co-stars. And I didn't have sex with Jace or any of my other security. In fact, I didn't have sex with anyone except you. Because we. Were. Married." She stared at him pointedly for a minute. "It was a vow I made. A promise. And I honored it."

"But now?" Zac seethed, glancing my way again. I clenched my jaw.

"What I do now is none of your business."

"Unless you're just continuing an affair that's been going on for years." Zac stood. "My lawyer thinks we have a good shot."

"At what, Zac? At ruining my life? At taking money and things that don't belong to you? Things that you didn't earn?"

"Putting up with your bullshit was work, sweetheart, believe me. I earned whatever I get out of this."

"'This was supposed to be a marriage," Juliet said quietly. "I see now it never was. Get out of my house." Pride and relief torpedoed through me.

"That's my cue," I told Zac, stepping closer.

"I can see myself out," he said, turning to move toward the front door. I could only imagine what he planned to do as he made his way through the house. He was probably going to grab a lamp or a painting as he passed through the entry way. "The way you came in," I instructed, moving to block his path.

"Brainless asshole," he said, glaring up at me. I was at least three inches taller than him and easily had fifty pounds of muscle on the guy. I almost wanted him to challenge me, but if I touched him, I'd likely be looking for another job. The firm didn't smile on killing former clients. Even if they were jerkwads.

I walked inches behind Zac as he made his way back to the kitchen door, where Chad waited. "Mr. Stevens is done here."

Chad grinned at him. "I trust you had a nice visit, sir?"

"You assholes," Zac said, and then he hustled down the driveway and back to his overpriced sports car, no doubt paid for by Juliet Manchester dollars.

"I love this job," Chad chuckled as I thanked him and went back inside.

Juliet was still sitting at the table, but her hands were shaking in front of her now. Elvis was asleep in her lap. I hated seeing her so shaken, hated that Zac had that power over her.

"You okay?" I asked.

Without a word, she placed Elvis on the floor, stood, crossed the room, and stepped into my chest. My arms went around her and I held her to me, comforting her, and taking too much comfort myself from having her there.

CHAPTER NINE
JULIET

"A sex tape right now will ruin you," Clarissa, my agent, said on the phone. "As will any entanglement that seems less than ... well, seemly."

"I need a seemly entanglement," I echoed.

"Or no entanglements at all," she mused, sounding thoughtful. "Though a fresh new relationship, one that has begun on the heels of your divorce—definitely not before—that could be a good thing."

Did I tell her? Could I mention Jace? My heart lifted. I cleared my throat. "There actually might be someone," I said, testing the waters. I had a feeling she wouldn't like it. I could already see how dating my bodyguard would play in the tabloids. So far this month I'd had a drug problem, thanks to a photo at the grocery store where I had on oversized sunglasses and a messy bun that was just a little too messy. And I'd also had a nervous breakdown. That photo had been shot in my driveway by a drone, I suspected. I was standing next to my car, my face leaning onto my arm. I remembered that day. It was just a couple days after I'd caught Zac. I had been crying.

"I have an idea," she said, and my heart sank. She'd ignored my words. Because it didn't matter if there was someone. She would tell me what needed to happen next. She would help me construct the façade I'd wear to keep the wolves at bay. She'd tell me how to act, who to be. Just as she had since my first movie had made me a star. "You and Ryan McDonnell had fantastic chemistry on screen."

Ryan was a nice guy—a good person. I'd filmed with him months ago, but the movie had just come out. We'd been photographed together at the premiere, arm in arm, and there had been several articles about the pairing on screen. Fans liked it. "Ryan?" I said thoughtfully.

"It's perfect. A movie star match will be just the thing to distract people from their belief that this divorce is shaking you to pieces. We can't really afford any more stories about you heading for rehab or breaking down. Your image is fragile, Jules. You're America's sweetheart, which is great, but it's not surprising they don't think you're tough enough to survive this nasty divorce. A sex scandal right now would destroy you. We'd have to rebuild from nothing. America's sweetheart doesn't make sex tapes."

I sighed. America knew very little about what its sweetheart did or didn't do. America didn't seem to care. "Clarissa, I don't know about Ryan. What if there was something real? Someone real?"

"If you haven't starred with him recently, I'm less interested. And this guy needs to be squeaky clean. Word on the street is that Ryan served in the Peace Corps, which is perfect. Like the military except you get all the service without all the killing and camo."

"So military service is bad?" I pictured Jace in his Marine Corps photo, looking hot and slightly deadly.

"It's not what people want for you, that's all I'm saying. Who is this guy?"

Jace's face flashed to mind as I sat in my bedroom, staring out at the branches of the old Oak that shaded my second-floor window. I saw the bronze skin, the sculpted lips, all the dark lashes fanning over his eyes.

"He's no one," I said. If I told her about Jace, he'd be thrust into a spotlight, even if she shot down the idea of us dating. She'd have him vetted—not the way he already had been, with a background check. She'd vet him for skeletons, past indiscretions, anything that could tarnish my reputation. And what Jace had already told me about his brother suggested it wouldn't go well. Besides, since Jace worked for Zac and me when we were together, it was a short leap to the conclusion that whatever lay between us might have started before the marriage ended. "Never mind."

"I'm calling Ryan's agent," Clarissa said. "You need to be seen together, as soon as possible."

"Why would Ryan agree to this?" I asked, thinking of the jovial guy I'd met on set. Ryan McDonnell seemed like a great guy. But he wasn't my type. Too pretty. Too ... movie star.

"Being linked to you could skyrocket his sagging career. And maybe we could throw him a bone—didn't Coppola give you carte blanche to choose your costar for the film you're doing next year?"

She had, and I'd relished the chance to actually choose something for myself, to make a decision for a change. Clarissa knew she had, I didn't even need to answer.

"So it's perfect. You can offer the role to Ryan if he's willing to spend some time playing love interest right now." She paused, and I could hear her tapping keys, clearly making notes about everything she'd just decided. About my life. "Plan a weekend away or something, a way for you and Ryan to be spotted."

"I don't want to go away," I said. "If I go anywhere, I have to attend my grandmother's ninetieth birthday party in a week, and I was going to skip that. I'd hoped to lay low."

"Low is the opposite of what I need from you right now. Where is your grandmother?"

"Maryland." Dread bubbled in my stomach.

"Not exactly a hot spot for paparazzi. What part? Beltway?"

"Kind of," I said. Gran lived nowhere near the beltway, but Clarissa's dictatorial tone was irritating. I felt like a petulant child, since that was how she was treating me.

"Okay, fair enough. No private jets. Go commercial. Be seen."

I rolled my eyes. This was going to be beyond painful. The cameras, the fans. And it was exactly what Clarissa wanted. "Okay."

"I'll have Ryan call you today to set things up."

"Okay." My heart sank. In the past week, I'd lived in a

quiet bubble with Jace, our evenings spent getting to know each other bit by bit, the potential and promise of something glimmering just outside our easy togetherness. It was slow and careful, the opposite of everything else my life had been.

"Stand by," Clarissa said. "We'll get through this Jules," she added. As if any of this was about her.

"Yep."

She ended the call and I sat, staring out the window into a world that I wasn't allowed to navigate on my own. This house was a cage I'd built with fame and money, and my life felt like a role I'd been playing for too long. And it was about to get even more false.

CHAPTER TEN
JACE

The day Zac visited us, Juliet stayed upstairs for most of the rest of the afternoon, and I worried about where her mind might be. We'd run together that morning, but there was little else for me to do. I could hear her on the phone at various points, and recognized the sounds of her workout app and then the shower that followed.

I didn't want to be hyperaware of everything she did. I told myself it was my job—it was, after all. But it was also more than that. Since getting to know her a bit, since kissing her, holding her in my arms, it was as if our cells had aligned. I was so much more aware of her than I had been before. And it was almost physically painful to be apart from her. And though I thought about going to talk to her, the employer relationship we still shared made things more complicated than they would have otherwise been. I was at work. She was my client. It would be inappropriate to interfere.

I'd passed the day studying in the kitchen, taking breaks here and there to try my brother and check in with my mom.

Jarred was still MIA, which meant soon I'd need to go looking for him. I was afraid of what I would find.

By the time evening fell, I was beginning to wonder if Juliet had sneaked out somehow. She hadn't appeared for lunch, hadn't come down for dinner. But just as I was going to give into my concern and head up to check on her, Chad radioed from the front gate to let me know we had company.

"Movie star douchebag alert," his voice crackled from the walkie beside me on the table where I was closing up my books. The last visitor we'd had made Juliet disappear all day. I wasn't eager for another.

"Keep it down, moron," I said. Chad never stopped to consider that movie star douchebags were why he had a job. A damned good one. And he had no way of knowing if Juliet was nearby when he said things like that. "What's up?"

"Incoming. Ryan McDonnell to meet with Juliet."

I felt my concern tick up a notch. I had a schedule of Juliet's meetings, and today had been blessedly blank. Something was up. "Got it. Come in with him, okay? He's not on the schedule. I need to go up to talk to Juliet. Is he on your schedule?" I thought maybe I'd just missed it somehow, though the day Chad was more on top of things than me was the day I'd have to quit.

"Negative."

A moment later, Chad escorted a man through the front door and into the formal living room just to one side of the door. I'd seen the guy before, plenty of times. He was a B-list Hollywood action star. I knew he'd been in a few things, nothing huge. And I was pretty sure his association with *Charade of Stones* would haunt him forever. Even though his character had a decent ending in that long-running series, fans were pissed about the way the whole thing had wrapped up, and there'd been plenty of backlash. And flying monkeys, for god's sake.

The guy was good looking, I supposed. He declined a chair, stood by the hearth instead, examining the photos Juliet had there. I'd looked at them plenty of times—nothing that told you anything about her life, really. One photo of the woman I now knew was Gran, but other than that, it was all glad-handing with other stars. Probably pretty interesting for a guy like McDonnell.

I took the stairs quietly and knocked on Juliet's door. "Juliet?"

The door opened and Juliet stood on the other side, stealing my breath. Her hair was piled on top of her head, and she wore a light pink sweatshirt that fell off one shoulder, revealing skin that looked smoother and softer than rose petals. I swallowed hard. "You have a guest downstairs. Mr. Ryan McDonnell."

She didn't say anything for a long moment, just looked up at me, like she was deciding something. She held my eyes and my heartbeat thudded into a rapid-fire rhythm. Something was up. Before I could figure out quite what, she stepped close to me, one hand reaching for my face. She cupped my cheek, and lifted up on her toes. My body instinctually followed where she led, and a heartbeat later my arms were around her, my mouth on hers. Her tongue pressed past my lips, sweeping my own, sending a signal of pressing desire through every cell in my body.

And then, as quickly as it began, it was over. She stepped back, wiped her mouth with the back of her hand and adjusted her top. I let my hand linger on her shoulder, rubbing a finger over that soft smooth shoulder. I'd been right —that skin was like heaven.

"I have to do something," Juliet said. "If Ryan agrees."

Was she signing on for a film? Telling me we were going on location? "All right."

"I don't like it. I don't think you will either."

That wasn't good. Worry sprouted roots in my gut. "Okay."

"But it's just a strategy. It doesn't mean anything, okay?"

Her blue eyes stayed fixed on me, waiting for a response. But I didn't know what to say because for one thing, all my thinking at that moment was occurring in the wrong head. For another thing, the woman was not making sense. "Gonna need more than that," I told her, unease working through every vein in my body.

She laughed, her posture relaxing a bit. "You'll figure it out. Basically I have to pretend to be in a relationship with Ryan for a while. To distract the media."

A vague hazy red haloed my vision as my mind threw images at me of what "pretending" to be in a relationship would look like. "What?" The word was more of a growl.

She put her hand on my chest again. God, I loved it when she did that. "Jace, it's not real. Just remember that, okay? It's just for the press. And only for a little while."

The fact she felt she had to justify it to me should have

made me feel good. It confirmed that I wasn't losing my mind. Although, that kiss a second ago confirmed it too. There was something here. Wrong side of the tracks or not, there was something here. I just needed to figure out if I was willing to risk my job over it. I kind of already knew the answer.

"Okay," I managed, forcing myself to remember there was something between us, something real. I took deep breaths, in and out.

"And we have to go to Maryland. Next weekend. Okay?"

"We, you and him?" I hated this idea, the thought of her out of my sight. There was no way she'd be going anywhere without security.

"We, all of us. There's a party and my agent has set up a magazine feature." She said this slowly, like she was asking my forgiveness as she did it.

"Fine." A mass of anger and jealousy twisting inside me was making it hard for me to speak. And movie star McDonnell was waiting. "Your guest," I reminded her.

"Right. We'll talk later, okay?" She smiled weakly at me and then went downstairs, Elvis trotting at her side and shooting me a glance over his little doggy shoulder as if to say, "you coming?"

I followed.

CHAPTER ELEVEN
JULIET

Ryan McDonnell stood, shifting his weight back and forth and stretching out his arms as if trying to work out a kink, in the middle of my formal living room. I swallowed hard, hating what I was about to ask Ryan, hating what I knew it would do to Jace and me. Chad stood in the doorway, watching him with interest.

I nodded at Chad, who winked at me and then turned, returning to his post outside, I assumed. I heard Jace come down the stairs behind me, and knew he would stay nearby. Jace was like my security blanket. My hot, muscular, sweet security blanket.

"Hello again, Ryan," I said, greeting my former co-star with a hug as he kissed my cheek.

"Juliet, good to see you," he said. "You have a beautiful home."

"Thanks very much," I said, refraining from adding the part about how Zac would like to take it from me. "Can I get you a drink or something to eat?"

He shook his head. "Nah, that's fine. My agent said there was some kind of deal to discuss? Oh hey, who's this?" He bent down to offer a hand to Elvis, who snuggled the offered hand and then promptly sank to the floor on Ryan's foot, asleep.

"Uh, that's Elvis. He has a bit of a sleep issue."

Ryan stood and smiled a little uncomfortably as he carefully slid his foot out from under Elvis's fat little snoring body. Jace stepped into the room, lifted Elvis gently and carried him to the corner to deposit him in his electric blue satin dog bed.

"A sleep issue, huh?"

"Narcolepsy. Doesn't hurt him as long as he doesn't fall asleep in his water dish."

"Aha." Ryan's mouth formed a half smile, and I knew he was picturing this. Poor Elvis.

"Anyway, yes, the deal. Thanks for coming." A little lump formed in my throat. I'd hoped maybe this could all be worked out at the agent level, but it seemed I'd have to lay out the ridiculous plan myself. "Yeah, there's something I'd like to ask you. Will you sit?"

Ryan sat on the couch, and I took the wing chair across the coffee table, perching myself on the edge and crossing my ankles. How did you ask someone to pretend to be your boyfriend?

God, my life was weird.

"So," Ryan said, his dark eyes full of concern as his brows came together. He leaned forward, resting his forearms on his thighs.

"So," I echoed.

Talk, Juliet.

"So here's the thing." I laid out the blackmail plot Zac was involved in, the painful settlement he was demanding, and the potential media fallout. I made sure to be clear that while it would certainly affect my career, it could blow back on some of my former co-stars too, especially Ryan, since we'd been romantically linked in a few articles. Purely speculation, but still, I thought it might motivate him to agree.

"That's awful," he said. "I'm sorry you're dealing with all that. What can I do to help?"

I wrung my hands in my lap and then forced myself to take a breath and pretend to be relaxed and nonchalant about this whole thing. "Well, my agent has had an idea. One that could help us both."

"Okay." Ryan looked uncertain, and I didn't blame him. This was all so weird.

It was now or never. I dove in. "We wondered if you might be willing to play a little role. Be my boyfriend for a weekend event, just for the press. We'd let ourselves be photographed together, stir up media speculation over the relationship, and capitalize on the chemistry we had onset. Hollywood loves that sort of thing, and my agent thinks that a juicy new love story will overwhelm whatever scandal Zac can stir up in the background."

Ryan pursed his lips, his lids dropping over the thoughtful eyes for a moment. "And that's good for me because ..."

I worried I was offending him, but forged ahead. "Sorry,

right. Well, my agent is pretty sure she can get the director of my next film to cast you as the male lead."

"So you're bribing me with a role? Because you feel sorry for me after that Antarctica disaster?" He grinned as he asked this, letting me know he wasn't offended. His last movie, some kind of pirate zombie thing in Antarctica, had been awful.

"Would it work if I was?" I tilted my head, put a little flirt in my voice. I needed him to say yes, even if him saying no would be a relief in some ways.

"It might. Honestly, between that and *Charade of Stones*, man ..." he trailed off, rubbing a hand over his jaw.

"I know it's not the easiest thing to agree to. Not ... normal. But I guess Hollywood isn't really a normal people kind of place, right?"

He laughed. "Definitely not."

"Oh, and there's one more part. The event. I have to go home to Singletree, Maryland next weekend for my Gran's ninetieth birthday party. Clarissa has set up a magazine inter-view to happen out there—a 'Juliet's roots' kind of thing. Would you be able to go as my date?"

Jace coughed from the doorway, and my heart twisted a little bit inside me. I glanced to where he stood, but could only see his shoulder in the shadowed dining room. I wanted to be with him, not in the middle of the Juliet Manchester telenovela that was my ridiculous life.

"So I pretend to be falling for America's favorite actress for a while, take an all-expenses paid trip to Maryland next weekend, and get a great role in a movie?" Ryan's uncertain smile cranked up to a grin.

"Not sure about the 'favorite' part, but the rest sounds right." A thought occurred to me as I glanced at Jace again. "Do you have a girlfriend, Ryan? Someone who might be hurt by this pretense?"

He laughed and shook his head. "Nope. I'm free and clear in that department."

For a brief second, I'd thought maybe we could still get out of this stupid plan, but it seemed we were diving in head-first. "Oh, okay." I felt awkward suddenly, waiting for him to decide.

"I guess we'll let our agents work out the details?" he said. "I'm sure there'll be something to sign?"

I sat up straighter. "So you'll do it?" Something like relief rippled through me.

He nodded, getting to his feet. "I'm happy to help, Juliet. And I guess it's helping me too. It's a win-win, right?"

I wasn't so sure. Jace's dark eyes flickered through my mind. "Yeah, I think so. I hope so."

"Then I'm in." Ryan hugged me lightly, kissing my cheek again. "See you soon, okay?"

"Yeah. And thank you." I opened the door for him, and watched as he walked down the front path, confident and strong. Ryan McDonnell was a good guy. It would be easier if I really did want to date him, but I didn't find the spark of interest inside myself that burst into flames whenever Jace was nearby. There was no use fighting it. I wanted my bodyguard. And I decided right then that tonight, before this insanity kicked up a notch, I was going to have him.

CHAPTER TWELVE

JACE

I could feel myself clenching as I listened to Juliet and Ryan talk. He was so agreeable, so easy to get along with. And the guy was handsome, too. Of course he was willing to play the part of Juliet's boyfriend. Hell, she could ask any red-blooded human male on the planet and he'd say yes.

I'd say yes.

Only, I hadn't been asked. And I wouldn't be.

Instead, I'd stand by and watch while another guy—another lucky clueless guy who'd had every opportunity gift-wrapped for him, including this one—got to touch the woman I wanted for myself.

But this was what I'd signed up for.

My jaw was aching by the time I heard the front door click shut again, and I knew I'd been grinding my teeth. A shitty habit, but it was better than destroying things, and right now I wanted to tornado through this fancy dining room and rip the place apart.

I heard Juliet come back into the living room and forced

myself to release, to take a deep breath. I wondered what might happen now. Would we talk about this? Was there anything to talk about? All I could imagine was pulling her into me again, holding her close and assuring myself I hadn't imagined what I'd felt with her, hadn't imagined that just maybe something could happen between us.

"Jace?" her voice came through the quiet room. "I'm going to head up for bed."

Disappointment washed through me unexpectedly. What had I thought was going to happen? She needed to focus on planning out her fake relationship. I needed to get a grip. "Okay," I managed, wishing I were a better actor.

"I'll take Elvis up. Maybe you can go ahead and shut down the house, and then you'll be off the clock, right?"

"Sure," I answered, beginning the process of checking the perimeter as I did each night. I radioed Chad to let him know I was shutting down inside. He'd keep watch until the overnight shift replaced him out front and then he'd be off the clock too, out in the guesthouse.

I walked through the enormous first floor of the house, checking windows and switching off lights, forcing myself to calm down, to breathe. By the time I'd set the alarm and begun climbing the stairs, I'd just about talked myself into a state of rationality.

But when I opened the door to my room, any semblance of calm I'd achieved washed away as my heart rate skyrocketed and my vision tunneled.

Juliet was there, on my bed.

Soft candles glowed on surfaces around the room, and

music played from a bluetooth speaker on the table, something soft and low. Norah Jones, maybe? I didn't spend much time trying to figure out what I was hearing because my body was too busy reacting to what I was seeing.

My beautiful blond client was leaned up against the headboard of my bed. She wore a red silk nightshirt with long sleeves and little white buttons down the front. It ended just at the tops of her thighs, and her long slim legs were out in front of her. She was smiling at me—uncertainly. Shyly. Like she wasn't sure if this was okay, like there was a chance I might tell her to leave.

"Hi," I managed, as every cell in my body flared and pulsed. She was perfect, laid out for me like an offering on my bed. But, I told myself, she was still a client.

No matter what had happened before, we still hadn't slept together. I could argue that I hadn't really crossed a line. Taking a step closer now could change everything.

"Hi," she said, her voice a soft breath that moved hot into my mind and then exploded there, sending shards of fire through me. "Is this okay?"

At a complete loss for words, I blew out a long breath. "Yeah."

"Then maybe you could come a little bit closer?"

I blinked hard, just to make sure I wasn't hallucinating. Maybe I was just dreaming this, while in reality I was downstairs destroying the dining room in a fit of jealous rage? Juliet moved on the mattress, and the squeak of the bed assured me this was real.

I toed off my shoes and closed the door, twisting the lock.

Then I turned back to her and took a deep breath, finally crossing the room to stand next to the bed.

Juliet looked up at me, and I was nearly leveled by what I saw in her eyes. Hope and a little fear, maybe. As if this famous movie star was every bit as nervous about what might happen here as I was. I pulled my T-shirt off over my head and sank to the edge of the bed. She reached for me, and I scooted closer, pulling her into my lap as our mouths connected.

There was no uncertainty in the kiss, and all the restraint we'd both practiced in the past fell away as quickly as Juliet's red nightshirt and the belt around my waist. We kissed and caressed and undressed, and a few minutes later, I held her in my arms, every inch of her perfect form pressed up against me, my rigid cock between us against the soft flesh of her belly.

I should have been more careful, should have been thinking about my job, my family. But all I could think about was that I was really here, every part of my body pressed against Juliet's soft yielding skin. There was no turning back now.

We didn't speak, but we did hold ourselves there for a long moment, each of us lost in our thoughts, or in each other, as our chests moved in unison, breathing in the heady anticipation of what was surely to come next.

Juliet's hands skimmed my back and sides, her cool fingers coming to rest just above the throbbing heat between us, teasing my stomach.

"Can I ...?"

I grunted some answer that I hoped was a yes, barely able to speak because my mind was so far gone. Just holding this woman, just feeling her next to me, against me, had me feeling like I was flying. And when her fingers wrapped around my cock, I could have died a happy man right there.

But it got better. She began to stroke me, lightly at first, and then with more confidence, gripping my shaft hard and kissing me in time to the motion.

My own hands found her perfect ass and pulled her closer, my fingers working their way toward the wet heat I could feel coming from her.

"Is that okay?" she asked, her words swallowed by my complete focus on her hands, her fingers, my desire to make her feel every bit as good.

"God yes, that's perfect," I said. But I couldn't reach her in the position we were in, so I pressed her to her back, losing the delicious tension on my cock for what felt like an eternity until her hand made its way back, enveloping me in warmth again.

I cupped her, letting her heat seep into my palm and then beginning a slow steady rub with three fingers, feeling the little bead beneath her skin as I kissed her softly.

She moaned beneath me, her own hand losing some grip as I let my fingers explore, testing her wetness and then moving deeper between her folds.

As she began to pulse her hips, pressing up into me, I slid a finger into her and took a moment to appreciate that this was actually happening. Warm happiness filled my chest. I took a deep breath, and then added a second finger, loving the way Juliet sighed beneath me.

I'd just begun to fuck her with my fingers, in rhythm to her strokes of my shaft, when a faint buzzing noise joined the buzz in my head.

"Is that ...?" her voice was breathy, low.

"My phone," I confirmed. I was going to ignore it, and began the steady rhythm again, Juliet immediately relaxing into me again and her hand gripping tighter. I heard myself grunt in pleasure.

But my phone didn't stop. As soon as it quit ringing, it would begin again, and finally, with a frustrated groan, I rolled over and reached for my pants, in a heap on the floor.

I picked up the phone, intending to turn it off and throw it back to the floor, my cock and Juliet's wet heat driving me back to the moment before. But when I saw my mother's name on the screen, I knew I had to answer.

"Mom?" This couldn't be good.

CHAPTER THIRTEEN
JULIET

My entire body was a fiery line when Jace rolled away from me to answer his phone. I was thrumming in a way I never had with Zac, a way I didn't think I ever had before, and I was more than eager to find out what would happen if I gave myself completely to Jace, if I gave into the overwhelming desire I felt to have him, to be owned by him. I wanted to feel him inside me, to feel the security I experienced with him wash through me, push away all the uncertainties in my life.

But the phone wouldn't stop ringing.

And when Jace answered, "Mom?" I knew our night had ended.

His face telegraphed his concern immediately, his eyes going wide as his big hand clenched around the phone.

I watched him, pulling myself up to sitting and pulling my nightshirt over me from where it had been dropped at the head of the bed.

Jace was listening, nodding along to whatever his mother

was saying. "I'll be right there," he told her, and my selfish heart sank.

A moment later, Jace was dressed and standing beside me. I'd put my nightshirt back on, blown out the candles and switched off the music, as Jace told me apologetically that he'd have to go. I felt like a fool, even though I knew that were it not for the phone call, things would have gone exactly as I wanted them to. Still, the cold harshness of real life had spilled into the quiet room where my fantasies were playing out, and in the light, they looked silly and gauche.

"Sorry," I began at the same moment that Jace said, "I'm sorry." I felt like I needed to apologize, but I didn't know why.

We laughed, each of us sounding nervous now. So strange, when a moment ago, we'd been touching each other in the most intimate way possible.

"Hey," Jace said, stepping near enough to me that I could feel the heat coming off his chest. His arms wrapped me and the insecurity lessened, dissolved. "I'm really sorry about this. My mom needs me, and I have to go."

"Your brother?" I asked, wishing there was something I could do to keep him with me, selfishly wishing Jace would just send Chad or one of the other guys from his security company.

"I'm not sure," he said. "Some men came to the house, scared my mom pretty bad."

My selfish thoughts disappeared as worry replaced the want inside me. "Go," I told him, realizing I was holding him up. "I'll be fine."

He took another long moment to look down into my face,

and then he leaned in and kissed me softly. "I'll be back," he said, and it felt like a promise that we'd continue what we'd started. I hoped so. I was in much too deep to just walk away. I wanted him. I wanted to know him. I wanted to continue feeling like he saw something in me that no one else had ever taken the time to see, something real.

Jace let me go and a moment later I heard the door in the kitchen. I looked around Jace's room, and then sighed, collecting my things and heading to my own cold empty room at the end of the hall. The timing was off, as always. Jace was my bodyguard, and I'd just made a deal with Ryan to pretend to be my boyfriend. A man like Jace deserved better than the complicated mess I could offer him.

I spent a long night in my room, not sleeping, just listening to Elvis snore and thinking about what a tangled disaster I'd made of everything. Maybe going home would be good. Seeing my sister and Gran might help me put things in perspective.

Maybe I should forget the way I felt about Jace, let him do his job and stop putting myself first.

* * *

IN THE SOFT diffuse light of morning, I felt worse than I had the night before. Jace hadn't returned, and Chad was in my kitchen when I finally dragged myself down for coffee.

"Morning, Ms. Manchester," he said, peering at me over the tabloid he was reading.

"Hi Chad," I said, trying not to sound hostile. I wasn't fond of the blond bodyguard. But then again, he wasn't Jace, so it was inevitable he'd fall down in the comparison. Chad just gave off a creepy vibe. "Jace isn't back?"

"Not yet," he said. "He called an hour ago, asked me to take his place today."

My heart dropped in my chest. Was his mother hurt? I wondered if I should call him, see if I could help. "So he'll be gone all day?"

Chad raised an eyebrow over the magazine, cocked his mouth into a half grin. "You sound pretty disappointed," he observed. "Anything I should know about what goes on in here when I'm sleeping outside?"

Yep. It wasn't the comparison, I just didn't like Chad. "Are you supposed to speak to clients that way?" I asked him, adopting an offended tone and crossing my arms.

The grin dimmed a bit and he shook his head slowly, as if he'd already answered his own question, and was judging me. "Of course not. Sorry."

"Chad?" I said. "I think I'm fine in here today. You can just be outside, okay? I'll call you if I need you."

The grin fell completely, and Chad dropped the magazine to the table. "Supposed to have one guy in the house," he said.

"Not today," I told him, my tone still icy. "I want to be alone."

"Uh, okay," he said. "I'll let the guys know. We'll get an extra guy on the doors then."

"That's fine." I watched while he stood and lumbered back out the side door, relief washing through me when he was gone.

The day crawled by as I tried to look at the pile of scripts my agent had messengered over, but my mind was at war with my heart and it made it hard to focus.

There were a million reasons why I shouldn't feel the way I did for Jace, not the least of which was to protect him. He didn't need to be dragged into my messy life, with vengeful exes and fake relationships, the press watching my every move. There was little chance we could keep any real relationship a secret, and Jace would surely lose his job if we were found out, since the firm he worked for made it clear that fraternization compromised security and had each of us sign an agreement.

There was also the little matter of Ryan, who was supposed to be my boyfriend now. If the press fell for the Ryan scenario, and it turned out I was dating Jace, there'd be another scandal, and would feed right into the story Zac was trying to sell—that I'd been unfaithful to him first. That I was just a whore, an easy slut.

It wouldn't be fair to anyone to continue letting my heart push me at Jace. I needed to cut that off before anything really happened. Anything else.

I was in the den watching television with a glass of wine when the security radio blared with Chad's voice.

"Miss Manchester? Jace is on his way in. Just didn't want you to be alarmed."

I picked up the radio, feeling slightly guilty about judging Chad earlier. Maybe he wasn't so bad. "Thanks," I said, pushing the button on the side to talk.

I went to the kitchen, where I knew Jace would come in,

and my heart lightened when Jace's familiar smile greeted me through the glass. But then I remembered what I'd decided today, and I pushed my heart back into place.

"Hey," I said, opening the door. "Did you lose your key?"

He looked tired and it took everything I had not to put my arms around him. "No, I just didn't want to scare you. Figured I'd announce my entrance. Chad said you've been alone in the house all day, so having someone suddenly appear might freak you out."

He was always thinking of me, of how to take care of me. All the more reason I needed to protect him now. "Thanks," I said.

"You okay?" He asked, those dark eyes watching me closely as I moved to the counter, refilled my wine glass and sighed.

"Yeah," I said. I couldn't look at him. I knew my resolve would shatter and I'd throw myself at him again. "Everything okay with your mom?"

He didn't answer and I risked a glance at him. The worry I saw written across his face was almost more than I could take.

"Jace?" I moved toward him, forgetting my resolve. He needed me.

He snapped back to himself, the easy smile crossing his lips again. "Yeah. I just ... I need to figure out how to get her moved. To a better neighborhood, somewhere safer."

"She's okay?" Every horrible scenario I'd ever heard about flitted through my mind.

"Just scared. Some guys came looking for my brother.

Broke into the house. Threatened Mom. I guess Jarred owes them money." Anger and sadness shot through his eyes, and my heart ached.

I held the wine glass out to him, and he shook his head lightly. "Can I help?"

He shook his head again.

"Have you found your brother?"

"Not yet," Jace said, and it was more like a sigh. "And if those guys find him first, I probably never will," he said.

I couldn't imagine how I'd feel if Tess was missing, in trouble. He must be terrified, but like always, he stood there strong and stoic. "What can I do?"

"Nothing, Juliet. This isn't your problem." His voice was tired, and his eyes were sad.

"I could pay an investigator, or—"

"No." Jace cut me off before I could even finish, his voice hard. "We're okay. We don't need charity."

That hurt a bit, I hadn't thought of it as charity. I wanted to help, but Jace was too proud to accept anything I could give him. I also wanted to wrap myself around him, to comfort him, to take comfort myself, but Jace looked tired. "I'm gonna do the perimeter check and then go to bed."

"Of course," I said, disappointment flooding me even though I'd just decided today that it would be for the best if we didn't get any more involved than we already were. I watched as Jace locked the kitchen door, and then moved into the dining room. I turned, heading back for the television. I knew I wouldn't sleep again, so I did my best to lose myself in *Younger,* my latest TV addiction.

Despite my resolve to stay uninvolved, an hour later I found myself with Jace's file and the telephone at my ear, giving Jace's mother's address to the man on the other end.

"Okay, Ms. Manchester. So we'll monitor the place, and I've got a couple other guys out looking for the brother."

"Thank you," I told Paul, the proprietor of the other security firm I'd been referred to when I'd hired the company Jace worked for. I couldn't call Austin, Jace's boss. So I did the only thing I could think of. "Call me if you find anything?"

"Will do. How long till they move, you think?"

I stared at the open laptop, at the picture of the little Brentwood cottage I'd bought last year as a getaway when I'd needed to escape Zac for a night. "I'm not sure. Soon, I think."

"All right. We'll be in touch."

"Thanks." I put the phone down and sighed. Maybe inserting myself wasn't the right thing to do, but I couldn't be to Jace what I wanted to be, couldn't have him be anything for me. So I could be a friend, I figured. My money could help ease the situation that had creased his face with worry and brought sadness into those dark kind eyes.

Maybe, if I knew everything was okay with him, I'd be able to keep myself away from him.

Maybe.

CHAPTER FOURTEEN
JACE

Seeing the fear in my mother's eyes had drained me, and hearing her refuse to use my money to get a hotel room, at least for the night, had possibly broken my heart. By the time I left the little house, having filed the police report, installed a new lock on the busted front door and reinforced the windows, Mom looked exhausted. I'd sent her to bed and waited up, watching the news at a low volume until I was sure she was all right. If Jarred did come back, he wouldn't have the new key. But I was beginning to lose hope he might come back at all, and anger was replacing worry. How could he do this to us?

I'd left Mom sleeping with all the lights on and a note telling her I'd see her tomorrow. I had offered to stay all night, but she'd insisted I go back to work.

When Juliet had answered her door, seeing her beautiful face had felt like a relief. It had felt like coming home. And that wasn't something I could let myself get used to. What-ever we had, whatever might be happening between me and

America's sweetheart—well, that had an expiration date. She had her own problems to attend to, and Ryan McDonnell was going to be the guy to help her do it. I was the paid help, and I needed to remember that.

She'd looked disappointed when I'd let her know I was heading to bed.

But I couldn't worry about that. Not now.

I WOKE to the sun streaming brightly through the windows of my room, and a madly buzzing phone.

The number wasn't one I knew, but with everything going on in my personal life I couldn't afford to screen calls. I answered, trying to sound awake. "Hello?"

"Jace Morgan?"

"Yeah. Who's this?"

"Captain Andrews. LAPD. You got a brother? Jarred?"

Relief and worry spiked through me, forcing me to my feet. "Yes sir." My military background kicked in. The guy on the other end of the phone was probably just a regular guy, but putting the title of "captain" before his name when he'd identified himself had me seeing captain's bars and getting ready to salute.

"We've got your brother in custody. He's not in good shape though. Can you come down to First Memorial Hospital today?"

"He's in custody at the hospital?" I asked, feeling like this guy probably thought I was a little slow. I'd expected to hear

Jarred was in jail. Not the hospital. Any anger I'd felt at my little brother dissolved.

"Yeah, he got beat up pretty good."

"I'm on my way," I told him. "Anything else?"

"Nah, just come down here. We'll fill you in."

I didn't know what to feel as I pulled on my jeans and grabbed a shirt from the back of the chair in the corner. I had no idea what I was going to find at the hospital, but I knew I couldn't call my mother until I knew how Jarred was.

I'd have to ask Chad to cover for me again today. I was shoving my wallet and phone into my pocket as I came out of my room and nearly ran Juliet right over. She was just passing my door, dressed in yoga pants and a tight tank top that distracted me from my worries momentarily. God, she looked good.

"Hey," she said, her voice soft and light. "Everything okay?" She must've read the worry on my face.

"I'm not sure, actually. They found my brother."

Her eyebrows lifted hopefully. "Oh?"

"He got beat up. He's in custody but he's at the hospital. I need to go."

"Of course. Go. Want me to come?" Her hand was on my arm, and we were both looking down at her slim fingers laid across my skin.

I thought about having Juliet with me. It would feel good to have her at my side. Having someone else in it with me would be nice. But if that someone was Juliet ... I could already see the photographers, the regular people turning to stare. "Probably not a great idea. Thanks though," I told her.

She let me go, sighing lightly. "Of course. Yeah." A cloud passed over her face before she managed to pull the smile back into place. "Take whatever time you need. Call me if you want," she said.

"Okay. Thanks." I turned, heading down the stairs ahead of her. It felt awkward to just walk away from her, like there should have been some more official goodbye. But what? A hug? A kiss? All the things I wanted were impossible where she was concerned. It was better this way.

AT THE HOSPITAL, I gave my brother's name and was directed up to the third floor. His room was easy enough to find, it was the one with the police guard sitting outside the door, a sight that made it clear exactly how much trouble my brother was in. I identified myself and the guy radioed someone, the captain, I guessed. I was directed to wait.

"Can I see my brother?" I asked.

"Captain said you see him first." The guard sat back down and pulled his magazine back in front of his face.

I tried to tell myself Jarred must be okay—stable at least, and settled into a chair to wait. It wasn't long before another cop appeared, this one tall and thin with an air of authority that told me he was in charge, and after chatting with the guard, he turned my way. "Jace?"

I stood. "Yes sir. Captain Andrews?"

He shook my hand. "You know much about what's going on with your brother?"

"Not a lot," I said. "Can I see him?"

"Just a minute." He waved back at the chairs. "Just want to make sure you know he's in a lick of trouble."

I hadn't heard anyone use the term "lick" that way since I'd been a little boy in the south. It plucked at the chord of sentimentality that had been strumming inside me since I'd been thinking about my little brother, about better days. I squinted at the captain, waited for him to continue. "Yes sir."

"Officers rolled up on him running last night. A few guys behind, chasing him with pipes, boards. We got a couple of the other guys—your brother basically collapsed in front of the cruiser. Guys must not have gotten a chance to search him before they started beating the shit out of him, because he was carrying a good amount of heroin."

"Shit." I squeezed my eyes shut. Jarred had been arrested once before for possession. But this was more serious.

"We gotta charge him with trafficking. That wasn't for personal use."

"What's that mean?" I asked. "Jail time?"

"Depends on the judge. If it's a first offense, could be lighter, but the minimum is gonna be at least five years."

Maybe that'd be long enough to get him straight. If he could survive in prison. Shit. This might kill my mother. I didn't have an answer to the cop's statement, so I just let the news sink in. "Can I see him?"

"Yeah."

"There gonna be bail?" Everything inside me cringed at the idea of having to scrape together what would surely be thousands of dollars.

"Should be. We'll let you know."

I nodded, and we rose, Captain Andrews seeing me to my brother's door. "Hey," I said, turning back. "You said you got a couple of the other guys?"

"Yeah, they're already in the system. Dirty types, repeats. Your brother's lucky to be alive."

I thought about those guys having been to my mother's house first, and felt like the most irresponsible son in the world. "Captain?"

The cop raised an eyebrow.

"I think those guys visited my mom's house first, looking for Jarred. They broke a couple windows, scared my mom pretty good. I filed a report last night. In Inglewood."

"I'll pull it up and make sure it gets added to this incident."

"Thanks." I hoped the guys would be in jail for a while, at least long enough to get my mom moved somewhere safer.

I pulled open the hospital room door to see my brother— or the body of the guy who'd once been my little brother— bruised, bandaged, strung out, and painfully thin. He was asleep, but his forehead was covered with a slick of sweat and he was shaking beneath the thin blanket.

Despite every cell in my body screaming at me to back out, to leave him here because this wasn't something I could handle, I stepped closer to the bed and pulled up a chair. For a long minute I sat and stared at him, memories of us as kids flashing through my mind even though I didn't want to see any of them. My little brother, grinning at me as we explored the woods behind our house, his lanky limbs and mop of dark hair flopping into his eyes. I saw his trusting smile, the way he'd watch me and my friends when we wouldn't let him hang out with us. And every one of those memories suddenly seemed like a missed opportunity. If I'd said something different, let him tag along instead of telling him no ... If I'd been a more generous big brother instead of a selfish little shit, could I have saved him?

I dropped my head into my hands and let my heart shatter for a moment, let myself mourn for the innocence neither of us would ever manage again, for the way my mother's heart would break when she saw him like this.

"Hey," a hoarse whisper came from beside me and I forced myself to look up, to meet my little brother's eyes, to let him see that I knew I'd failed.

"Hey," I said, reaching out a hand to lay on top of his.

I should have done something sooner. I shouldn't have given up on him. This was my fault, and the guilt of it almost killed me. I dug up whatever set of balls had gotten me through the time I'd spent in Afghanistan and Syria, the iron will that had forced me to stay put when everything inside me screamed to run. And I held my little brother's hand and looked into those bloodshot eyes with as best a smile as I could muster. "We been looking for you, buddy."

His eyes slid shut again, and he let out a shuddering sigh. "I know. I fucked up, Jace."

I couldn't deny that, so I didn't try. All the anger I'd felt at Jarred slid away, replaced by a tenderness for this brother who'd always just wanted to be at my side.

"Is Mom here?" He asked after a few quiet minutes. My

eyes were on our hands, and for a second I didn't hear my twenty-something year old brother at all. I heard the kid I'd fished and hiked with, the little boy I was supposed to protect, to take care of.

"Not yet," I told him. I couldn't tell him those guys had come to her place first, looking for him. I couldn't tell him that she'd been in danger because of his choices. He looked too vulnerable, like one more thing might break him completely.

"Jace," he whispered. "How do you do it?" His fingers squeezed mine lightly and I met his eyes again, eyes so full of pain and misery I worried I might actually be swept away inside that whirlpool of hopelessness.

I knew what he was asking, though we had never talked directly about much of it. Jarred had been overseas too. He'd enlisted three years after me. Maybe because of me. Or maybe because kids like us didn't have a lot of other opportunities.

Only, the Corps that saved me from my shitty childhood, the service that gave me the opportunities I had now—the job, the GI Bill—that was the same Corps that had wrecked my little brother. I don't know what he saw over there. But I could guess, based on what I saw myself.

Whatever it was, his ghosts weren't banished as easily as mine, which haunted me still but kept to the shadowy murk of my dreams. Jarred's demons dogged him in daylight, forced him to seek out planes of reality where they couldn't follow.

I took a steadying breath, rubbed a hand over my face. "I

don't have any answers man," I told him. "But I should have stayed closer when you got back, made sure you were okay. We should have gotten you some help, someone to talk to—"

"Don't do that." His voice was stronger then, almost angry, and I looked up again to see some steel in his eyes. "You don't get to take this on."

"It's already on me," I said over his protests. "You remember what Mom told us when we went to see Grandma and Papa? When they decided we weren't quite good enough for them, for all our little rich cousins?"

He held my gaze, shook his head almost imperceptibly.

"We were both mad and hurt, we'd gone to Grandma's house and she turned us away—right after Dad left. And I don't know if you understood anything. I didn't at the time. I got that we were trash, weren't good enough for them, that Grandma was saying we weren't her people anymore. But it was about Mom more than it was about us. I know that now." I sucked in a breath, the shame of that day still washing through me, making me feel small and unworthy. "And as soon as we were back at the car, Mom grabbed us both—do you remember this part? You must have been six or so."

I remembered the hot car, the way the slick plastic seat had squeaked and stuck to my thighs. I saw Mom's eyes flash with anger, with hurt as tears stood in the corners, tears she wouldn't allow to fall.

"Maybe a little."

"She hugged us tight, and she was trying not to cry, her voice all shaky. And she told us we would always have each other. That we were brothers and that our most important job was to stay close, to look out for each other ..." I trailed off, realizing just how miserably I'd failed.

"You always did," Jarred whispered. "You always have."

I glared at him. I'd rather have him angry at me, I'd rather he had slapped me. "She told me I was older and so it was my job to protect you. To take care of you. You're my little brother." My voice broke on the last word and I dropped his hand and pushed out of the chair, turning toward the window. A storm raged inside my gut and my whole life raced through my mind, highlighting every missed opportunity to steer us in a different direction, choose a path that would have led somewhere other than here.

"You didn't do this. I did." Jarred was struggling to sit up, but a glance over my shoulder told me how much it hurt him. Those assholes probably broke some ribs, judging by the way he winced with every move. "I just ... I'm not like you. I'm weak. I couldn't stand it anymore ..."

"I'm not any stronger than you." I thought about how close I'd come to fucking Juliet, to sacrificing everything I'd worked for just because I couldn't control myself.

"Please don't say that. The only way I get through a day is by imagining that some day I'll grow up. That some day I could still be like you. Be strong and brave."

Shit. My heart was being slowly wrung out, twisted and pulled and warped, and I wondered if I'd be anything close to the man I'd come in as when I finally left this room. "We'll figure this out. We'll get you some help. Get off the drugs. Get a lawyer."

He gave me a look that told me he knew people like us didn't have what it took to get any of those things.

"We'll figure it out. But you have to get well."

His face crumpled for just a second, and it reminded me of every scraped elbow, every hurled word from bigger kids that I'd failed to protect him from when we were little, when the stakes were low.

"We can do it." I didn't know how, but I knew I couldn't fail him again. We were in it together. I had to try.

"Okay, Jace." He took a deep shaky breath. "I'm sorry."

I held his eyes a long minute, feeling the truth of his apology in my heart. "It's okay, little buddy. I need to call Mom." I stepped from the room, as much to call my mother as to collect myself. And when I had control of my breathing, of my guilt, I called.

CHAPTER FIFTEEN
JULIET

J ace came home late. I knew this because I wandered the house all day, trying to keep myself occupied as I pretended to be doing things other than waiting for him to return. In his absence, my house felt big and empty, and I began to wonder what I ever did here alone before Jace and I had begun ... whatever it was we were doing. When I'd been married to Zac, Jace had lived out back with Chad in the guesthouse. And I'd thought of him out there sometimes, but not like this. Now it felt like he was missing. Like he wasn't where he belonged, and I couldn't possibly relax until he was back.

"Elvis, this is bad," I told the pug as I sat at the kitchen counter eating yogurt at ten P.M.

My fat little dog made a grunting noise to acknowledge my statement, and sat down, staring up at me with his big round adoring eyes.

I took another small bite of yogurt, thinking about the situation I'd found myself in. Zac, Ryan, Jace. "Maybe it would be better if I decided to swear off men altogether," I suggested.

Elvis snorted.

"I know." I liked men. And I doubted either a sudden swing to women or celibacy would actually be any easier. I glanced around the dark quiet kitchen, the old fashioned clock over the door ticking loudly in the silence. "I just wish I wasn't so lonely," I whispered.

Elvis whined, tilting his head and sniffing at my ankles. I gave up on my yogurt, and lowered the spoon down to him, and the little dog sprang to his feet and licked the vanilla yogurt enthusiastically, making satisfied little snarfles the whole time. His little feet danced as his mouth worked and his big trusting eyes moved back and forth between the spoon and my face.

"Is it good?" I crooned, laughing at his little butt waggling in excitement.

After a few minutes, he'd finished the yogurt, and he staggered in a dazed circle and then toppled to his side, falling immediately into a snore-filled sleep.

"Aww, Elvis," I sighed. If only I could sleep so easily.

Though falling asleep anywhere and everywhere would probably not do good things for my career. It was okay for a pug, but less good for an actress, I decided. I put down the yogurt carton, left the spoon in the sink, and carried my dog up to his favorite jumpsuit-inspired doggy bed in my room. Then I headed back to the kitchen to start the dishwasher and try to get ready for bed.

I was just turning out the lights in the front hall, having

sent Chad out an hour earlier, when I heard the kitchen door rattle and then open. Fear forced its way into my bloodstream, sending my heart rate climbing even though my mind knew it was probably Jace or Chad. I hoped it was Jace, and I tiptoed to the hallway so I could see into the kitchen.

In the darkness, I could see a big dark form moving with the self-assured grace that could only be Jace, and my heart leapt in happiness, like Elvis with yogurt. I knew it was Jace.

I was about to go to him, unable to stop myself from greeting him happily after missing him all day—after the way we'd left things the night before—but something stopped me. Once he was inside, he locked the door behind him and then stepped to the counter and sat. He didn't turn on any lights, and I watched as he sank onto a stool in the darkness, pushing his elbows onto the counter and dropping his head into his hands in silence. I watched, waiting for something, some cue that it was okay to interrupt, but he didn't move, and with every second that ticked by, the anticipation and excitement thrumming inside me dulled into something else.

He was upset, tired. Sad?

His life was about things I didn't know about, things he hadn't told me. His family, his brother ...

Was my infatuation with him selfish?

I stood in the darkness, watching him sit stock still in my kitchen with his head in his hands, and insecurity and self-doubt threatened to drown me.

Who was I to push myself on this man? He had an entire life I knew nothing about, and just because he worked in my house, I'd made myself believe he would want some kind of complicated romantic—or sexual, at least—entanglement with me? He probably felt like he had no choice about it. If I came onto him and he turned me down, he might worry that I'd fire him.

I'd put him in an impossible situation. And now I'd spent an entire day moping like a lovesick teenager, waiting for him to return, so I could what? Force myself on him? Show up unwanted in his room again? Though, I reminded myself, it didn't feel like I was unwanted when I'd been there.

I let out a slow silent sigh, realizing how the life I led had tainted my objectivity. The entire world did not actually revolve around me. And I needed to give this man his space.

Slowly, silently, and with a heart that felt like a set of lead dumbbells strapped to my chest, I went upstairs to my room and closed my door.

Ten minutes later, I was going through the motions, readying myself for bed like an automaton. I needed sleep. And if I could sleep, then tomorrow this would be easier, I thought.

Elvis was snoring away, a fat little ball in his bed in the corner, and I took comfort in that. He was my normal, my every day. Me and Elvis against the world.

Too bad he was asleep half the time and would happily lick anything presented to him. He wasn't the most discerning partner—he'd eaten a helium balloon once before I could stop him when I took him on a walk—but he was mine.

Despite the fact I was in bed, teeth brushed, hair up, ready for sleep—physically, at least—I couldn't bring myself to shut off the light next to my bed. I was just about to reach for it when a quiet knock sounded at my door.

"Juliet? You up?" Jace's voice was a whisper like sandpaper against every cell in my body, and I was up instantly, awake and painfully attuned to the big man on the other side of the door.

It would be best to let him go. Not to answer the door. Pretend to be asleep. Let Jace have his life, and don't force on him the complications of my own.

I told myself all of these things as I crossed the room, laid a hand on the solid wood between us.

Let him go, Juliet.

On the other side of the door, I heard him sigh, a ragged exhale that tore at my heart.

I opened the door, knowing I was about to cross a threshold I couldn't recross easily. "Hi."

Jace stood like a tortured god in the darkened hallway. His dark eyes locked to mine, and they were full of pain and worry and sadness, even as his full lips lifted into a gentle smile. "You're up," he said, his deep voice rough and low.

"I'm up," I confirmed, my body pulled toward him like a planet into the sun's orbit. Everything in me was reaching for him, pushing me forward, but I kept my feet planted.

One big hand lifted, long fingers raked through Jace's dark hair, and he tilted his head to the side, looking at me with a hungry but careful expression. "Should I let you go to bed?" he asked, shifting his weight like he was about to leave.

"Come in," I said, taking a step back to make room for him. "Tell me about your day?" It was a question because that was all I could manage. He was under no obligation to tell me anything, and we both knew he should have probably kept a professional distance, said goodnight and moved on. But he'd knocked. And now he was coming inside. And energy rushed through my body like freeway traffic, starting and stopping and impossible to anticipate except for its constancy.

Jace looked at me for a long second once he was inside, saying nothing. The dark eyes scanned my body, and the gaze was like being raked over with some kind of toy, some teasing implement, erupting gooseflesh everywhere it went. When his eyes found mine again, there was a question in them, a plea, maybe.

All my earlier decision making flew out the window. It was nothing in the face of the very real attraction between Jace and me. It was just a bunch of suggestions, ideas about what would be right. But this? This thrumming pulse of energy between us? This was real. And good. And how could it not be right?

I pushed the door shut and then turned back to him, taking one deep breath and then diving from the edge of the precipice on which I stood and stepping into Jace's waiting arms.

He pulled me in, crushing me to him as if I held the cure to whatever was threatening him, as if I was the answer. And even as I lifted my chin and he claimed my mouth, possessive, deep and commanding, I wondered vaguely when any other man had ever made me feel needed and wanted this way. Like a woman, not a possession. Like a person, not an accomplishment.

I melted into him, opening my mouth and my body to the strong gentle touch of his hands, his lips.

Jace walked me backward, and my legs hit the side of my bed. I wrapped my arms around the strong hard muscle of his torso, and together we tumbled onto the bed. We moved on instinct, we weren't urgent or frenzied, but deliberate. We pulled, unzipped, unbuttoned, and soon the slide of flesh on flesh replaced any need for words. My body asked and his answered, his questioned and mine confirmed. Hands, mouths, hot searing skin and wet tight spaces aligned, until Jace hovered above me. His face was a mask of sensual focus, hooded eyes, flushed skin, full lips, and his chest rose and fell rapidly as he paused.

"Is this all right?" he asked, even as I reached for him, agreeing to it all, consenting to anything he wanted, desperate to feel him everywhere.

Jace stepped back and rolled on a condom, and when he positioned himself over me again, it felt like a homecoming.

He moved slowly, with deliberate care, and when he pressed inside me, I gasped at the feeling of utter completion that washed through me then. He pulled back, sliding slowly forward a few more times until his cock was buried inside me so deeply neither of us could speak or move. I held him, gripping him with every muscle I possessed, clinging to the mountain of muscle above me, around me, inside me, and my mind spun out like spiraling arms of joy reaching for something to ground it.

Full, full, full, it chanted. But the fullness I felt was beyond physical. Being joined this way to Jace, feeling his chest on mine and our breaths synchronized with our hearts, was unlike anything I'd ever known, and it redefined the idea of sex for me in that instant. This wasn't some base, primal conquest. It wasn't one person taking and the other giving in.

This was two people locked together in an exploration of the possibility that united, they were each more—stronger, freer, more entirely themselves even as they were part of another.

When Jace began moving inside me, I was already lost, my mind having detached in its futile efforts to categorize and understand the wild unfamiliar sensations rocketing through me. I was nerves and skin and breath, heartbeat and hot, wet need.

I moaned as the joy and want mingled and built inside me—a helpless passenger along for the ride. Jace brushed the hair from my face, stared into my eyes, and then kissed me, his body pumping into mine as every thrust ratcheted me higher.

With my legs wrapped around him, my body more open and accepting than it had ever been, I was wild, I was unbound. I was his.

I was arching up to meet him, my body and heart a swirl of sensation as I felt myself nearing some terrifying abyss, some place I'd never seen or imagined. But I knew that wrapped in Jace's arms, connected to him, it would be safe to fall, safe to let myself go completely. And when his rhythm began to break down, the grunts coming from him becoming more urgent, less controlled, I dug my fingernails into his back and held on with everything inside me as we flung ourselves together from the edge.

And my life shattered into pieces that flew out far and wide in a burst of light and air and sound, as my body exploded. And then, in a tangle of breath and sweat and sheets, it came back together and I felt myself release in a different way, letting go of so many things I'd held onto for far too long, letting go of things that would make it harder for me to hold Jace.

Jace's head was bent next to mine, his body still around me, over me, inside me, as he regained his breathing. His hands still held me, his skin pressed to mine everywhere in a slick constant kiss. After a few minutes, he slid to one side and I turned with him, not wanting the separation I knew would come.

We lay facing one another, our eyes open and hands moving slowly over skin for long silent minutes. Jace traced fingers over my lips, my cheek, down the length of my nose, making me smile.

I let my fingers explore his neck, the dip of his collarbone, the bulge of his shoulder. The beautiful Celtic knot inked into his chest.

Finally, I found my voice. "Are you okay?"

His eyes, always intense, had lost some of the pain I'd seen there earlier, and they met mine as he said, "yeah."

"Your family?"

"Not as good." In whispered tones, he told me then. He told me about his little brother, about seeing him broken and beaten, suffering through withdrawal. About his mother coming to the hospital and collapsing in a desperately sad pile next to her younger son's bed. About holding them both and feeling like they were already lost.

"Don't say that," I told him, thinking about what it would be like to find Tess that way. My chest ached.

"I don't know how to help him. But I've got to try."

"Will they put him in some kind of rehab while he's in jail?" I asked. "Or give him time to go through a program before, maybe?"

Jace's hand stilled on my arm. "I don't think it works that way. Maybe in prison they have something like that. I don't know."

I thought about the little house in Brentwood, about Jace's mom, and took a chance, knowing the proud strong man in my arms might accept my help if I could phrase it the right way.

"I don't know what to do about your brother," I began.

"Me either."

I put a finger on his lips, wanting to get the rest out before he stopped me. "But maybe your mom would be better in a safer neighborhood. Maybe she could move somewhere you wouldn't have to worry about her, somewhere closer. What if—"

He pulled my hand away from his mouth and gave me a sad smile. "I can't afford more, Juliet. I'm doing everything I can for her. I reinforced the window locks and replaced the deadbolt yesterday."

I wanted him to listen, to let me help. "I have a house in

Brentwood. A cottage really, small. Two bedrooms. I don't use it."

"No." His face turned hard.

"It's just sitting there empty. It's a great neighborhood." I didn't understand his refusal.

"No." He dropped his hand, began to move away.

"Wait, Jace." I pulled him back to me, stared at his face until he met my eyes again. "Please let me do this."

"Juliet—"

"Listen," I said, my voice harder than I'd intended. "I'm like this ineffectual flower kept in a box. I can't do anything, I can't affect anything. My life is about pretending—that's my job. And my job makes it so I can't have a real life—I can't leave my house, I can't have any real influence on anything important, I can't do anything. But I can do this. I can help. Will you let me? Please?"

He stared at me, his eyes unblinking for long seconds, and then he closed them and let out a breath. "No, Juliet. I can't let you do that."

"What would your mother say? Would she say no?"

I watched his brow crease, his eyes squeeze harder as he thought about her, and I knew he was close to saying yes.

"Don't be proud, Jace. Please let me help. If your mother was in a safe place, you could both focus on taking care of your brother." I waited for his final answer, feeling like everything depended on his words.

"I pay you rent," he whispered, his eyes still shut.

"No, don't—"

"I'll do it if I pay you rent," he said, opening his eyes to fix me with a determined stare. "I can't handle charity. I know you have a lot to give, that you support those women's shelters. But I'm not like that ... I can't be a charity to you."

"You're not, Jace."

He squeezed his eyes shut. "I want to say no, but I can't. It's my mom. So please let me pay rent. I know I can't pay what you'd rent it for to someone else. But it can't be free."

"Okay, sure." I tried not to let the relief I felt turn into a wide smile. He was going to let me help—I was going to be able to actually DO something. Something real.

He sighed, and the fight all went out of him. I felt it in the way his limbs loosened, the eyes lost their fire. "God I'm tired," he whispered.

And for the rest of the long night, I held him, sensing that as much as I'd needed to feel powerful and capable for once, Jace needed to feel like he could finally let down his guard.

We spent the night in a kind of reversed state of being, and I guarded him fiercely, keeping him close in my bed and warding off whatever demons might keep this strong capable man from the sleep he deserved.

CHAPTER SIXTEEN

JACE

I awoke in Juliet's bed, sunlight filtering in like fairy dust through the thin gauzy shades over her window. The night before rushed back, the pain, the worry, the fear, and finally the release I'd found in Juliet, in her understanding. Her companionship.

Juliet was facing away from me, her back rising and falling in a soft steady rhythm as she snored.

I pushed myself up on an elbow to consider her. She was delicate and fine, soft and gorgeous. And she snored like a squirrel trying to suck chocolate pudding unsuccessfully through a straw. Loudly. With a lot of saliva involved somehow, making the sound especially wet and slurpy.

A smile pulled at my lips as I thought about the incongruity of that—perfect Juliet sounded like a drowning rodent when she slept. And I loved it.

I closed my eyes again, remembering what she had looked like beneath me, my arms still tingling at the feel of her there between them. She was soft and forgiving, but when I thought about our conversation before we'd gone to sleep, I realized she could be fierce too. And I'd drifted to sleep in the circle of her arms, feeling guarded and watched over. I hadn't felt that way since Mom had sat next my bed when I was a kid. Like it was someone else's turn to keep watch. Like I could finally breathe easily.

The slurpy snores halted and I opened my eyes. When they didn't start again, I turned my head, worried. Was Juliet suffering from sleep apnea? Had she quit breathing?

I dropped a hand onto her shoulder softly, rolling her to her back so I could see her face.

But Juliet's eyes had opened and she was smiling at me, a lazy beautiful smile full of sleep and memories of the night before. My heart filled with warmth.

The snoring sound began again.

And then the snoring turned into a snarfing, slurping sound that morphed into a low-throated grumble. And it was most definitely not coming from Juliet as she said, "Good morning."

I moved close to her side, glancing over the side of the bed as I did, and finally remembered Elvis was here. Snoring. The sound was far less charming when I realized who was actually making it. I wrapped an arm around Juliet and tugged her tightly against me. "Morning."

"Sorry about the snoring," she said. Her voice was light and soft, and I let it wrap around me like a warm blanket, reassuring and sweet.

"I thought it was you, actually," I told her, my lips at the shell of her ear.

She stiffened in my arms. "Seriously? Jace!" She laughed, and her body relaxed again, little shivers moving between us.

"I forgot your narcoleptic pug was in here." I nibbled softly on the flesh between my lips.

She released a little moan, breathy and so fucking hot, before she managed, "I don't snore, do I? And if I did, it wouldn't sound like that."

"I wouldn't know," I reassured her. "I slept more soundly last night than I have in years."

Juliet made a little noise in the back of her throat that sounded like satisfaction. I wasn't sure if it was because she was glad I'd slept well, or if her pleasure was coming more specifically from what my fingers were doing between her legs, as I'd just slipped them down her hip.

She moved her ass against me as I stroked her, pressing herself against my throbbing cock, which had woken up about the same time I had, both of us delighted to find that we were still in Juliet's bed.

I kissed and sucked at Juliet's neck as my hand continued its exploration, and I enjoyed the feeling of having her trapped against me, my arm caging her against my chest as she moaned and squirmed up against me. The little noises she was making were doing all kinds of things to my body, sending shivering spikes of excitement through me and making my balls draw up tightly as I remembered what it had felt like to plunge inside her the night before.

"Mmm," she moaned. "More." Her voice was languorous and low, her word stretched out on the unfilled minutes of a morning with no schedule before us. I was only too happy to comply with her request.

I let my hand slip from her mound, sliding it over her hip and behind her to grasp my needy cock. I fisted it a few times, letting her feel the motion against the skin of her naked butt, and then I released myself, using my hand to press her gently forward, halfway onto her stomach. When she'd rolled a little, I let my fingers slide around to her hot wetness, and she lifted a knee, laying almost on her stomach and opening herself to me from behind.

She muttered something sleepy and sexy, her face pressed into the pillow as I fingered her.

This. God, I could do this every day, I thought, as dirty thoughts and images flickered through me, sending my want for her shooting higher.

My cock was heavy and full and aching with the closeness to Juliet, to her waiting willingness. I rolled to the nightstand, where there was another condom, and rolled the rubber over myself. I took my cock in my hand again and rolled nearer to her, sliding down enough to notch myself against her waiting entrance. And when I began to push inside her from behind, the mound of her perfect ass at my stomach, I nearly lost it right then. She moaned and whimpered, and once I'd pressed myself fully into that hot tightness, I leaned forward to take her mouth again. Her head was turned so I could kiss her over her shoulder, and as I did, I let my hand slide around her waist again, and then lower, finding the spot between her legs waiting for my fingers.

She cried out when I found it, and I moved in and out

gently, my own hand locking her body to mine in the perfect position beneath me.

It didn't take long for her to find her release, and once I was sure she'd come, I clamped my hand around her soft stomach and drove into her as hard as I dared. The angle kept her legs together between mine, and it was like being inside a tight wet clamp, wedging myself into a delicious space that was just barely big enough to accommodate me. And it was so fucking hot I only needed a few more thrusts before I felt everything in my body stiffening, tightening, coiling for release.

"God, yes," she moaned, feeling how close I was. "Do it, Jace."

Those last words sent me right over the top, my whole body shuddering my release as her body lay soft and firm beneath me, her entrance gripping me tightly as I came.

We both lay there for a long moment, breathing each other in, letting our bodies and minds unspool. It felt like being caught in a time apart from the real world, and we both knew that once we got up, once our feet hit the floor, reality would rush back in.

And I was no longer sure what my reality should look like.

Were Juliet and I together? What did that mean for her agent's plan for Ryan McDonnell?

And if I was going to allow her to take care of my mother, give her a place to live out of the goodness of her heart, what did that say about me? And how tightly did it bond me to

Juliet? If something went wrong between us, what would happen to Mom?

It was too hard to think about those things while Juliet lay wrapped tightly against me. I kissed her shoulder and rolled away, nearly stepping on a pile of Pug as I dropped a foot to the hardwood floor. He dodged with a grunt and I muttered, "Sorry, Elvis."

"Did you step on my dog?" Juliet asked, her voice lacking any real concern. The evidence of Elvis's continued existence could be easily heard. He was on his feet, whining and slurping his desire to be escorted outside.

"Negative," I said. "He's here, in all his pugly glory, waiting to go out."

She rolled over and shot me a brilliant smile, her pink cheeks framed by all that golden hair, and my heart stopped beating for a moment as I looked at her. "I'll take him out in a minute," she said. "But first, tell me you're okay." She sat up, and her brows pulled together over those deep ocean eyes. Juliet was worried about me.

It had been a while since anyone worried about me.

"Yeah, I'm okay." I stood, pulling my jeans back on. "Maybe a little unsure about all this." I gestured between us.

She nodded, her eyebrows pulling together. "Let's just enjoy it?"

"I did enjoy it," I assured her. "I guess I'm just not sure what it means. If it means anything."

"It meant something to me," she said, scooting close to take my hand and hold it between hers. "It meant a lot to me."

My steely determination was nothing in the face of her soft skin, her shining eyes. "To me too."

"Then let's just see where it goes," she said. "I like you Jace. I like you in a way I maybe haven't ..." she trailed off, leaving me desperate to hear what might have come next. "I just don't know ..."

"Your life is complicated right now." I suggested this, waiting to see if she'd tell me what was on her lips or if she'd take the out.

"It is. So is yours."

The eager excitement I'd felt about the thought that we were on the same page dampened a bit. "Maybe it's not the best time to do ..." it was my turn to trail off.

"Jace," she said, her voice nearly a whisper. "There will never be a good time. And being with you has been the first time I've felt like I'm really myself in ... maybe years. Can't we just let it be whatever it is? Enjoy it?"

God, I wanted to do that. But everything I'd ever done had been planned, strategized. There was a purpose to my actions, and those actions led to a result I'd pre-determined. And this thing? This living breathing desire I felt for Juliet Manchester? I didn't have a strategy to manage it. I didn't even know what it was.

"Don't overthink it," she suggested. "Please don't. Because if you do, I'm terrified you'll decide it's too hard, too uncertain. And I don't think I could take it if you told me that," she said.

"Okay." My mouth agreed before my mind even engaged. Because clearly, my dick and maybe my heart were driving my mouth. My brain was like a good friend who we'd stopped consulting because he just made things too damned difficult. He was the guy we didn't call when we were planning a fun night out. He was the wet blanket.

Elvis let out a pained groan, and Juliet slipped out of bed, pulling on light grey sweats and doing something magical with her hair and hands that resulted in a perfect messy little bun on top of her head. I stared at her, amazed. In about thirty seconds, she'd gone from sleeping beauty to awake, upright, and gorgeous.

Juliet Manchester had some kind of magic. And I wanted to understand it better.

LATER THAT DAY, I was at Mom's house. She'd packed her clothes into duffle bags and suitcases, and now her hands were fluttering as she coughed and paced, watching me pack up the boxes I'd brought in the back of the Uhaul.

"I don't understand," she was saying as I wrapped dishes in paper and stacked them in the box. "Did you win the lottery Jace?"

In a way I had, I guessed. "No Mom. Just figured out a way to keep you safe. To make things better for you." It felt like a lie. Juliet's money was going to make things better for Mom. And even though I'd tried, I realized I couldn't turn that down anymore than I'd been able to turn down a chance to take her to bed.

"But Brentwood? Jace, I'll feel like the lady from the stix over there. What will the neighbors think?"

In a way, it felt right. Like Mom should be in a nice place, should be somewhere that would make her own family jealous. "I don't care what they think. I care that you're safe." The kitchen was the last room I needed to pack, and as I finished up, a knock sounded at the door. "Jace?"

Jack, one of the other guards from Juliet's, had agreed to help me move the furniture. "Hey Jack," I said, calling through the locked security door. I moved to unlock it and let him in. "Thanks for helping, man. This is my mom, Renee."

Mom's hands were still fluttering, only now she was touching her short gray hair, brushing it out of her face, acting like a teenaged girl in front of Jack. "Hello," she said.

"Jack and I work together, Mom. He's going to help me move the furniture."

"Oh, how nice," Mom said, smiling up at Jack, who was intimidating in size. The guy had been a linebacker in college, but had blown a knee out just before the NFL draft and lost his shot. He'd been working security ever since. I guessed he hadn't been in college for the degree, but we'd never really talked about that. "Are you from Los Angeles, Jack?" Mom asked him as we moved into the bedroom to pick up the mattress.

"No ma'am," Jack said. "Grew up on a farm in Nebraska," he told her with a broad smile.

"Oh, that's nice," Mom said, and then she launched into a coughing fit that doubled her over and sent her scurrying to the kitchen, embarrassed. I pushed down the worry that rose in me. One thing at a time.

"Your mom's a nice lady," Jack said. "She sick?"

"Yeah."

Jack just nodded, keeping inside whatever he might think or feel about my mom, about my family.

We moved and lifted things into the truck outside, Mom trying to keep up a conversation with Jack the whole time. I realized Mom was lonely. She rarely left the house and Jarred was never around. Especially now.

By six o'clock, Mom was fluttering around the new cottage, exclaiming over the window coverings, the little patio out back surrounded with flowers. Juliet had moved her things into storage, but refused to call off the gardener or housekeeper, saying she'd be paying for those things whether anyone was living in the cottage or not. As much as I hated the charity, I felt relief too, that Mom would have more time to rest. Maybe make some friends. Now I just needed to figure out how to get her to go to the doctor.

I ordered food in, and we spent that first evening at the cottage sitting on the back patio, listening to sounds that were very different than those in Inglewood. Instead of planes approaching LAX, we heard the distant sounds of steadily moving traffic. Instead of sirens and the bass pumping from some passing car, we heard birds and the occasional dog barking.

Mom was smiling at me across the table. "You always take care of me," she said.

I didn't want her to cry, and I still needed to get to the hospital today to see Jarred, so I pushed my chair back and stood. "You deserve more, Mom. But I hope this will be a good change."

She stood and pulled me against her, her frail body like an insubstantial bunch of sticks pulled against my chest. "I love you, son," she whispered against my shoulder.

"I love you too, Mom. I'll be back Sunday, okay?" I told her. "Call me tomorrow and tell me how you're doing. If you need anything."

She nodded, the tears ready to fall, and I let myself out feeling like I was still carrying something heavy. Only there was no place to put this load down or unpack it.

Jarred had looked worse than ever when I'd finally gotten to the hospital but the doctor assured me he was actually getting better.

"Withdrawal is neither quick nor easy," she had said. "But we'll keep him here until he's through the worst of it."

"Thanks." I had no idea what to expect once he was moved to county jail. I just hoped he was strong enough to survive there until we could get through the mess he'd made.

Juliet was waiting for me at the top of the stairs in the darkness when I returned, and without a word, she stepped into my arms and held me.

"Are you okay?" she whispered finally.

"Yeah." Being in her arms made me feel like less of a liar.

She pulled away from me, looking up into my face for assurance, and I wondered what she saw there in the shadowy darkness. Whatever it was, I was happy for it, because she took my hand then, and pulled me into her room, shutting the door as Elvis curled into his satin bed and taking me to hers.

CHAPTER SEVENTEEN
JULIET

J ace was quieter the next day or two, and each day he asked Chad or Jack to take over part of his shift so he could go to the hospital to see his brother and stop by his mom's new place—my place—on the way back. I didn't mind having Jack inside the house. There was something comforting in his presence, something calm about the atmosphere around him. Chad was still not my favorite, with his penchant for tabloid magazines and the interested looks I caught him sending my way sometimes. But if it made Jace's life easier, I would put up with Chad.

As long as Jace was with me when he got home. And for those incredible, perfect days, he was with me.

"Hey," he said to me one morning after we'd run. Since I wasn't working on a movie, we'd been able to get out to run a little more often, and I enjoyed being out of the house with him, feeling like we existed somewhere besides the rooms of the property that was both fortress and jail to me. "Would you want to meet my mom?"

My heart had leapt into my mouth, making it hard for me to answer. It felt important, it felt like a turning point. One that was about to be interrupted by my plans to begin a fake relationship with someone else. "Yes. Definitely."

"Ready in an hour?" He'd grinned as he said it, like the fact I wanted to meet his mom made him happy too. And that made me ecstatic. I wanted to make Jace happy, I realized. Whenever I could.

We'd gone in the security company's dark car, me sitting in the back behind tinted windows, wearing a ball cap and dark sunglasses that covered half my face. It was a private enough journey, from here to Brentwood, but the last thing I wanted was cameras interrupting what seemed like an important event.

When we pulled up to the familiar cottage, there were pots of overflowing Geraniums on the doorstep and the garden beds out front looked manicured and perfect. A woman knelt in front of one of them, a broad-brimmed hat on her head. She turned, squinting at the car as we parked at the curb.

"Mom's been gardening a lot," Jace said, shooting me a smile that made even my teeth feel glad. A little bundle of nerves popped around in my stomach as we got out of the car.

We approached the woman and she stood, wiping her hands on her jeans. Jace's mom was little, I thought with surprise. She couldn't have been more than five-foot-two, and she smiled up at us through a lined face that held dark coffee-colored eyes' that were an exact match to the ones I adored. "Hello," I said.

"Mom," Jace said. "This is Juliet. She owns the house, and I work for her."

Jace's mother smiled broadly then, reaching out a hand to shake. "It's wonderful to meet you, Juliet. I feel a little silly inviting you into your own house, but come inside."

The house looked so different without my overstuffed furniture and meaningless decor. It looked lived in and loved, even if there were still a few boxes here and there, when before it had only been an impersonal escape. "The place looks wonderful Mrs. Morgan," I told them both.

"Call me Renee," she said, taking off the big hat and setting it on the back of the couch. "Can I get you coffee? Tea?"

We accepted coffee and the three of us sat down, but just as we were beginning to talk a bit, Renee erupted into a coughing fit that went on much longer than it seemed like it should. Jace had said nothing about his mother being ill, but this didn't sound like a cold.

"Are you sick?" I asked when she'd recovered a bit.

"No, no," she waved my concern away.

"Yes," Jace said, his voice flat and ominous. "She won't do anything about it."

I glanced between them, sensing this was an old fight. But I didn't like the sound of the cough at all. Still, it wasn't my place to say anything else. Not right now.

We stayed for an hour, talking about Jace's brother Jarred and how they were when they were little boys—Jace the protector, even then. We also talked about their hopes that Jarred might escape the grip of drugs this time, even if it did have to happen in prison. Jace said Jarred had tried to quit several times before, going cold turkey and visiting a free counselor, but each time he'd relapsed.

"It's so nice to meet you," Renee said later, as the mugs sat empty on the coffee table and Jace leaned back in the couch, finally relaxing a bit. "I can't thank you enough for allowing me to live here. The neighborhood, the quiet ... the garden ..." tears were welling in Renee's eyes, and I was embarrassed suddenly that a house I didn't even live in could mean so much to her.

I leaned forward and took her hand. "I wish I could have helped earlier. I'm so glad you're happy here."

She ducked her head and wiped at her eyes. "You must think I'm such a failure," she said quietly.

Jace sat up straighter. "Mom, what? No."

She shook her head, still not looking up. "Can't even take care of myself," she whispered. "My boy... the drugs..."

"Mom," Jace's voice cracked along with my heart. I thought how easily any family could find itself in this situation, how it could be my own Gran sitting here, feeling like a failure.

"No," I said, forcing my own voice to be strong, cheerful, reassuring. "No, Renee. If there's one thing I learned from my Gran, it's that we don't always control what happens in our lives. We can only control the way we weather the things that happen, we can only try to hold onto ourselves through the hard stuff."

She looked up at me, then her eyes darted back down to her hands.

"And you've done well, I'd say." I paused, and Jace dropped a big hand on my knee, a silent thanks. "Jace is an incredible man. And I haven't met Jarred, but I'm willing to bet the drugs don't define him. We all make mistakes, but I'd bet that Jarred has just as true and strong a heart as either of you. And that's something a mother can take credit for."

Renee wiped at her face and then smiled up at me, and Jace squeezed my leg lightly. His tender touch made me feel like we were a real couple, like I could be part of this family. I had a sudden longing to introduce him to Gran, to Tess.

Soon, we were heading back home, but I felt like something had grown inside me, made more space. In a life where so much of what I saw and did was a construction, merely make-believe, it was incredible to spend a day feeling like part of the real world, like a part of something that mattered. I liked Jace's mom a lot. And I wanted to help her.

"I have a doctor who makes house calls," I told Jace in the car on the way home. "I can send him over to see her."

Jace looked at me for a long second without speaking. Then, as if it was hard for him to do it, he said, "okay."

IT WAS JUST the two of us in the house those evenings as darkness settled outside, swathing the property in dark drapery and silence, and what felt like privacy. Jace set the walkie talkie nearby, but kept it turned down low so if anyone outside needed to reach him he was still there, but Chad's incessant chatter was less irritating at low volume.

We ate together, talked in my room or his, and spent a lot of time in bed.

It was just a few perfect days and nights, hiding from reality with a man who really saw me, who wanted to really know me. A man who didn't care how well my last movie did, but who wanted to know about me as a person.

Only, it couldn't last.

When I hadn't made weekend plans to go to Maryland by Wednesday, my agent called me to ask.

"Juliet, this is what we got Ryan on board for. And the magazine piece is all set up. You need to go. Make a long weekend of it. See your family."

I sighed and moved away from Jace, staring up at the ceiling. Ryan. Right. I hadn't spoken to him since he'd been at the house. My stomach churned as I glanced at Jace and then sat up, wishing I could stop time from advancing so we could continue this, continue pretending real life could ever be this good. "I know. I'll go. I'll buy tickets today."

"Leave tomorrow. Alison Sands from *Hollywood Entertainer* wants to speak to you Friday morning and take some pictures, and then return Saturday evening for the party."

The party. Gran. The magazine. My disaster of a brewing scandal. Ryan.

Real life came rushing back and smashed into my chest like a train, forcing a deep sigh from me. I heard Jace roll toward me and felt him put a comforting hand on my back.

"Okay. We'll head to Maryland tomorrow." I put down the

phone and texted my sister to let her know I was coming out. I didn't give her any specifics, since I didn't have them yet. Then I texted Ryan McDonnell, asking him to be ready to go tomorrow. He had already known the date of the trip, and his reply didn't indicate any surprise at being called last minute.

"Taking a trip, huh?" Jace's voice came low and deep like rocks tumbling over one another, and my stomach leapt in response. I turned my head and then gave up the pretense of getting up and crawled back into bed, pushing myself along the ridges of hard muscle of his body as he wrapped me in his arms.

"I'll need security," I murmured into his chest.

He didn't answer, and when I pulled back my head to look up at him, my hair on the pillow between us, his eyes were cloudy and worried. I wondered what he was thinking, how he would handle seeing us play out the pretense of this fake relationship. But I wondered if he was worried about more than that, about his family.

"You thinking about leaving your mom? Your brother?" I should tell him I didn't need him, that he should stay here. But the thought of spending the weekend across the country, out of his arms and away from the sense of complete understanding I felt around him was almost impossible to bear.

He chuckled then, and some of my worry skittered away. "No. I should be thinking about them. But I was thinking about you. About how things will go out there. With him."

"Ryan."

A look of distaste curled Jace's lip, wrinkled his brow. "Him. Yeah."

It wasn't right, but my heart warmed at the look of jealousy on Jace's face, and when his arm tightened around my waist ever so slightly, I smiled. "It's just pretend."

"So if we go to Maryland, what will that look like? At night, will you be in my bed?"

"Of course I will," I said quickly, but then my mind began to work through the idea. It would depend, I guessed, on how far I had to take the pretense with Ryan. Did I have to make my sister and Gran believe we were together? Gran had a tendency to blurt things out, and if she blew my cover while the magazine people were around ... I looked into the dark eyes I'd begun seeing in my dreams, tightened my grip on the body I felt even when he was away from me. "Oh shit. Actually ..."

"That's what I figured. You'll need to make them all believe it. And if you're with me ... if you even look at me ..." He trailed off, the storms rolling back across his face. He closed his eyes. "Even the idea of him putting his hands on you ..." Jace pulled me more tightly to his body, and I let my hand slide between us, grasping him gently and stroking until he let out a pained groan.

"This," I told him, continuing the motion and then sliding myself over him until we were lined up, until I could feel him right against my entrance. "This is what you need to remember. I'm yours," I told him, sliding myself down his length as he blew out a sharp breath. We'd abandoned condoms when I'd told him I was on birth control and my doctor had confirmed I was clean, despite Zac's best efforts.

"Fuck," he groaned, the sound coming from him like an involuntary prayer, rasping and pained and desperate.

As I moved, I whispered to him. "I want you to think about this while we're there. About what's real. Because being with you? It's the first time I've ever felt like there's something real in my life, something that matters, something I can't give up." I spoke as I pressed my hands into his chest, moving in rhythm, and his big palms wrapped the sides of my hips, holding me there and guiding me.

Jace opened his eyes when I'd stopped talking, stopped making promises. And the look in them sent flames racing down my spine, bursting to life at my center and in my chest. Want, need ... something else ... At that second, I knew I could live the rest of my life happily if only Jace would look at me like that now and then. Like I made the earth turn for him. Like I was important. Like this was everything.

"Yes," I whispered as he began thrusting up beneath me, holding me with his huge hands so he could use me the way he needed to. "God, yes."

I ground myself on top of him, seeking the pressure I needed to release, never dropping his gaze as every cell inside me seemed to align with him. I was making him a promise with my body, with my heart, and I was sealing it with the shared release we found as we stared into each other's eyes.

And though neither of us said the word, I was certain as Jace held me fixed with his hands, his cock, his eyes—that what passed between us was the culmination of a year of quiet confidence and a couple weeks of building trust. It was the outcome of quiet nights sharing truth and long days spent believing in one another. It was something more than employment or protection and it lived outside the complications that lay between us.

Jace loved me. And I loved him.

And it wouldn't matter what ridiculous charade we had to go play for the world to see.

Love was strong. I was sure of it.

CHAPTER EIGHTEEN
JACE

Juliet and I packed, my efforts taking about fifteen minutes before I went in to watch her struggle to decide what she needed over the course of several hours. When she'd finally finished, she had several hard suitcases and an overnight bag.

"Think you forgot anything?" I teased.

"I'm terrible at packing," she moaned. "I know it."

We'd be gone four days, but she was bringing half her closet.

"The weather in Maryland is unpredictable. And I don't know how I'll feel," she added.

"My clothes never seem to care how I feel," I told her, laughing.

"I mean I'm not sure what I'll feel like wearing," she said, poking me in the chest and then dropping another hand low to give me a teasing squeeze.

"Don't start something you can't finish," I warned her.

In the past few days there'd been a lot of finishing. For both of us. But I'd begun to see that the more I had of Juliet, the more I wanted of her. Every time I held her in my arms, my mind started working through future scenarios, ways we might be able to make this thing between us work in the long run, while my heart just hammered out words that echoed inside my skull relentlessly. Words like: Forever. More. Love. Mine.

She'd smiled up at me then, the smile that made my heart melt and my dick into a steel girder at the same time. "Soon. We'll find a way, I promise."

I carried her things downstairs, and we waited for Ryan to arrive.

When Chad radioed that McDonnell was there, the warm intimacy between us stilled. And when Juliet pulled open the front door and her movie star "boyfriend" gave her a casual hug, I took a step back, physically and emotionally. This weekend would not be easy. I would need to hang back, stay in the shadows. No matter how much it hurt.

We took two cars to LAX Thursday night. Jack and Christian had taken an earlier flight to Washington DC so they could arrive at the house in Maryland a couple hours ahead of us. They'd need to check the property, identify security risks and set up the patrol and response plans before Juliet and Ryan arrived.

McDonnell left his car at Juliet's house, and the two of them rode together in the back of a dark Town Car one of the other guys from the firm drove. A second car waited just behind it, this one for me and Chad.

"Ready for this?" Juliet had asked McDonnell when he'd arrived, black bags slung over his shoulder and a shit-eating grin on his face. Of course he was ready. All you had to do was look at Juliet to see that any man with blood in his veins and two brain cells to rub together would have been ready in a heartbeat. My blood raged inside me and I found myself needing to count to ten and take calming breaths more than once in the fifteen minutes we spent packing up their car.

And as I packed her into a car with Mr. Perfect Hollywood, Ryan McDonnell, Juliet's promises were all I had to keep me from going Hulk on the car and ripping the roof off to get to her. I forced myself to keep my eyes away from the windows because if he touched her—if I saw him touch her—there was a chance I'd kill him.

I took small consolation from the fact that Elvis was currently in Brentwood with my mother, undoubtedly being spoiled rotten. It was ridiculous, but the fact that my mother had Juliet's dog—it was like part of her was being kept by part of me, and nothing between us could break as long as a narcoleptic pug was with Mom.

Grasping. Straws. Yeah, I knew it. It was all I had.

JULIET HAD DRESSED CASUALLY, but had refused the baseball cap and shades I'd suggested would help stave off attention, telling me the whole point of the farce with her and pretty-boy was to be seen.

Still, I wasn't quite prepared for the crush of paparazzi

already gathered at departures when we arrived. There were always crowds around Juliet, but this was excessive—someone had tipped them off. Chad and I had to play offensive line, holding back the crowd and directing luggage handlers as the movie stars made their way through the terminal.

"Keep moving," I growled at McDonnell at one point, when he looked around, acting surprised to see all the people focused on them, and then he stopped to stare at Juliet.

He didn't keep moving, and my skin tried to crawl right off my body as I watched in horror while he put his hands on her and she rose up on her toes to kiss him.

This was not a peck.

This was not chaste.

Movie-star-asshole-douchebag McDonnell had his hands all over Juliet and his tongue in her mouth, and I swear to God, I could not hear for the sound of the blood rushing violently inside my head. My skin was burning and if I clenched my fists any tighter, I was pretty sure every bone in my hands would actually break.

Flashes were firing, and reporters were calling out questions as passersby took video of that asshole groping Juliet like she belonged to him. Like he had the right.

Fury was suddenly my new religion and I was ready to throw myself on its altar and use McDonnell for a human sacrifice.

As they broke apart, Juliet's eyes found me, and she held my gaze for a long second. When her eyes met mine, the searing want and need I felt for her leapt up to join the jealousy spiraling inside me and I actually felt sick. Like I might need to sprint off to find a potted plant. Maybe I could just vomit into McDonnell's suitcase.

Steady, Jace, I told myself. *They're acting. That's what they do.*

I took a deep breath, telling myself this was just for show, it was fake, and we continued moving through the airport, finally coming to the gate just in time for boarding to begin.

Chad didn't seem to mind the excitement or the fact that McDonnell kept a possessive hand on Juliet's waist. He even leaned into me when they were finally done searching for one another's tonsils for the cameras and said, "Shit, I've got a chub just from watching that. I'd like to give her a little boink some time. Did you hear her tell him to put his hand on her tit? Maybe she's some kind of domme, huh? Into kinky shit, you think?" He moved away to push back a photographer who'd stepped too close, and it was a good thing because I'd been about to shove my fist down his throat.

On the plane, Juliet and Ryan sat side by side in first class, and Chad and I sat right across the aisle from them where we'd be close enough to intervene if needed. I was relieved to see Juliet pull out a little pillow and go immediately to sleep while McDonnell flipped through a magazine he produced from his bag. I couldn't help eyeing him, trying to understand more about the man who'd just had his hands all over the woman I was pretty sure I was falling in love with. He seemed completely unaffected by the kiss they'd shared. Not that I'd expected him to pass out or anything, but the dude did not look like a guy getting ready to score. He wasn't paying much attention to Juliet really; his focus seemed totally absorbed by the—was that a cooking magazine?

We landed at Dulles and repeated the LAX scenario almost to a tee. McDonnell groped Juliet again while I struggled to keep myself from murdering him, and soon we were back in two town cars, driving south for what felt like centuries before finally pulling up in front of a huge white house lit up by spotlights where it perched on a riverbank looking like something out of *Gone With the Wind*.

"Who. Is. That?" Chad asked in an appreciative voice as we peered out the windows. There was a woman standing on the front steps, gazing out toward us. Chad let out a low whistle as he took in what had to be Juliet's sister. Annoyance flared in me. We were here to work, not to ogle Juliet's sister. Or Juliet, for that matter. The woman on the steps had long dark hair and a pretty face, and she smiled as Juliet emerged from the car and moved to embrace her. Jack stood on the porch just behind her, and there was something moving around at his feet, flapping and jumping. Was that a chicken?

Once introductions had been made, and Jack had explained that the chicken was a pet who had taken a liking to him, Juliet's sister Tess waved us into the house. "I've set up a few rooms this way for your security," she told Juliet.

Juliet glanced back at me with those big blue eyes, and I thought there was some kind of apology there, though it was hard to see in the low light of the front parlor. McDonnell stood at her side, and I stopped myself from cringing visibly as Tess motioned to a stairway, telling them their rooms were that way. We wouldn't even be sleeping in the same part of the house, I realized, disappointment landing like a stone in my gut.

"Perimeter security is non-existent," Jack said, stepping close. "I did a check of the house, and the structure is secure enough, no vulnerable ingress points as long as we keep watch front and back. The night of the party will be a little more complicated, but I've got the CONOPs set up here." He handed me a sheet of paper as Juliet and McDonnell disappeared up the stairs, leaving us in the front room.

"Yeah, okay," I said to Jack as the chicken I'd seen on the porch let out a loud shriek, making me jump.

"What the fuck is this?" Chad asked him, pointing to the bird, which was now standing on Jack's shoe.

Jack sighed and rolled his eyes, rubbing a hand through his hair. "Dude, I don't even know. This bird like adopted me or something. It won't leave me alone."

Chad burst out laughing and I elbowed him in the ribs. It was pretty late, and I knew Juliet's grandmother was probably sleeping somewhere nearby.

"Did you set up a watch schedule?" I asked Jack.

"Yeah. Chad and Christian on first watch," he said.

"Thanks a lot," Chad muttered.

Jack ignored him. "You and me on second."

That meant I'd have a couple hours sleep, which I was glad for, though I wasn't sure sleep would be possible, given the furious rush of my blood at the moment. Jealousy didn't look good on anyone, I knew, but I couldn't stand the fact that Juliet had just disappeared up the stairs with McDonnell.

Were they sleeping in the same room? How far were they going to take this farce?

"Yeah. Good."

"I'll show you the rooms," Jack said, leading us into the east wing of the house, the chicken dancing at his feet as he moved.

CHAPTER NINETEEN
JULIET

I followed Tess up the stairs with Ryan, every tiny cell in my body screaming to go back down, to go wherever Jace was going instead.

But we were basically onstage now, and I needed to follow through with the plan. We were here for a reason—to offer the press something besides my messy divorce and scandalous sex tape—and if we pulled it off, it would work well. But if we screwed it up and somehow revealed that this was actually a ruse, it would just give the media more fodder to use in their efforts to paint me as a sad, desperate star on her way to financial ruin, rehab, mental collapse and cinematic obscurity. We'd raised the stakes by taking on this act. And now we had to go through with it and do it convincingly.

And that meant staying away from Jace for the weekend. My heart surged in protest as I thought about it.

As Tess pointed us to our (thankfully separate) rooms, Ryan said he was hungry, and Tess agreed to help him find something to eat. But before she'd gone downstairs with him, we'd had a few minutes together as she helped settle me in my room.

"So this thing with Ryan," she said, smoothing the duvet as she talked. "Is it pretty ... uh ... serious?" Her voice was a little bit unsteady, and I wondered if she could possibly still be entertaining the crush I knew she'd had on Ryan a few years ago, when *Charade of Stones* had just begun and he'd been in some silly movie called *Meet me in Manhattan* that Tess had loved.

I hated having to lie to my little sister. It definitely wouldn't do anything to help us close the distance that had grown between us over the past few years. "I don't know," I said, a nervous laugh escaping my mouth.

She was giving me a look like she was trying to figure something out, tilting her head to one side and squinting at me. "What aren't you telling me?" she asked.

Oh shit. I'd been here five minutes and Tess was about to figure it all out. "There's nothing to tell, Tess," I said, forcing my voice to be light. "Zac was a shit, and now I'm seeing Ryan." I turned away from her, unzipping my bag. "I'm exhausted. I'm going to bed. We'll talk tomorrow."

I wanted her to stop asking questions. My mind was churning over how I might be able to go to Jace without the rest of the security team catching me, but I didn't even know which room he'd be in, and Chessy seemed to be hovering around the security team that had come earlier. She wasn't a quiet house chicken and I didn't need her throwing up some kind of alarm if I went down there.

"Good night," Tess said, leaving my room and shutting the door behind her.

I picked up my phone and texted Jace.

ME: Top of the stairs. Second door on the right.
Him: Your sister and McDonnell are up. Too risky.

I SANK ONTO THE BED, a deep disappointment mixing with the exhaustion in my bones and making me feel heavy and hopeless. What had I gotten myself into? How could I possibly be around Jace for four days without letting on the way I felt about him? My body was magnetically drawn to him, my heart aligned to him like he was my true north.

That night I slept fitfully, tossing and turning. I was in an unfamiliar bed, in a house I hadn't slept in for years—one that creaked and moaned with the slightest breeze. One in which I couldn't be myself, where I'd always felt the weight of my parents' deaths like a physical pain inside me.

This was the place we'd come to live after they had died. And I loved Gran. But she wasn't my parents. And I knew that Tess had gotten over their loss more easily—she was younger when it had happened, after all—but for me, the emptiness I'd felt when Mom and Dad had died had never really filled back up. From that point on, I had always felt like I was looking for something to replace their love, to soothe the gnawing emptiness I felt inside.

For a while, the excitement of Hollywood had been a

good distraction, but once I'd settled into my success, the hole had opened up again. It was a gaping cavern just as wide as ever. I'd married Zac thinking a family of my own would be the answer, but Zac didn't want kids. And the hole gnawed itself even bigger inside me.

The thing was, in the last few weeks, as Jace and I had spent more time together, I hadn't noticed it as much. The pain had faded. It might have been the distraction of something new, but I thought it was more.

And now, being here, being away from Jace, I was empty again.

* * *

THE SUN WAS bright in the morning, and I got up early, thinking I might go down to the river and stretch a little bit. Southern Maryland did offer some benefits over my home in Los Angeles, the biggest one being the fact I could actually go outside alone, go for a walk without worrying about being accosted or swarmed by photographers.

I pulled on some yoga pants and a long tank top and went downstairs, carrying my flip flops in my hand. The house was quiet, and as I passed the entrance to the east wing, I wondered where Jace might be.

I hated that we hadn't gotten a chance to talk after the scene at the airport. I hated that I didn't even know which room he was sleeping in. Had he tossed and turned all night too? Was he still okay with everything or might he be thinking this was all just too much?

I went into the kitchen and brewed a pot of tea, standing in front of the counter and staring out the window at the big sprawl of the yard, the slope of the bank down into the lazy river below. My eyes swept the dominating green of the landscape, finally coming to rest on the incongruity moving over the lawn. A black-shirted man in jeans, walking near the back porch.

My heart hammered in my chest.

Jace.

I made two cups of tea and carried them out to the back porch. "Hey," I called softly down the steps, drawing his attention.

His face had been stony and serious, but when he turned to look at me, a smile spread over those full lips that made my heart clench inside my chest.

"Hey yourself," he returned.

"I made you some tea," I said.

He glanced around, as if looking to see if anyone was nearby, and then came up the stairs and onto the porch. "Thanks." He accepted the mug I held out to him.

"No one else is up," I told him, setting my own mug on the table.

He stood a couple feet from me, around the curve of the big table. He seemed to think about my statement for a minute, then put his own mug down and stepped closer, scanning the yard and peering into the kitchen through the screen door as he did so. "Is that an invitation, Ms. Manchester?" he asked, his voice a growling whisper that made my stomach drop because it made me think of the other times he'd used that voice.

"I miss you," I whispered back, stepping closer to him.

We both glanced around, but there was no one nearby to see anything they shouldn't.

Jace reached a hand to me and I took it. He tugged gently and I was in his arms a second later, the vacancy in my heart suddenly full again, my mind calm and my body screaming for him. I pressed myself against him, loving the warm solidity of him, the smell of him, the way he held me exactly right. I took in a few deep breaths, assuring myself he was there, this thing between us was real. And then I tilted my head up to look into his serious face with the high cheekbones, the full lips, those dark dangerous eyes I loved.

He leaned down and pressed his lips gently to mine. For a moment, time froze and we held ourselves still, breathing together, being together. Then something snapped and he pulled me roughly to him, his mouth devouring mine, our tongues tangling and teasing until we finally broke apart breathless, our eyes still locked.

"This weekend is going to be difficult," he said.

That was an understatement.

I brought a hand to my lips, missing him there already as I stepped back to a respectable distance in case anyone might step out of the house. "It will," I agreed. "But it's not real Jace. You have to remember that. This," I said, motioning between us. "This is real."

He blew out a long breath between pursed lips, as if calming himself, centering himself.

A loud squawk came from the lawn around the side of the

house, and we both turned as Jack appeared, Chessy hot on his heels.

"That chicken is ... interesting," Jace said, his voice amused.

I laughed, the tension between us fading. "She is," I said. "She seems to like Jack."

"She slept outside his door," Jace told me.

This was new. Chessy had only been around the past couple years, and I'd been here once in that time, with Zac. He'd been so offended by the idea of a house chicken that we'd had to keep her out in the coop with the other chickens while he'd been here, though she didn't get along well with the ladies of the coop and she squawked continuously, upsetting them all the whole weekend. Tess said none of them would lay eggs for weeks after we'd gone. I wanted to tell her I was pretty sure Zac had that effect on everyone.

"Morning," Jack called as he passed.

"Good morning," I called back.

He disappeared again, around the other side of the house, and I looked back to Jace, trying to figure out how I could find time with him, how we could make the best of this. "Come to my room tonight," I said.

He nodded once, then picked up his tea, sipped it, and then went back out onto the lawn, taking up his watch again in the shade of the big oak.

I sat on the porch and watched him, stoic and proud and strong. And so handsome it broke my heart to look at him and know I couldn't touch him.

CHAPTER TWENTY
JACE

The morning passed in a swelter of humidity and sunlight, my guts twisting into a painful knot any time I let myself think about McDonnell and his perfect straight-toothed smile being anywhere near Juliet.

Standing watch, unfortunately, gives you plenty of time to think, and as I finished my shift, I tried to tell myself this was what she had to do. It was to protect her. It wasn't about us.

By the time Chad and Christian appeared to take over, I was bleary-eyed and ragged, and it had little to do with the time change or the long night, but I still went gratefully to my room.

During the day, all four of us had areas of responsibility, but I already knew this weekend was going to be calm from a crazy-fan perspective. The house in Maryland was secluded, and the dense woods around it, along with the river on one side, made it fairly inaccessible for your run-of-the-mill photographer or star-struck nut job. Still, it paid to remain vigilant, and I had no intention of letting my guard down during our time here.

It was lunchtime when I came back out of my room, having taken a shower and tried hard to talk myself out of strangling McDonnell the next time he touched Juliet.

"Hi there," said a bright voice in greeting as I stepped out onto the back porch, following the sounds of dishes and the smell of food. Juliet's sister, Tess, had risen to greet me as I'd come out.

"Hi," I said, shaking the small hand she'd reached out to me.

"I'm Tess," she said, "and this is my grandmother, Helen." She waved at a woman with gray hair piled on top of her head in a messy bun, wearing a bright pink sweat suit, complete with a thin gold chain that held a tiny clock face. I recognized Gran from the photo at Juliet's, though in that picture she'd been wearing a dress.

"Hi," I said again. "Nice to meet you both." Gran was exactly as Juliet had painted her for me.

"There's some food on the counter in the kitchen. You're welcome to grab a plate," Tess said.

"Thank you," I said, unsure what the expectations were for staff versus those who lived here. The place reeked of old school southern tradition, and I imagined it might have been the kind of place that had a separate servants' dining room. I looked around, and spotted Chad at the table inside, wrapping his sizable mouth around a cob of corn. "I'll eat inside," I told them.

Gran didn't say a word, just swirled a brownish drink and

eyed me under her lowered brow. I had the feeling the woman didn't miss much, and a little spark of worry flared in me for Juliet.

I ate quickly, sitting across from Chad, who made inane conversation the whole time we were in the kitchen.

"Some place, huh?" he asked.

I grunted a response as I took a bite of my sandwich.

"Seriously fancy, right? Like old money fancy."

I didn't know what to say to that, so I just took a sip of sweet tea instead.

"And the sister?" Chad blew out another low whistle, signaling his apparent appreciation of Tess's looks. "Good genes in the family, man. But that old lady ..."

"Shut it," I growled. Tess and her grandmother were sitting not twelve feet from us on the other side of a screened door. They didn't need to hear the paid help's opinions of them. "We're here for Juliet. Pay attention to her."

"She's upstairs with McDonnell," Chad said, and my blood instantly ignited. "Hot shot movie stars don't get out of bed until noon, I guess." Chad shoved half a chicken breast into his mouth, which I hoped would keep him quiet for a few minutes while I dealt with my irrational anger.

I knew Juliet hadn't slept in McDonnell's room. I'd seen her out here this morning. Kissed her just this morning. Heard her reassuring words only a few hours ago. I told myself that whatever she was doing upstairs with him now wasn't what Chad was insinuating, and managed to take a few deep breaths and continue eating.

I cleaned my plate a few minutes later, and with a nod

and a thank you to Tess and Gran on the back porch, headed out to make a sweep of the perimeter.

When Juliet and McDonnell emerged a few minutes later, it was as if my entire body aligned with her gravitational pull instantly—as if she were the light I had to keep close to. I wished, for the weekend at least, that I could turn off my sharply tuned awareness of her, but I couldn't. When she was nearby, she was all I could focus on.

I roved nearer to the edge of the porch, meeting her eyes briefly as I took up a post close enough to hear what was being said.

Gran was talking to Juliet. "So you can't screw things up too badly, I'd guess, on the heels of that last asshole, Juliet." She was talking about Zac, and I had to keep myself from nodding my agreement.

"Gran!" Juliet cried, sounding surprised and a little bit amused.

"I'm pretty sure I told you back then that Zac was a moron, but no one ever listens to me," Gran went on, sounding bitter and then sipping the fresh drink in front of her. "Just wait, young man," I glanced behind me to see her addressing movie-star McDonnell now. "Once you hit a certain age, everyone assumes you've got a few connections unhinged up here and they pretty much ignore everything you say."

I had the sense Gran didn't have any loose connections.

Jack wandered close then, the chicken in hot pursuit. "This fucking chicken," he hissed as he passed me, "will not leave me alone!"

"Chessy!" The old woman yelled form the porch. "Leave that poor man alone!"

The admonishment did no good, and Chessy continued tracking Jack's every move as he headed down toward the water, maybe planning to try to find out if chickens could swim.

"Well, if you listened to me," Gran went on, still talking to Juliet. "You wouldn't have married that idiot in the first place. And please tell me the media was wrong about the settlement you're giving him. My whole guild is talking about it. That numb-nuts didn't deserve a cent. That moron was a couple beers short of a six pack. Hope you're firing on all cylinders, cuz he certainly wasn't. So. The settlement?"

I wished I could go up there, rescue Juliet. But this was her family. She would know the best way to handle them and their questions. "Did you say guild?" She asked.

"Yes. In the game," Gran answered. "Settlement. Talk, young lady."

"I don't think you can 'young lady' me anymore, Gran." Juliet was quiet a moment and I wondered if she would tell them about the blackmail—but that would mean telling her family there was a sex tape. "I'd rather not talk about it," she said. "It's not final, and it's just ... it's hard."

I risked a glance at her then, but her eyes were locked with McDonnell's, and anger flooded my system when I saw his hand on her arm.

How the fuck was I supposed to do this? I could barely breathe when the guy was within two feet of her, and I was supposed to stand by while they pretended to be a couple for a magazine shoot? I'd have a heart attack.

I moved around to the front of the house, stepping close to where Chad sat in a rocking chair and managing to form actual words. "Switching spots. You go out back."

Chad frowned up at me, but stood. "Whatever you say, man."

When he was gone, I dropped into the chair he'd vacated and gave myself yet another calming talk. They were actors. They were acting. I knew Juliet and I were together.

Didn't I? I thought I did.

After a few minutes, I was breathing normally and even felt like I could think straight. I'd made a few sweeps of the front yard when my phone buzzed in my pocket. Mom.

My worry ratcheted up again. "Hey, everything okay Mom?"

"Hey honey. Yes, actually. I have good news."

I needed good news. The last time I'd checked in, Jarred was suffering tremendously with withdrawal symptoms, and the hospital had been sedating him to keep him from hurting himself. We needed a better answer, but the administrators there were going to release him in another two days, and he'd be out on bail until his trial. Mom had managed to get a bail bond with the money I'd been saving over the past few years. It wasn't a lot, but thankfully Jarred's bail was pretty light. "What's up?"

"I found a treatment center for Jarred. There's a wait list, but they'll take him in a couple weeks, they think."

That wasn't good news. Jarred needed something immediately. "Mom, what will he do for the weeks between being released from the hospital and the time the center can take him?"

"I'll keep him here."

I screwed my eyes shut, rubbing a hand across my head, which had begun to ache. "It's not gonna work, Mom. He'll be out looking for a score the first night."

"He promised me he wouldn't. We agreed. He'll just stay in the house. I'll watch him. It'll be different this time, Jace." Mom's voice was full of the desperate desire to believe these words were true, but we both knew they weren't. I'd done enough research about heroin recovery to understand that the first few weeks were critical, and Jarred didn't just need to be kept away from the drug, he needed intense therapy to help him relearn how to experience emotions on his own— that was the key to real recovery. We had been through this— and failed—before.

"Mom," I breathed, feeling helpless. "He can't stay there. He needs a rehab center that can take him immediately. Not in two weeks. It'll be too late."

I heard the hope leave my mother with her next sigh. "I know," she said, her voice cracking. "But the state-sponsored centers are the only ones we could afford, Jace. Those other places ..." she trailed off. She didn't need to finish the thought. They were expensive. And we didn't have it.

"I'll figure it out," I told her, my heart dissolving to dust as I uttered what was essentially a lie. I had no means of scraping together the money it would take to get my brother admitted to the kind of facility that would take him immediately and keep him for the amount of time it would take to truly give him a chance. That kind of place was for rich people—socialites. And movie stars. I cringed at the thought of Juliet finding out about this. She'd try to fix it. And then I'd owe her more than I could ever pay her back. I couldn't tell her ... I needed to figure this out on my own.

"This little dog sleeps a lot," Mom said, her voice tired.

"He's narcoleptic," I told her. "Just make sure he doesn't fall over into his water bowl and drown."

"Oh!" She sucked in a little breath. "Okay, yes, I will. We've been getting along well. It's nice having him here, actually."

Mom needed a dog, I thought. Maybe I could find her one. It felt good to discover something I might actually be able to do. "Did the doctor stop by, Mom?"

"Oh yes, she did," Mom said. "She took some things to a lab and is supposed to call me."

"Okay, good." It was good. But it was one more thing I'd allowed Juliet to do for me. "Well, I'm actually working, so I should go. But I'll call you tomorrow, okay?"

"How is Juliet?" Mom asked. We hadn't told her there was anything going on between us, but Mom's question suggested she already knew. It would have been a relief to talk to her about it, but I couldn't. Especially not right here. "She's a lovely girl."

"She is. She's fine."

"Okay honey. I'll talk to you tomorrow."

We hung up and I called the hospital where Jarred was being held, and basically threatened the discharge nurse when she confirmed they were planning to release him in another forty-eight hours. "You keep him there as long as you possibly can," I'd growled at her. "If you let him go, you might as well just shoot him as he walks out the door," I said. I shouldn't have been telling her. She wasn't the one in charge, but I hoped maybe she could do something.

The nurse had said that she would see what she could do, but I already knew we'd need to find something else. Fast.

CHAD and I took up positions inside as the afternoon went on, and Juliet wandered through the front room at one point, eyeing Chad suspiciously. She stopped in front of us, and I had the sense she wanted to talk to me, but with Chad right there, she couldn't.

"Have you seen Ryan?" she asked us. I swallowed down the ire that crept up at her asking about Ryan.

"Think he went for a run," I told her. We were supposed to be keeping track of both stars, but Juliet paid us, so we kept closer tabs on her.

"Okay, thanks," she said, casting a look over her shoulder as she disappeared back up the stairs. I wished I could follow her.

Chad made no effort to hide the way he watched her head back up the stairs. "What I wouldn't give for five minutes with that ass," he said.

My hand was bunched in his shirt before I'd even had time to think about what I was doing, Chad's face pulled close to mine and my other fist next to his jaw. "If you ever lay a finger on her, I'll kill you," I told him in a whisper.

"What the fuck, man?" Chad's face ricocheted between surprise and concern. "Just a comment," he said, pushing me away with his hands on my shoulders.

I released him and stepped back as he stared at me. "Keep it professional."

"I don't know what's going on with you, but you better get it under control, Jace." He shook his head and smoothed his shirt out. "Shit, man."

I forced myself to breathe, and by the time Ryan McDonnell strolled by, I had myself mostly under control.

"Hey," I said to him as he walked by, partly proving to myself that I could be civil.

"Hey," he said back, turning with a smile. "It's Jace, right?"

I couldn't explain why, but knowing he knew my name gave me a small bit of satisfaction. I nodded and angled my head at Chad. "That's Chad."

McDonnell's face took on that shiny movie-star grin. "Thanks for being here, guys. Looking out for us."

As if we were here for him. "We're here for Juliet," I told him. There was no way I wanted this guy believing we worked for him.

He looked appropriately embarrassed, and I took a little bit of joy in it. "Right, yeah. Just ... thanks."

Chad chuckled, enjoying the star's embarrassment, no doubt. "Any time," he said.

"Juliet was looking for you a while ago," I told him. And then I forced my breathing to stay steady as another man climbed the stairs, no doubt heading to the bedroom of the woman I believed I might love.

The rest of the day was painful, standing in the shadows as the family and McDonnell moved here and there, and images of my brother's broken and frail body flashed through my head. My mind fluctuated alternately between desperate fear for my family and jealous rage over the situation with Juliet. I wanted to be at her side, to have her with me. Instead, I couldn't even find a moment to ask her how she was doing, to hold her hand and make sure she was okay. I didn't know if she'd heard anything more from Zac or her lawyers, if maybe they'd found a way to squash that moron so she could drop this pretense with McDonnell.

Gran didn't seem overly charmed with all of her sudden company, either. We all sat around the big table on the porch at dinner, and she erupted in complaints that we weren't entertaining enough.

"I expected tales of Hollywood insanity," she said at one point. "You two have to be the most boring movie stars there are. What are those magazine people going to talk to you about, your crocheting strategies?" She'd excused herself from the table after referring to the four of us bodyguards as "gorillas" a couple times, and gone back to the room where I'd learned she played video games most of the day. I suspected she did some other things in there too, based on the cloud of marijuana smoke that wafted from beneath the door of the room. Gran was not your run of the mill grandmother, that was for sure.

As the evening wore on, Jack asked if Chad and I would

be willing to take the first overnight shift. "I need a break from this chicken," he said, gesturing down at where Chessy stood on his boot, her head laid against his shin.

"Maybe you should just stop fighting it," I suggested. "She loves you. Be happy."

Jack sighed. "Right." Then he turned and went into his room, pulling his foot in last and using the door to basically scrape the chicken from his leg. She squawked and hollered angrily outside the door until he pushed a pillow out for her. It must have smelled like him or something, because she pecked at it a few times, and finally settled on top of it, keeping watch on his threshold like a dedicated guard chicken.

"Oh man," Chad laughed. "I'll get the perimeter. I like the smell of the air out there. Less chickeny."

I was relieved. If Chad was outside, I wouldn't have to sneak around too much to get up to Juliet's room. And I was desperate to see her.

When the house was quiet, except for Gran screeching in her little back room, I headed up the stairs. I tried to be as quiet as I could, but a two hundred and twenty pound guy on two hundred year old stairs was bound to make some noise. Still, if I'd ever needed to sneak, it was now. If we were caught together, it wasn't just my job, but Juliet's entire career. And maybe Ryan's too. At the top of the stairs, I turned, knocking lightly on the second door, as Juliet had instructed.

The door opened a crack, and Juliet's beautiful face appeared in the glow of golden light from within.

"Jace," she said, her voice happy and relieved. Her hand found mine, and seconds later we were pressed together, her back to the closed door and our bodies reminding us how perfectly we fit.

There were no words between us for a while, as we stripped off our clothes and found our way to Juliet's bed, each of us being as quiet as we could be.

I wanted to memorize every inch of Juliet's body, and the sound of her quiet moans as I slipped down beneath the covers, licking and kissing my way to her sweet center and giving her every bit of attention I'd been dying to give her all day. Feeling her pulse and release around my fingers as I sucked and kissed her was possibly the best moment of my life, though when I sank into her a few moments later, feeling her tight warmth envelop me, I revised that opinion.

Every minute with Juliet was the best moment of my life.

When the frenzy had stilled and we lay in each other's arms forehead to forehead, I finally felt like I could breathe.

"God, I missed you," I told her.

"Me too. I hate this, Jace. I know it's awful ..."

"Watching you with him ..." I couldn't even continue the thought.

"I know. But it's just a couple more days. Let's talk about something else." Her hand rubbed a soothing line up and down my arm, over my shoulder, and I closed my eyes, letting myself relax. "How's your mom? Your brother?"

Tension seeped back into me. "Let's not talk about that." There was no solution there, and I didn't want to waste the few minutes I had left with her on something so awful. "Mom says Elvis is good company."

She laughed lightly. "He's a good little guy." Her bright blue eyes fixed mine. "Tell me what's going on with your brother, Jace. I know you're worried. Don't keep it from me."

I sighed and pulled her closer, telling myself not to tell her, not to pull her into this. But the comfort of having her in my arms, having her soft body so near to mine and her sweet voice encouraging me to share was too much. I started talking, and then I couldn't stop. I told her about the rehab center, about what would happen if the hospital released Jarred to my mother, about how he'd relapse and Mom would blame herself. "It's impossible," I told her. "And there's nothing I can do to stop it. I already scared the shit out of some poor hospital administrator and a discharge nurse, neither of whom have any real control over this."

"Aren't there rehab centers that don't have wait lists?"

I squeezed my eyes shut. If I told her the truth, I already knew what would happen. She'd try to fix it. With money, which was like water to her. But on top of everything she was already doing for Mom, it would be way too much. And how could I hold my head up around her if I let her save me over and over again? I was a strong capable man. I could figure this out. "Not an option." I prayed she would leave it alone.

"That's insane. I know someone who just went into one a week ago, and she hadn't even planned it the week before that. It was like checking into a hotel. They can't all be over-crowded."

"I don't know," I said. "I don't want you to worry about it."

"Don't be ridiculous, if I can help, I will."

I let her go, sat up. I hated charity, ever since I'd been old enough to understand it, what it really was. We'd worn our cousins' hand me downs when we were little. But that last time we'd visited, before we'd been asked politely to leave, my cousin had made fun of me for wearing his old shirt. I would never forget that feeling, the shame of accepting someone else's castoffs. Charity made it impossible to hold your head up high. "Don't, Juliet. You've done enough."

She pulled the sheet up around her and sat up, turning toward me. "Jace. This is life or death. If I can help, it could save Jarred's life." She stared at me, and I knew she was right. Was I willing to risk my brother's life for my own pride?

"It's too much, Juliet. The private places are tens of thousands of dollars. We just ... my family ..." I trailed off. There was no point telling her we didn't have it. She knew that. I stared at my hands in my lap. My stupid, strong, ineffectual hands, callused from work and war and fighting but incapable of making the kind of money that would save my family. "I can't let you do it."

Juliet reached out and took one of my hands in hers, held it in the warmth of her palms. "Jace, you don't understand. I want to."

Charity. All I could think about was how this was charity. How it made me smaller and her bigger. How it ruined the equilibrium that was already hanging by a delicate thread between us. But it was my brother's life.

I couldn't speak. I just shook my head, wishing I could change anything at all.

"It's just money." Her voice was a plea, and I knew she believed her words. Because to people who had money, that was all it was. To people who didn't? Money was like water in a desert. Fundamental and scarce. And impossible to hold in your hands.

"If you do this, it'll ruin everything." The words slipped out, and I knew they needed context, but my mind was so ragged I couldn't add it. I couldn't make her see how her help made me feel small, how it emasculated me, how being saved by the woman I was falling in love with made even my love seem powerless and ineffectual.

"Why?" She asked. "Why can't I help?"

I thought about my brother's laughing face, the one I'd seen as a kid. I thought about the scraped knees I'd been able to bandage for him, the tears I'd wiped away when the kids on the bus had bullied him. I thought about how I'd knocked down the kid who'd been about to punch him after his first day in high school—when I'd been a senior and he'd been a freshman, how I'd saved him over and over. And how I couldn't save him now. Except by swallowing my pride and saying yes. Giving up my own sense of self to preserve his life.

"Okay," I said finally. And then I stood, dressed, and left the room before Juliet could say anything else. She watched me, asking me to stop, to talk, until I reached the door, and then I heard her soft voice. "Jace?" But the door was already closing between us.

"I can't," I managed. Maybe loudly enough for her to hear.

I was blind with anger and humiliation as I descended the stairs. Which was why I ran directly into Chad as he crossed the darkened front room.

For a moment we just stood facing one another in the darkness. I could practically hear the wheels turning in his thick skull.

"Everything okay upstairs?" he asked.

"Yeah."

He looked between me and the stairs for a minute. "Maybe everything is more than okay, eh?"

I stared at him, wishing I could set him on fire with my eyes. I was already full of shame and anger, and now a deep gnawing worry crept into the mix. Chad was an idiot, but he could certainly figure this out. And if he told Austin, if I lost my job right now, just when I needed money more than ever... "Everything is fine."

"You getting cozy with the boss, Jace?" His eyes narrowed as he thought about this. There'd been plenty of evidence back in LA, if he'd cared to see it. But now he was thinking about it, and I had no doubt he'd figure out that Juliet and I were involved.

"She's with McDonnell. You know that." I could barely force the words out. My mind was spun out, exhausted. I wasn't sure I even cared if he knew. I'd get fired, but maybe then at least I wouldn't have to see the look I knew I'd find in Juliet's eyes from today on—the look that told me I was less than a man, that I was someone who couldn't take care of his own, someone weak.

"Maybe she's with you too, eh?"

"She's not." I told him, my hands in fists so tight they ached. "I'm going outside." I pushed past him, aware that I'd done nothing to tamp down his suspicions.

Maybe it didn't matter anymore.

CHAPTER TWENTY-ONE
JULIET

Having Jace's permission to help his brother set me spinning into action, though I hated the way he'd left. I understood too, though. He was proud. It was part of what made him the man I cared about. He'd told me straight out how hard it was for him to accept help, but this was important. Finally, I felt like I could do something to show the man I was falling in love with that I cared—that I'd do just about anything for him. I wanted to be able to demonstrate what he meant to me, and though money was just money, if I could help this way, I was glad. I wanted to make his life easier if I could, give him one less thing to worry about, since at the moment I was only adding to his worries with all the crap with Ryan and with Zac.

Jace had stood by, hadn't complained as I'd asked him to pretend with me. He was loyal and steadfast—like Elvis, except with less snorting and a better command over his autonomous nervous system. Jace was my rock, and I was going to do whatever I could to show him what it meant to me.

I dug around in my email, looking for the name of the place Audra Harbinger had checked into a few days ago. I'd heard about it from a mutual friend I emailed with now and then, another actress. And after a few minutes of digging, I found the email.

"Hollybrook," I whispered, pulling up a browser. It was perfect.

It was late in Maryland, but earlier in California, where the center was located, so I called. And they had a spot for Jarred, for a significant price, of course. My heart lifted and I felt some of the tension float out of me. We could get him in. They'd pick him up from the hospital when he was discharged—Jarred wouldn't get the chance to fall down again. We could save him.

I was smiling when I'd finished arranging everything, and despite the hour, I picked up my phone to text Jace and let him know.

Me: The place is called Hollybrook. It's in the mountains near Lake Arrowhead. They'll pick Jarred up when he's discharged. It's all arranged.

Me: You'll just need to call to let them know the planned release day and time. Here's the number: 909-555-1945

I watched my phone for a response, and though three dots danced for a moment as if Jace was typing, no response came. I pushed away the disappointment—what had I expected?

After fifteen minutes, I forced myself to stop staring at the phone and go wash my face and get ready for bed. When I plugged in my phone and laid down, he still hadn't answered. And I tried not to think about him being angry, him holding onto his pride so tightly he wouldn't see I was helping out of love, because I cared. I didn't let myself think about the possibility that maybe I'd just made a choice—helping his family over having him.

He must have fallen asleep, I told myself. He'd respond when he woke up for his watch shift and there'd be an answer when I woke up.

Sleep came quickly once I'd closed my eyes. Between my confusion over Jace's hot and cold responses and the stress over my own messed up life, I was exhausted.

And my dreams were full of dark chocolate eyes and big warm hands, Jace's low rolling laugh. I refused to address the nagging worry that maybe everything that had felt so right could already be broken. I'd been trying to help. How could that have ruined anything?

I woke up early and checked my messages. There was no response from Jace. Still.

But I had a string of texts from Zac.

ZAC: *I've got three guys willing to testify against you. Double the settlement if you want to keep the video out of the press?*

Zac: *I'm not the only cheater here, Juliet.*

Zac: *Answer me...*

.   .   .

M**Y LAWYER HAD ADVISED** me to ignore any contact Zac made, so I took a screenshot and forwarded it to her.

Quick, efficient, businesslike. If only his words didn't affect me at all, but they did. Reading the vindictive and demanding texts from my ex made my head ache and my chest feel hollow. How could I have been so wrong about him? There had been a point where I thought he'd loved me for me.

He'd been so gracious and attentive when we'd first met. But soon after we were married, his attention was definitely more devoted to my income than to me.

But even when things were good, he'd never made me feel seen the way that Jace did. I tried to imagine Zac being happy to spend a night in, to play Mastermind by a fire with me, but I couldn't. Zac wanted to be seen, to go out, to be at the right events with the right people.

I sighed and rolled out of bed, taking the time to shower and get dressed, since the magazine interview was this morning at nine.

I couldn't help but worry about Jace's silence. How would I spend the day pretending with Ryan for the cameras, if Jace was angry or hurt? We needed to talk, but I didn't know if there would be time now.

Downstairs, the house was quiet, and I went into the kitchen to start the coffee maker, looking out over the back lawn in hopes of seeing Jace, but he wasn't there. I watched the coffee brew, letting my mind wander aimlessly as worry twisted inside me. Worry over Zac. Over Jace's silence. Over my ability to pull off this thing with Ryan.

When the coffee was ready, I poured a cup, so caught up with what was going on in my head that I didn't even notice Chad appear behind me.

"Got a cup for me?" he asked, startling me as I turned. My breath caught and I gasped as I sloshed coffee over the edge of the cup and my hand.

"Shit," I said, turning back for a towel to mop up the mess.

"Sorry," he said, stepping closer to me, crowding me a bit into the counter as he reached for a paper towel and then knelt down to mop up the puddle I'd made. He stood again, still in my personal space, and grinned down at me, an odd look in his eye. "Didn't mean to scare you."

I slid sideways to get away from him a bit, laughing nervously. "No, it's fine. I was just miles away in my own head. Didn't hear you come in." I motioned to the coffee maker and cups. "Help yourself."

Jace and Chad seemed to work the same shifts most of the time, so I glanced into the hallway, expecting to see Jace nearby, but the front room was silent. A tiny finger of unease crept up my spine, but I told myself to ignore it. I'd been alone with Chad lots of times. He was harmless. Just creepy.

"So," Chad said, seemingly in no hurry to get to whatever station he'd been assigned for the morning. "Long night?"

I smiled at him, my mind beginning to churn over his strange behavior. "Um, no, not really." I could hear a steady beat coming from the basement, along with irregular sounds that told me my sister was awake, and beating up the old punching bags she'd hung down there years ago. I was about to turn toward the basement stairs when there was a knock at the front door.

Chad put his coffee cup on the counter, and pushed past me in the hallway. "Duty calls," he said, his hand brushing me —maybe accidentally—as he went by. I recoiled from his touch and followed him to the front door, hearing the conversation as he opened it.

"Good morning. *Hollywood Entertainer* to interview Juliet Manchester and Ryan McDonnell? Are we at the right house?"

I glanced at my watch. They were early. Really early. I moved up next to Chad. "Good morning. Glad you could make it," I said. "Please, come in."

Chad motioned the crew into the front room, and I spotted Jace outside, talking to one of the cameramen, as the reporter came up the front steps, her red bob bouncing as she walked. A little stone of concern lodged itself inside me. He was up. And he hadn't made a point of responding to me? "Good morning Juliet. Wow, this is beautiful."

"Hi there," I said, reaching out a hand to shake. "You're Alison, right?"

She beamed, as if pleased I had recognized her. "I am," she said. "And I'm so happy to be here." She looked around. "We'll need some time to get the room set up. This is where you want us?" She stood in the front parlor, which Tess had said was where she thought the interview should take place.

"If that will work," I told Alison, wishing they had not popped up so early and needing to let Tess know they were here.

"Perfect."

"Excuse me," I said. "Chad can help you if you need anything." The driving urge to get away from Chad was still lingering in my chest, and I slipped through the basement door and down the stairs, relieved to get away from his odd energy.

As I fled down the steps, I could hear Tess breathing out quick hard breaths as her fists and shins struck the heavy bag hanging from the ceiling. "You're still beating the shit out of these bags, huh?" I asked her stepping into the padded space in the center of the unfinished basement.

"Keeps me in shape," she said, smiling. "Gets my mind to still a bit."

I raised an eyebrow and stepped closer to the bag. A still mind sounded pretty good right then. Between Zac and Jace, and Chad's weird behavior ... and the magazine people arriving early, I could only wish for a still mind. "Dad would be happy," I said. He'd taught her to box when we were young and she was getting bullied a bit at school. Mom had hated the idea, but Tess had always been physical. "Maybe I could use that." I tapped the speed bag with my fist, watching it bounce.

Tess watched me with big observant eyes. "You doing okay?"

I shrugged and punched the heavy bag, hard. Pain flared through my hand as the bones inside of it smashed into what felt like concrete. The bag barely moved. "Ouch. Shit!" I looked over my knuckles to make sure they weren't bleeding or obviously broken.

"You need to wrap your hands if you're going to hit that hard." Tess held up her own wrapped hands, and then switched off the music and picked up her drink. I zoned out while she tidied up and got ready to come back upstairs. She bumped my shoulder. "You sure you're okay?"

"I'm great Tess, really." I couldn't tell her anything, no matter how much I wanted to talk. I would have loved to tell her about Jace, about the way my heart squeezed when he was around. Or to get her advice about Zac, or even Chad and his weird behavior this morning, but I couldn't. I couldn't do any of that without jeopardizing the delicate tower of lies I had built to protect myself. And at this point, telling her the truth would hurt Ryan too. His career depended on this link to me, as stupid as that was, and the last thing I needed to do was affect one more person's life in a negative way.

"Ryan seems nice," she said, her voice soft and careful.

Right. I was supposed to be dating him. I was supposed to gush over him, be lovestruck. I tried to channel my feelings for Jace into my voice. "He's a good guy." It was the best I could do.

"So you've just been seeing each other a couple weeks? I mean, you weren't seeing him before ... you know ...?" My sister was asking me if I'd cheated on Zac.

I tried not to let my anger at the question show. It was a natural thing to be curious about.

I turned and we started up the stairs, and I almost wished I had cheated on him since I was going to pay for it either way. "No. I would have been faithful forever. Even though things ... " I thought about the distance between my husband

and me even before he decided to betray me on the island with my chef. "Things had gotten harder," I said. My voice cracked.

"Jul," Tess said, her tone soft and understanding. "I'm so sorry."

God, I wished I could really talk to my sister. I needed a friend to confide in. "There's so much I want to tell you," I said instead.

"So tell me."

"I can't. The magazine people are here." It was as good an excuse as I could come up with, and as I pointed to the front parlor as we came up the stairs, it was a good distraction. Tess immediately spun up into stressy-Tessy. Chad stood right in front of us, grinning at me in a creepy way.

"Crap," Tess said. "They're really early."

"It's good," I told her. "Maybe we'll be done early." And then I could finally talk to Jace.

"I need to shower. I wanted to be ready. I had a plan." Tess sounded mildly panicked.

"It's fine, Tess. You don't have to wait on anyone." We stepped past Chad and Tess looked around, taking in the people milling around the front parlor.

"I got this," she said, and my sister went into hostess mode.

* * *

Soon, Ryan and I were sitting next to the window, with Alison in front of us, perched on a stool like an over-alert seagull, waiting for either of us to drop something it might grab and digest. Jace had come into the room a few minutes after we'd been seated, and his eyes had glanced over me as if I was just another piece of furniture in the parlor. They'd hung for a moment too long, however, on Ryan.

A little jolt of satisfaction popped to life in me, as much as I didn't want it to. He hadn't returned my texts, he hadn't spoken to me since last night. At least that lingering glance, in which his eyes had darkened with what looked like anger, meant he did see me. He did care. In some way, at least.

I sighed, but just as I was telling myself to relax, Chessy skittered into the room, flapping her wings and chattering. Jack stepped in just behind her, looking exasperated.

Alison turned her head in horror, and Jack mouthed "sorry" to her just before Chessy shrieked and launched herself at Alison, maybe deciding she was a rival for Jack's affection.

"Chessy!" Tess screamed, sprinting into the room after the chicken, pulling her from Alison's legs, where the chicken was trying to peck her to death. Alison was teetering on top of the high stool, her legs pulled up under her. At least if she decided to write about our crazy chicken, she'd have less space for delving into my life.

"What is that thing?" she hissed.

Tess managed to grab Chessy and held the irate house chicken to her chest. "This is Chessy," she said, as if it was completely normal to have a house chicken attacking guests.

Alison hadn't relaxed any at this explanation. "Why is it inside?"

"She's an indoor chicken," Tess said. She glanced at me, but I couldn't offer any help and Alison did not look mollified. Tess's eyes rounded and she gave me one last pleading glance before she said, "It's very trendy here in Maryland."

I nodded helpfully.

"Really?" Alison asked, relaxing slightly.

"Oh yes," Tess said, evidently getting comfortable with her insanity. "You should see all the fancy ladies out at lunch with their hens in designer bags. I'm surprised they're not doing it in California yet." I cringed, but Tess barreled ahead. "It's a nod to environmentalism and the humane treatment of animals, and antibiotics ..."

Antibiotics?

"Interesting," Alison said. I stared at her as she jotted down Tess's muddled explanation.

"I'm sorry, I thought Chessy was out of the way," she said, taking Chessy toward the kitchen.

"Sorry," I added, leaning in toward Alison. I wondered if insane chicken husbandry was going to make it into the article. Now all we needed was Gran ambling in, smoking a joint and screaming at children in her online game.

"Not to worry," she said. "Very interesting."

I could feel Jace watching from across the room, his eyes heavy as they took in the way Ryan and I sat close together, our legs touching.

"So tell me," Alison said, looking up at us then. A wiry man with glasses and a camera was filming us from just behind her. "Tell us what it was like, when you first knew you had more than just onscreen chemistry with Ryan McDonnell." She raised her eyebrows and grinned, as if imagining herself with Ryan.

I wanted to tell her she had a shot, that she could have him. I forced myself to keep my eyes from Jace, standing dark and handsome in the far corner of the room. "It wasn't love at first sight really," I said. "I mean, I'd seen Ryan of course— who hadn't? He'd been in every amazing action movie I saw." I turned to look at Ryan, doing my best to force all the feelings I had for Jace into the look, to make it convincing.

Ryan smiled his easy grin. "It was more like complete adoration at first sight," he said, pulling my hand to his lips. I still wasn't used to him touching me like this. It felt stiff and unnatural, and I tried not to cringe away. He wasn't repellant —not like Chad. Just ... he wasn't Jace.

And then it came, as I knew it would. "Are you willing to talk a bit about Zac Stevens? Your divorce and the rumors surrounding it?" Alison's face morphed into something like an eagle's, sharp and anticipatory.

"Um," I managed. Very smooth. I glanced at Jace, met his eyes and felt heat rush through me. I was blowing this. Falling apart.

Ryan saved me. "We don't need to drag her through that," he said, squeezing my hand.

I cleared my throat. "It's fine," I said. "What do you want to know?" If I was really the victim here, there was no reason I shouldn't be willing to answer at least a few questions.

Alison went on to ask about the rumors of Zac and one of our house staff, and I told her that it had been me who caught them together, and that was how I knew for sure it was true. That question didn't surprise me. I hadn't wanted to talk about it, but I'd been prepared for it. The next one? Not as much.

"And there are other rumors. About the settlement. That Zac has a tape he's threatening to release?"

I felt myself stiffen. No one was supposed to know about the tape. My agent had assured me that paying Zac off would make it go away. But Alison knew. How did she know?

"That is something I can't discuss," I made myself say. "The settlement is still being sorted by the lawyers, so I'm not able to give you any specifics, I'm afraid." I pushed down the fear that was racing up my throat, making my hair feel like it was standing on end.

"And the blackmail rumor?"

Ryan proved that he'd been the right choice for this job. "I think we can find other things to talk about, can't we? No one in the midst of a divorce wants their dirty laundry aired. Not even America's sweetheart," he said in a way that was both sweet and threatening at once. Maybe he was a better actor than I'd given him credit for.

"Right," Alison said, and she smiled back, clearly ready to move on.

I bumped Ryan's shoulder in thanks, relief washing through me.

Alison went on with her questions, sticking to recent films and upcoming plans, and I felt the room chill noticeably when Chad took Jace's place by the door and Jace disappeared, heading for the kitchen. I managed to stay where I was, but I had to actively restrain myself from following him.

I needed to talk to him, find out if maybe he just hadn't seen the messages I'd sent. Or learn if there was something else going on.

The few times I'd met his eyes over the reporter's, they'd seemed sad, haunted, even. But Jace's eyes were always dark and expressive. Maybe I was misreading things. Maybe everything was fine.

But I had a creeping suspicion that everything was not fine.

CHAPTER TWENTY-TWO
JACE

I watched Juliet and Ryan answer questions for the magazine and take photos all morning, feeling sick in a way I never had before.

McDonnell's hands were all over the woman I'd begun to think of as mine, and the way he touched her was so easy, so possessive, even I was believing they were a couple. And that, combined with Juliet's texts about Hollybrook, was turning my stomach and tunneling my vision in a way that darkened everything I looked at. The gorgeous blue-skied Maryland day, the greenery leaning over the shore of the river, even Juliet, who always reminded me of light and air—it was all tinged with blackness as the ichor inside me tainted my world.

The photo shoot would have been hard enough to handle on its own. The reporter had them rolling on the lawn together, her hair falling down around his shoulders as she straddled him and leaned down over him, giving me flashbacks to times when that hair had tickled my skin, brushed my cheeks as I buried myself inside her. They posed near the river, next to the house, with Gran and Tess (Gran complaining the whole time), and just the two of them.

And fuck, if Juliet wasn't a good actress. Part of me wondered if there really might be something going on with them, but I quashed it as quickly as it had been born. For all the things I was already questioning—my masculinity, my ability to be an independent adult in a world that revolved so completely around resources I didn't have—I wasn't questioning Juliet's loyalty. And I knew she wasn't with McDonnell, no matter how convincing the act.

But maybe she should be.

As the morning wore on and I stood near the back porch keeping an eye on things, my mother's smiling face kept sweeping through my consciousness. How different she looked in the cottage in Brentwood, how much more relaxed and happy. Juliet had given her that. She'd given her a safe place to live, a place where she could relax and garden, and live the life she deserved. Juliet had made sure she'd seen a doctor. And now Juliet was busy saving my brother too. And it was all nothing to her.

So how could I explain that those actions, actions that were easy for her, things she could control because of her wealth, they were impossible for me? And having them handled so easily, as easily as sweeping some dust off the table top or picking up a gallon of milk, it made my entire life feel petty and small. I couldn't begin to dream of setting the people I loved up the way she had. She'd been able to manage everything simply because she decided to. Things I would have spent the rest of my life trying to find the resources to make happen.

How was I supposed to reconcile my ego and my pride with the fact that I'd never be able to take care of my family that way? And how could I ever hope to take care of a woman like Juliet?

I wasn't sure I could.

I'd spent the whole night looking for some alternative to Hollybrook for Jarred. I'd talked to the hospital staff, worn tracks all over the internet trying to find some other way, something I could pay for, but it didn't exist. There was nothing I could find that would offer the same immediate care, at the same level of quality. I just didn't have the money to make it happen. And I hated myself for it.

The only option I could come up with was to take two weeks off work and be Jarred's babysitter until the spot opened up at the state-run facility. But as Mom had intimated, that wasn't a sure thing. They might have a place for him. It depended on lots of factors, evidently. Hollybrook was a sure thing. If you had the cash, at least.

In the meantime, Chad was getting on my nerves and I was close to clocking the guy. He'd been giving me creepy grins all morning and I kept replaying the way he'd asked me the night before if I was getting involved with the boss. I didn't like him, but I also didn't think he was an idiot. It was only a matter of time before he decided to talk to Austin, and then I was surely going to lose my job. And now that I'd spent my savings on Jarred's bail? There wasn't much hope to hold out for ahead.

But maybe it didn't matter—I wasn't sure anything else would be happening between Juliet and me. How could I ever hold my head up, knowing I needed her to take care of me?

I was a fucking Marine.

And I couldn't take care of my family.

THE MAGAZINE PEOPLE FINALLY LEFT, and lunch was served on the porch. Ryan and Tess were leaving the property, and while I didn't think it was a good idea for him to be off running around Maryland, I also didn't work for him. If Juliet was here, the team stayed here. But Chad and I had a few hours off the clock, and I had a lot of thinking to do.

I'd flopped back on my bed and had begun a serious study of the plaster ceiling when a knock came at my door.

"Jace?" Juliet's voice was on the other side. I hated the excitement that glowed in me at the sound of her voice. I'd been avoiding her all day, I should have just continued. But that wasn't the mature thing to do. I needed to face my problems.

I was on my feet, opening the door, before I thought better of it. She came inside and I closed the door behind her, hoping Chad wasn't around. "Did anyone see you?"

She shook her head. "No, I checked to make sure no one was around." Juliet gazed at me for a long second, but when I made no move to get closer, she let out a long breath and then turned, looking around the room before finally settling on the end of the bed. "Is everything okay?"

I didn't trust myself. If I went on instinct, we'd already be in the bed, my body seeking the same intoxicating comfort I'd found with her the night before—and all the nights back at her house in Los Angeles. But I couldn't let that happen now. I sat in a chair in the corner of the room, and kept my eyes away from the puzzled look that appeared on Juliet's face.

She spread her hands on her thighs, dropping her head for a minute and both of us staring at her hands, her pale skin white on the denim of her skinny jeans. "We told Tess the truth," she said quietly. "About me and Ryan. So you don't need to worry about keeping up the pretense with her." She glanced at me, dropped her eyes again. "Gran doesn't know still."

"Okay," I said. I didn't want it to, but a little spark of hope ignited at that revelation. If she told Tess it was all an act, then maybe that validated us a little bit? "Thanks for letting me know. I don't think I'll tell the guys. Just let them keep things as they are until we head back."

"Sure," she said. She got to her feet, took a step toward me, and then seemed to think better of it. She stopped in the center of the room. "Have I done something wrong?" Her voice pulled at something inside me, made me want to reach for her, comfort her.

I let out a slow exhale. "No." How could I tell her that every wonderful thing she'd done had been right—but that it all made it impossible for me to look her in the eyes? "The things you've done for my family ..." I swallowed hard and forced myself to look at her. To thank her properly. "I'll never be able to thank you for what you've done. Moving my mom, helping my brother ... I don't have the funds or the words to repay you. I'll never be able to repay you. That place, Hollybrook. I looked at it online, talked to the administrator there." I swallowed some of my humiliation and went on. "It costs more than I made last year, Juliet. I can't ... I don't..."

"You don't have to repay me, Jace." She sounded surprised that I'd brought it up.

"Of course I do. I can't let you—"

"You didn't let me do anything," she interrupted, her voice stronger now. "I did something because I wanted to. Because I care about you, and that means I care about your family. If you saw someone lying in the street, would you help them up, or just walk by, knowing you could have stopped them getting hit by a car?"

I looked up at her. Her cheeks were blazing pink and her eyes were wide as she waited for an answer. "This isn't even close—"

"It's the same thing," she said. "I'm not the kind of person who can just ignore something like that."

"It's tens of thousands of dollars, Juliet."

"Which I can easily afford."

"And I'll never be able to." That was the simple truth of it. I dropped my elbows to my knees and bowed my head.

"What difference does it make?" She asked, stepping closer to me. "Jace, why does it matter?"

It made all the difference in the world. To me, at least. But maybe to her, it really didn't matter. Could I live with that disparity? When I didn't answer, she went on, dropping a cool hand to the back of my neck, leaving it there.

"I can't even leave my house anymore," she said. "I can't have a relationship without it being put under a magnifying glass. I can't grocery shop, go to a restaurant. My life is not my own. And you know what? That's okay. That's the deal I made. And as annoying as it is to live my life like a hermit, afraid to take a wrong step or give someone the wrong idea, I get paid pretty well for it. Maybe that's ridiculous, but that's how it is. Money is the one thing I do have. And if I can use it to make your life easier, to help the people you love, then why wouldn't I do that?"

I let my head roll back and forth, stretching the muscles of my neck under her hand. She would never understand.

"Jace, let me help."

"I don't have a choice," I muttered, my shame beginning to morph into something closer to anger. I stood, her hand falling from my neck as I turned to face her. "I have to accept your help, no matter how small it makes me feel, because I don't have any other choices."

She stared at me, her shock at my angry tone written in the wide eyes, the little round O of her mouth. "You're angry that I helped?"

"No," I said, rubbing my neck and pacing away from her. "How could I be angry at that? I'm grateful. But ... really, when you offered, what choice did I have?"

"You could have said no," she whispered. I could feel her eyes on me as I paced back and forth next to the bed.

"I think I did."

"And I didn't listen. But I couldn't let you say no, not really. Did you really mean it?"

Those words stopped me. "No, that's the point. Don't you get that? Saying no would have killed my brother. Maybe my mom too."

"So why are you angry?"

"Because it's made everything impossible between you and me," I told her.

She shook her head, the light hair sliding around her shoulders. I had a sudden vision of myself wrapping all that long hair around my fist, pushing her to her knees and her mouth taking me, me thrusting into her, spurting out all the venom and anger I felt at the world, the universe, in a hot rush of release.

"I can't even look you in the eyes now," I admitted, stopping myself pacing. "I'm supposed to be the one to help them. To save them. But I couldn't do anything, and here you were with all your money, so willing and sweet."

She made a scoffing noise of disbelief. "You're angry because I was willing and able to help."

"I'm angry that I needed you to." The words came out hard and cold. "I'm not angry because you helped. I'm angry that I couldn't. That I couldn't save them, I didn't have the resources. Without you ... well, my family would be in a terrible situation."

"Why? Because you have some ridiculous idea that because you're a man, because you're a Marine—that you shouldn't ever need help? That you should always be able to handle things?"

I didn't answer as the truth settled over me like a scarf woven from stones. I believed exactly what she'd said. That I was the man, that I was the Marine, that all of that together meant I should be able to solve any problem that came my way.

"It shouldn't matter where the money came from," she said. "Just that it came."

"Right." I felt the fight leave my body and resignation take its place.

"So you can't even look at me now?" Her tone was a mix of anger and distress, and my heart twisted in response. "Jace."

I wanted to reach for her, wanted to throw her on the bed and never let her go. But I couldn't make myself move. How could I expect her to ever look at me the same way again? "Whatever was between us," I managed to say. "It won't be the same now. It won't—"

Juliet didn't let me finish. She stepped into my chest, pressing her mouth to mine and kissing me almost violently. She pulled me into her body, wrapping her arms around me and claiming my mouth, finishing the kiss with a painful bite of my lower lip. She glared up at me and then sank to her knees, her hands going to my waist.

"No," I said, my mind racing, shame and desire flooding me, confusing me.

"Shut up." She had my fly open, her hands slipping inside my pants, finding me already hard.

"Jul—" Her name got lost as she took me into her mouth, and my hands went into her hair. I wrapped the long silk around my fist, realizing this was exactly what I'd pictured just moments before, the image turning to reality and nearly sending me off right then. I stared down at her, fisting her hair and pulling her head back and forth as she licked and sucked and moaned around me. "Fuck," I whispered.

Juliet didn't say anything, and if she minded the way I was moving her head, or pushing myself into the back of her throat, her protests sounded a lot like moans of satisfaction. One of her hands gripped my base as the other cradled my balls, and every thought in my mind had scattered, lost in the dark want that was filling me as I felt the tingling begin at the base of my spine. I was angry. I was desperate. I was hurt and ashamed. And all of it was being literally sucked from me by the hot wet mouth of the woman I knew without a doubt I was in love with.

Juliet Manchester, America's sweetheart, was on her knees for me as I fucked her mouth until her eyes watered.

Her hand left my cock and slid around to grip my ass, pulling me deeper still, and that did it.

Maybe shame was the prevailing emotion when she'd come in, maybe I'd felt like something less than a man before. But having her on her knees with my cock shoved halfway down her throat did a hell of a lot for my ego. And as I erupted inside her, grunting in an effort to keep from shouting, I thought there was a chance things could still be okay.

CHAPTER TWENTY-THREE
JULIET

I was angry at Jace. Even as I took him into my mouth, my own body igniting with want and need for him as he thrust over and over into my throat and I egged him on, I was still angry.

Money was the only thing I actually had—and it couldn't replace freedom or respect, but it was mine and I'd earned it, and I wouldn't apologize for that.

And I wasn't about to apologize for helping the family of the man I loved. But it felt like the money—the help—had wound its way between us like a poisonous serpent, tainting what had been perfect and sweet.

After I'd released Jace and wiped my mouth, gotten back to my feet, he'd pulled me into his arms gently, those big dark eyes still full of pain even though the lines on his face had relaxed.

"I'm sorry, Juliet," he said in a whisper. "This is hard for me. All of it. Watching you with him. Pretending I don't care.

And then having you sweep in and rescue me like I'm some helpless princess ..." he trailed off, squeezing his eyes shut.

"Princess," I repeated, the irony of this huge man calling himself a princess striking me as funny. "Put your ego aside, Princess," I told him. "If you can. Because that's the only thing screwing this up right now."

"My ego, about a million dollars, a vindictive ex-husband, a pretty-boy movie star who's gonna lose a hand next time he puts one on your tit, and the fact you're my client. That's all that's screwing this up," he said, his tone bitter.

"Is that all?" I tried to keep my voice light as I realized how many things were actually stacked between us.

Half his mouth curled up into something close to a smile as his hands rested warm and firm on my back. "Yeah. And don't call me Princess again."

I laughed, pressing my cheek to his chest and trying to memorize the way it felt to be in his arms, the scent of him. As we stood there, I heard the front door open and close outside Jace's room, and then open again a few minutes later. I was about to figure out what to do next—dinner, more pretending—when I heard the door open yet again, and then heard Ryan and Tess talking as they moved past the east wing.

"I swear," Ryan's voice said. "I told you the truth. If Juliet's got someone in her room ..." I stepped back slightly and looked up at Jace, who was clearly listening too, his dark eyes serious, focused on the door.

"Ryan," Tess's voice came, sharp and angry. "You're the only guy here."

"We're sleeping in separate rooms."

"Doesn't sound like Gran is talking about sleeping," Tess said. Gran? What had Gran said? Had Gran heard me having sex? Mortification flooded me.

"You know," Ryan said, his voice becoming fainter as they moved through the house. "There is the security team." I felt Jace stiffen.

Tess's voice was louder now, filled with mocking disbelief. "Juliet is not getting together with a bodyguard."

Jace's arms fell, leaving me cold as he stepped back. The look on his face told me that might have been the last straw, the tiny barb that made the wounds to his ego mortal, unre-coverable.

"Jace," I whispered, staring up into those pain-filled dark eyes, wishing they would dance and gleam as they had the first few nights we'd spent together in the safe bubble of my house. The tone in Tess's voice, the complete dismissal of the idea that I would get involved with someone like Jace, revealed both my sister's opinion of what was important to me in people and also the other part of what was bothering Jace—the belief that he wasn't good enough.

"She's right." He frowned down at me. "This is ridiculous. You're fucking Juliet Manchester, and I'm ... I'm a broke former Marine who can't take care of his own family, let alone a woman like you."

I gaped, my body chilling as he put a hand on the door-knob. "It doesn't matter," I said. "I don't care about any of that."

"That's what people tell themselves sometimes," he said.

"That's how they sell books and romantic movies." He shook his head, a mirthless smile pulling his face into a painful expression that broke my heart even more. "But we live in the real world. Where I'll never be able to pay you back for what you've done, and neither one of us will ever be able to forget it."

"Jace." I stepped toward him, and he actually put up a hand to keep me back, stopping me in my tracks.

"Go find a movie star to love, Juliet. Someone like you. And one day you'll look back and you can congratulate yourself on the way you took care of that charity case that one time. That poor helpless idiot, Jace."

"What?" I felt the blood drain from my face. "Is that what you think of me?" I hated him in that instant, as he stood there self-righteous and innocent, playing the victim. The reason I'd found my way to Jace, to his arms and his bed, was because he saw me—really saw me—in a way no one else had ever been able to. He had never cast me in the role of superficial starlet, had never made me feel two-dimensional and insignificant. He'd seen the woman behind the cardboard cutout.

But clearly, I'd been wrong. He saw me exactly as everyone else did. A shallow movie star. A name.

That's all I'd ever be, I realized, wishing I could undo everything and never move away from Southern Maryland. I hadn't been happy here, but at least I'd been a human being. I moved past Jace, stepping out the door as he pulled it open and forcing myself not to look at him.

Chad was emerging from the room next door at the same

moment that I stepped out of Jace's room, and for a second, we both stopped.

"I had some business to discuss with Jace," I told him.

"Right," Chad said, nodding as his lips pulled into an ugly grin.

I went to my room and stayed there, fuming and crying, until Tess called up that it was time for dinner, and then I went downstairs, girding myself. I'd still need to play Ryan's girlfriend for Gran, a task made harder by the way my heart ached for Jace. I hoped he might be outside during the meal, somewhere I could forget about him for a while.

But he wasn't. As we sat around the dining room table, Gran smiling broadly at one end, Jace hovered in the doorway, his black-clad shoulder coming into sight now and then as he shifted his weight.

The meal was a painful blur of polite conversation, and when it was over, I was relieved. Ryan stood, reaching for my plate. "I'll get these," he said.

I forced a smile at him. "So polite."

As Ryan left the room, Tess burst out, "Gran, at the table?" I looked down the length of the dinner table to find Gran industriously rolling a joint on the cherrywood top.

Gran shrugged and gave Tess a wink. "Big raid in an hour."

"Get it out of your system tonight. Tomorrow you have to dress up and be the center of attention and act like a proper old lady."

Gran sighed. "I'd kind of hoped I'd keel over before then. I guess there's still tonight. Sometimes wishes come true." I thought about that. It didn't feel like it to me. Then Gran continued, "You got to kiss your Hollywood crush, after all."

I felt my brow wrinkle in confusion. What? I swung my gaze to Tess, who was staring at me, pulling her lower lip between her teeth. "Jules," she whispered.

Ryan had just come back into the room, and I looked between them, my mind working over what I'd just heard. Had Tess been getting together with Ryan? Even though she'd believed he and I were together? Would my own sister do that? "You kissed Ryan?" I said, before I could figure things out.

Gran leaned back in her chair, watching this exchange with something that looked like pleasure.

"What? No," Tess said, too quickly. "I mean ... no, he's your boyfriend, right?" That, I knew, was for Gran's benefit. We wouldn't even be able to touch the real issue with Gran here —the issue being the fact that Tess was just one more person who saw me as something less than an actual person, someone she could just step around if I was in her way. "I mean, he was in your room last night," she went on. "Moaning huskily, right Gran?"

What was she even talking about now? I glanced toward the doorway, long enough to see that Jace had moved closer and was watching all this. The mention of Ryan being in my room had turned his expression to stone.

Gran looked stricken. "I wasn't eavesdropping," she said, her voice shrill, telling me she had probably been standing in the hallway with a glass pressed to my door as Jace and I had sex. "I couldn't help it. You were so loud. I haven't heard those noises in this house since I quit watching Erika Lust films." She shot me a look that dared me to complain, and then stood abruptly. "I'm expected elsewhere." She walked out of the room, passing Jace on her way.

"What the hell is going on?" I asked Tess. Then I shot a glance at Ryan. "Are you two hooking up?"

"No," Tess said.

"Yes," Ryan said.

For fuck's sake. I dropped my head into my hands. I couldn't accept my sister piling on at this point. Everyone in my life had assumed I was just a pretty face, just someone who could read some lines and scoop up some money. Then I was supposed to go home and be happy with my lot in life, be happy that people expected me to stick to a script, never have any genuine thoughts or emotions of my own. That allowed them to just move around me. "Seriously?" I asked her.

"Jules," Ryan said, his voice low, intimate. "I didn't plan it. It's just ... I think there's something here." He waved a hand toward my sister.

My mind rolled, anger and hurt mixing inside me. Jace, Zac, this ... I couldn't take it. "Yeah, something's here," I spit at Ryan. "My little sister's here. And she doesn't need you barreling into her life and screwing everything up, just to leave when your next movie role takes you to Timbuktu." I channeled the tiny bit of my anger that had erupted on Tess's behalf. She didn't know how Hollywood worked, she wasn't equipped to be involved with Ryan.

"What are the odds there'll be another movie in

Timbuktu?" Ryan asked, grinning. "I think it was just that one—"

"No." I interrupted him, getting to my feet. I felt like I was going to explode, and seeing Jace hovering there, listening, only confused issues more. "You don't get to charm your way out of this one, you ... you ..." Words failed me as tears pricked the backs of my eyelids. I was angry at Jace. I was angry at Tess. I was angry at Chad with all his knowing looks and suggestive smiles, and I was angry at Ryan for taking advantage of my sister. "Man!" I finally found a word to hurl at someone and it wasn't even half of what I'd hoped.

Tess looked disappointed at the insult, and said, "Not much of a burn." Then she shook her head and went on. "Listen, guys. Let's just pretend none of this happened. If you're hooking up, that's perfect. That's what you want everyone to think anyway, right? And you'll be gone in a couple days, and Gran and I can go back to our regular lives. Whatever happened between me and Ryan, which was pretty much nothing, was just a lighthearted fling. It was nothing."

"Um," Ryan said, sounding hurt.

Jace's body had gone rigid in the doorway. Perfect. Now he thought maybe I was hooking up with Ryan. I stepped closer to Ryan, unable to get hold of the chaos inside my chest and head. "No. Look. You're here because I'm doing you a favor," I told him, pointing a finger at him. "I didn't bring you here to charm the pants off my naïve little sister and break her heart. That's not what this is about. This is about—"

"You." Tess said, spitting the word at me as she stood. "Everything is about you. It always has been. Right, Jules?

And this, this weekend—which was supposed to be about Gran, by the way—has become a media circus so you can show the world that Juliet Manchester is just fine after her nasty divorce. And what makes a woman fine? Another man, of course! So you picked one off the man tree to help you out, and we all have to play along, right?"

Shock ran through me. What? On top of everything else, Tess was calling me selfish? Hadn't I called myself the very same thing earlier? Maybe that's all I really was. A selfish empty-headed starlet who ran around hurting other people and not even realizing it.

"It's so hard for you to imagine that maybe someone might actually be interested in me, isn't it? It's just completely outside your realm of experience. After all, what do I have to offer? I'm the short one, the fat one, the unpopular one ... I'm Juliet Manchester's little sister, right? That's all I've ever been, and with you around, it's all I'll ever be."

Confusion washed through me, gushing over whatever logic or sense I had. I shook my head, managing to clear it slightly. Whatever was coming out of Tess's mouth didn't feel like it was about this weekend. Or about Ryan. It felt much deeper and older than that. Tess thought I was selfish, self-centered. She thought having me around made her life harder, worse. She thought I wanted the spotlight all the time, that I needed it. How could I explain how wrong she was? "No, Tess ..."

"Let's just get through tomorrow night's charade and then you can all go back where you belong," she said, turning. "You can take your fame and your angst and your enormous security guards and just go home. Both of you." Tess turned and left the room, flying past Chessy, who squawked in a chicken version of a fist bump as I sank back down at the table.

Ryan stood still for a second, his hands spread on the white tablecloth as he leaned his weight on them. "Juliet. I'm sorry," he said quietly.

I didn't know what to think. I was upset, but as I pieced through the feelings zipping around inside me, I realized I wasn't angry at him, not if he really cared about Tess. "You just met her, Ryan."

"I know. It's insane. But Juliet," he stood up and looked at me, wearing the most open and honest expression I'd ever seen. "I think I'm in love with her. I've never felt this way."

I knew that feeling. I hoped maybe it would work out better for Ryan than it was working out for me. I sighed. "Go get her, Ryan. But if you hurt her ..." I barely had the strength to make the threat.

"You and Gran will team up to remove my balls," he suggested.

"Something like that." I had no doubt Gran knew more about what was going on than I did. I'd been so wrapped up in my own world. In Jace.

Ryan left the room and I sat at the table for a while, comforted in a strange way by Jace's silent presence in the doorway. I looked over at him, but if he had thoughts about everything that had just happened, he wasn't sharing them now. He stood silent, his back to me, both of us sharing the pain and hurt that might as well have been a canyon between us.

CHAPTER TWENTY-FOUR
JACE

I listened as Tess and Ryan revealed their relationship, and tried to understand whether Juliet was angry, or jealous, or ... what. At first, it seemed like she was angry. She wasn't with McDonnell, but she didn't want anyone else to be either? But then, as her sister rambled, furious, I realized it wasn't about McDonnell. It was something else, something older, that lay between Juliet and Tess. My heart ached, listening to Juliet's pain, and I wanted to step into the room and tell Tess she was wrong about her sister, that Juliet was caring, giving, that she cared too much about other people, even.

Of course Chad had no such thoughts, apparently—he felt sympathy for no one. He stood in the hallway, having been summoned from his post by the front door when the voices escalated around the dinner table. He leaned casually against the wall, just out of view, and chuckled at the misery of those in the dining room, raising his brows at me as if to say, "rich folks have issues too."

When things had settled down, he returned to his post, brushing a bit too close to me and bumping my shoulder on his way by.

"Watch it," I growled.

"We all should," he returned. Was that a threat?

Gran had escaped back into her gaming lair, and Tess headed upstairs as soon as the argument had ended, followed soon after by Ryan.

I waited, but Juliet sat still at the dining room table for a long time, her head in her hands. I wanted to sit down beside her, talk to her, but I couldn't do that with Chad lurking nearby. Instead, as our shifts came to an end and I handed off duty with Jack and Christian, I went into my room and sat on the end of my bed for a while, staring into the paneled door and trying to unravel my own feelings.

I was certain I was falling in love with Juliet, if I wasn't there already. But I was equally certain it would never work between us. How could it, when there was such an enormous disparity there? Maybe she was right, maybe it shouldn't matter. And I guessed maybe if I could solve everyone's problems with a wave of my hand, by writing a check or just calling my bank, maybe I'd actually believe it didn't matter. But the reality was that it did.

To me, at least.

I heard the house quieting around me, heard the settling creaks of the old foundation, the sounds of faucets in distant corners upstairs being turned on and off. I heard the cicadas out my open window, their chorus joined by frogs and other night creatures all creating a thrum of constant sound that seemed to be getting louder and louder until I thought it might drive me insane. I pushed to my feet and was out of my room before I'd decided on a destination or thought much about anything besides the misery welling inside me, keeping the beat with the Maryland night.

Sounds were coming from the far corner of the house, punctuated by Gran's occasional cackle or curse, and though I was pretty sure she wouldn't appreciate the interruption, I followed them anyway, but lingered right outside the door. Gran sat at her computer, very active in the big gaming chair, which rocked with her movements as she navigated across the screen with her mouse. She wore a giant headset, and had a joint smoldering in a nearby ashtray. I wasn't scared of much, but Gran made me a little uneasy.

"Fucking children," Gran spat at the screen as I hesitated. "Next time you ask me to group with you, check your birth certificate first. If you haven't turned eighteen yet, move along. And quit asking me for my Judgement armor. You have no idea how much actual money I spent to get gold for this set, you little nincompoop!" The old woman dropped her headset into her chair and spun, spotting me immediately. "Come on, gorilla," she said, as if she knew she'd find me loitering behind her. "Let's get a drink."

I glanced around, but I was the only gorilla she could have been referring to. For a second I thought she was demanding I take her to a bar or something, but she floated past me in her fluffy brown wombat slippers and headed for the kitchen. "You coming?" She called back.

I followed her, confused and off balance.

"Which one are you?" She asked, pausing at the kitchen counter and turning around to assess me.

"Jace, Ma'am."

She took a long moment, scanning me from head to toe, her eyes finally coming back up to rest on my face. "You're the one Juliet has the hots for, right?"

A distant squawk from the house chicken was timed perfectly, as if to confirm this. Which was fine for Chessy, but I owed it to Juliet not to discuss this, didn't I? I rubbed a hand across my jaw, my mind twisting more slowly than normal after all the muddle of the day. "I mean, no," I started. "She's dating Mr. McDonnell."

"Bullshit," Gran said. She turned back to the counter and opened up a cabinet, revealing an impressive liquor collection. "You like bourbon, Gorilla?"

"It's Jace, Ma'am."

"Answer the question. You're off the clock, right? Though honestly, I can't figure out what you henchmen think you're guarding us from all the way out here. Rabid groundhogs, maybe. That's about as spicy as it gets down this way."

I had seen several groundhogs on the property, especially at dusk, now that I thought about it. None of them had been foaming at the mouth that I'd noticed, however. "Um, sure," I said.

"Sure, you think we're all in danger from infected whistle pigs, or sure, you like bourbon?"

"Bourbon, Ma'am."

She sighed dramatically and turned to face me, the sequins on the arms of her purple sweat suit catching the light and twinkling like glitter. "Quit calling me ma'am. Makes me feel old. I can't drink with someone who's calling me ma'am all the time, dammit." She turned back around and began pulling bottles from the cabinet and placing them on the counter. "Just call me Gran, like everyone else," she said.

"Sure," I agreed, feeling like we'd reached some kind of settlement. I leaned against the doorway, watching her. I liked her tell-it-like-it-is attitude, and wished my own mom had a little bit more of whatever it was that made Gran tick. But there was a lot to like about my own mother's quiet sweetness, too.

"Now where did Tessy hide it?" she was asking, rising up onto her tiptoes to try to see into the back of the cabinet. "Harambe, is there a jar back up in there? You're like a skyscraper, you should be able to see back there."

I frowned at her latest choice of moniker—wasn't Harambe the poor gorilla they shot at the zoo? Gran was far from PC, I wasn't sure why I was surprised. I decided not to say anything, but stepped forward and pulled a jar from the back of the cabinet, where I had no doubt Tess had tried to hide it. "Is this ..."

"Moonshine. You got it." Gran cackled with delight and then pulled two small glasses from another cabinet. "You and me, Ivan. One shot and then I'm going to teach you to make a Manhattan. The right way."

Gran was not asking me. She was telling me. And since I was tired, and my head was a mess, I just nodded when the old woman handed me a shot of clear liquid that smelled like jet fuel mixed with peaches.

"Maryland's finest."

I sipped at the liquid as Gran pounded hers. It actually wasn't bad, despite the burning sensation it caused in my throat. I swallowed the rest and put my glass on the counter next to hers.

"All right," Gran said, pulling a shaker from the sink and rinsing it out. "Now, most people make a Manhattan with Rye. What about you, Gulliver?"

"It's Jace," I said, though I was beginning to admire her creativity. "Unless you want me to call you a Lilliputian."

"Ha!" Gran laughed. "So you do have a personality. And you've read *Gulliver's Travels*! I guess I can use your actual name. I was running out of giant and gorilla names anyway. I was going for King Kong next, though. Kinda sad I'm not gonna get to use that one."

"You can call me Kong if it makes you happy," I told her, earning a smile.

"Jace works too," she said.

"I make a Manhattan with Maker's Mark," I told her, gesturing at the low square bottle.

Gran turned to me with a raised eyebrow. "That sounds good," she said. "You make it, then. I'm old. I'll sit and watch. But narrate while you do it. I'll pretend you're a cabana boy, waiting on me in my private Caribbean cottage." She raised an eyebrow and gave me a lecherous smile before the expression fell from her face and she let out a sigh. "Never mind, pretending to flirt is exhausting. Just make the drinks, KoKo."

I laughed, relaxing a little for the first time all night.

"Okay," I said, moving to the counter as Gran took a seat at the table.

"Make two," she said. "When you're done we're having a chat."

"Two parts Makers," I said, narrating what I was doing as I poured and mixed. "One part sweet vermouth, and I'm going to use these spiced orange bitters. A couple drops of cherry juice and two Luxardos per glass. Sound good?" I glanced over my shoulder and Gran gave me a huge toothy grin.

Once I'd shaken the drinks and poured them out, I served her one and joined her at the table.

"Cheers," I said, raising my glass.

"Chin chin," she said.

We both sipped and Gran closed her eyes for a long second after taking a drink. Then she bobbed her head once and regarded me through narrowed eyes. "Yes. I like it," she said. "You're all right, Kong."

Pleased to know I'd passed some kind of test, I leaned back a bit, enjoying the sweet burn of the drink as I waited for Gran to tell me what we were going to talk about. I already knew it was going to involve Juliet, I just wasn't sure what she knew or what she might think about it all.

"So," she said. "You don't seem like a complete moron."

A chuckle escaped my lips at what I perceived to be a compliment. "Thanks?"

"But you're sitting in the kitchen, drinking with an old lady, while Juliet is upstairs, upset."

There was no use pretending Juliet was with Ryan, I guessed. "It's complicated," I told her.

"Oh for fuck's sake, you people and your complications." She took another sip, put her glass down, and leaned forward, fixing clear blue eyes on me. "Life is short, Kong. I know I make old look good, but not everyone is so lucky. And if there's one thing I know about Juliet, it's that she won't be alone for long. She hates being alone. That's why she chooses idiots to keep her company. She figures anyone is better than the silence of her own mind." Gran leaned back again, crossed her arms. "She still have that ridiculous narcoleptic dog?"

I smiled, thinking of Elvis. "She does."

"Surprised she didn't insist on bringing the mutt along."

"He's with my mother, actually."

That stopped Gran cold. Her mouth dropped open. "So. This is serious then." Gran watched me carefully, then took another long sip from her glass. "Tell me."

It wasn't in my nature to talk intimately with people I barely knew, but Gran's invitation—and the Manhattan, and maybe the moonshine—came at the right time. I needed to talk. So I did. I told her I loved her granddaughter. I told her it had been me in her room. When I'd finished, wrapping things up with my confusion over my own feelings, the way Juliet's generosity made me feel small, Gran just nodded.

As she drank the rest of her cocktail and picked up the toothpick holding the cherries, she seemed to be thinking. "Gender roles," she finally said. "When will we ever really be able to let them go?"

I didn't have an answer, so I sighed, finished my own drink, and waited for her to go on.

"If it had been you saving her family," she said, "we'd have no issues here. If the man is the one with the money, the one who rides in and saves the damsel, everyone's just fucking peachy."

She had a point.

"But you, Grape Ape ... you and every other hulking mountain of man in this country and most of the world ..." she shook her head and looked down at the table, as if disappointed in my reaction before she'd even finished talking. "You can't accept that a woman might be capable of giving you something you couldn't get yourself. And your ego won't let you just say thank you."

"I want to. I know I should ..."

"Look," she said. "This is not complicated. Juliet has a generous and lonely heart. When she sees someone she can help, she helps. She spends half her time and money trying to save the battered women of the world. If you've spent any time with her you know that."

I did know that. I'd gone with her a few times over the last year to the shelter she supported in Hollywood, and I'd heard a few of the conversations she'd had with her accountant as she'd walked through the house. She gave generously.

"And if you leave her," Gran went on, "because she helped, you'll just be proving what she already believes. That she is destined to be alone no matter what she does. Let me ask you this. If she hadn't helped, could you be together then?"

I thought about that. How I would have had to scramble to try to keep Mom safe, to keep Jarred clean. I wouldn't have had the resources to do either, and I would have been looking for ways to manage. There wouldn't have been time for Juliet. And being near her, surrounded by wealth while my family suffered would be nearly impossible. "I don't want it to be about the money."

"But it is," Gran finished.

"It is."

"Kong, here's the truth. Money is just lubrication. It makes things move more easily, but man cannot survive on a diet of KY Jelly alone, right?"

I wasn't sure if Gran had just made a sex lube analogy or if I was just drunk. "Weird analogy, but okay."

"Why would you resist the lubrication if someone's willing to squeeze some out for you?" Gran shot me an impish smile.

"We're going with this KY Jelly thing, huh?" I threw back the rest of my drink, fortifying myself to discuss lube with a ninety-year-old woman.

"I'm on a roll," Gran said. "Why shove things in, causing pain and complications, when you can just accept the glide and move forward? Juliet's just smoothed the way, taken care of the sticky issues so you can keep things moving."

I frowned. Was it as simple as that? Had Juliet just eliminated barriers to our ability to be together? Was sexual lubricant really the right analogy for this situation?

"Give Juliet a chance to be an actual person. Don't make her about her money," Gran suggested. "If you do that, you're no better than that pooptaco, Zac."

Let her be an actual person, I thought. God, had I made

her all about her money? I had. That's exactly what I was doing. I nodded, realization dawning. "You're right."

"Little known fact, Harambe," Gran said, standing. "I'm always right."

"I'll remember that," I said.

Gran shuffled toward the doorway, her fuzzy slippers making a swooshing sound against the tile floor. "Be sure to hide the moonshine, or Tess will have both our hides in the morning," she said. And then the old woman was gone, and I was left to clean up.

CHAPTER TWENTY-FIVE
JULIET

I sat in my room late into the night, thinking. If I made a list of days that ranked most crappy in my life, this one might not have made the list—it turned out I'd had a lot of crappy days—but then again, it wasn't going to rank among my favorites either. I'd tried to do something nice, to show Jace I cared about him, about his family, and it had blown up in my face. And then Tess had accused me of making everything about me.

For pretty much my whole life.

By the time dinner was over, I had needed some quiet time, some time alone. And as much as I wanted to dive into the shelter of Jace's arms, I wasn't sure those arms were the safe place they'd been before. I wasn't sure where I stood with him at all. I went upstairs, feeling heavy and worn out, like the dinner conversation had sucked the energy out of me, left me empty.

My room was quiet and soothing, the rosy light coming from the corner lamp cast a glow across the floor and the bed.

I took a deep breath as I closed the door behind me, looking around. This room had been mine since we moved into this house with Gran when I was a little girl. I remembered Gran on a ladder, painting the walls pink because that was what I'd had at home. She'd brought my fluffy bedspread and all the stuffed animals from my room at my parents' house, and done everything she could to make it feel like home. But I'd felt as empty back then as I did right now—like maybe somehow the world was too big for me, like I just didn't fit into it.

As I'd stepped in from the hallway, I'd heard a giggle from Tess's room—Ryan was in there, I supposed. And I knew I should be happy for them, happy someone was finding the world a little easier to navigate than I did.

After I'd brushed my teeth and washed my face, I curled up on my bed, pulling one of the frilly pillows against my chest and pushing my nose into its soft edge.

It was time to take stock, I figured. The recent events in my life—Zac cheating on me spectacularly and now blackmailing me, Jace essentially telling me he felt differently about me because I had more money than he did—they seemed to be sending a message I needed to absorb. The person I was, or the people I'd been surrounding myself with —it wasn't working.

I squeezed my eyes shut tighter, my heart twisting inside my chest. Who else could I be?

Jace's rejection was the hardest to swallow because I'd actually believed that to him I wasn't just some movie star.

He'd made me feel seen in a way no one ever had, not even my own sister.

But something had gotten broken along the way.

I was just beginning to sink into my self pity, feeling the waves of despair lap around me, when my phone chimed with a text. I nearly ignored it, figuring it was Zac with more threats, my agent checking in, or the lawyer telling me how much she thought it was going to take to pay Zac off for good. I sighed and rolled across the bed to pull the phone from my nightstand.

Jace: Any chance you could come to my room?

A smile came to my lips before I remembered the words we'd had earlier in the day.

"Go find a movie star to love, Juliet. Someone like you. And one day you'll look back and you can congratulate yourself on the way you took care of that charity case that one time. That poor helpless idiot, Jace."

Anger and hurt flared in me again. But so did hope. Maybe he'd changed his mind. Why was he texting me? Could I forgive him? I just didn't know. The small hope his text had ignited was delicate. I didn't think it would survive any more misunderstandings. I needed to be alone, to regroup.

Me: I don't think I can take any more today, Jace.

Jace: I owe you an apology. Let me make it in person.

I sighed and rolled onto my back, staring up at the ceiling. My heart was already rushing down the stairs, flying toward him. But my rational mind was blaring out warnings about trusting men who had already hurt me.

Me: Okay.

I would go. I would let him apologize.

Because even though I was angry and hurt, there was something else.

I was in love.

The house was quiet except for the occasional scratch of Chessy's feet on the planks of the back porch outside, where I guessed Jack must have been on watch. And Gran's sporadic cries as she battled whatever enemies she faced in that game she loved. I was pretty sure she was too old to be behaving the way she did, but then again, I wasn't one to tell people how to manage life.

I was failing at it.

Jace's door was cracked, and my heart rose into my throat as I stood outside. I felt fragile and knew I couldn't take much more. I wanted to fall into his arms, to feel the heat and comfort of him, but I couldn't survive him taking it all away again. I took a deep breath and pushed the door lightly, calling quietly inside, "Hey. It's me."

When I entered, he was in the center of the room, barefoot and painfully handsome, his eyes locked on me. "Hey," he said, not moving from the spot where he stood glued.

I shut the door and waited uncertainly just inside. "You wanted to talk to me?" I wrung my hands together, completely uncomfortable in his presence suddenly, unsure what to do with myself. I wished I could be the woman I'd been earlier, the one who'd refused to hear his excuses, the one who'd taken him in her mouth because she was commanding and in charge. Was this what it would be like with us now? Maybe whatever had been here was already broken.

"Juliet," his voice was part plea, part prayer, and my chest constricted with his tone. I stayed where I was and waited. He sighed and dropped his head into his hands for a moment, looking so much like a tortured god, standing there with the overhead light catching strands of his ebony hair, making his light skin glow.

"I'm so sorry," he said after a minute, looking back up at me. He reached both hands forward, and stepped toward me slowly, stretching out to me. My hands lifted from my sides, reaching for him. When our fingers brushed, my skin lit up, goosebumps flying up my arms in a chain reaction started by his touch.

He held my hands gently, gazing down at me with the dark soulful eyes I knew I'd imagine every single time I needed to portray a woman in love. "The things I said earlier," Jace said, his voice a husky whisper. "I didn't mean them. I was an idiot. My ego was hurt. I thought I should be able to take care of everything myself—you, my family. It was hard to accept that there are some things I just can't handle alone."

I dropped his gaze, stared at our hands intertwined. "And you can accept that now?"

"I'm working on it," he said. "I think money is hard for people who grew up without it, who don't have it."

I didn't want to talk about money, but I knew it was critical to him, that it was at the crux of this issue. I made myself look up at him again, wanting him to know I was willing to listen.

"But maybe money is just like sexual lubricant."

I dropped his hands. "What?" Was this some kind of weird foreplay? We had a lot to figure out before I could get into a conversation about sex. And lube.

"Shit. No. I mean ..." He took my hands in his again.

Confusion must have been written across my face, and a little laugh escaped me. "Why are you talking about sexual lubricant?"

Jace's perfect mouth lifted on one side in a doleful half-smile. "Someone else used that analogy once. Someone much smarter than me."

I still had no idea where he was going with that. "Okay."

"What I'm trying to say is that the money isn't the key thing here. It just allows us to focus on the important stuff, keeps us from having to worry about other things."

"Right," I agreed, still confused about the sexual lubricant thing.

"And I also need to say thank you."

I cringed. I didn't want his thanks. I wished we could just take all of it—the money, his family—and hide it somewhere far away. I didn't want him grateful or indebted. I only wanted him. "You don't have to."

"I do. My family is better off for me having met you. I'm better off."

I sighed. "Because of the money." Disappointment washed through me. Jace just wanted to say thank you for the things I'd done for his family. I began to pull my hands from his, but he clamped his fingers down more tightly.

"Not for the money. For being you. You've made me a

better man," he said, pulling me a little closer. "Not only have you helped my family immensely, but you've made me look at things differently, understand that we don't all live in a cookie cutter outline in the world, a place set for us at birth."

"Of course not," I agreed. Wasn't I in the midst of trying to break out of my own mold? I had to believe this was true.

"There's more though," he said, his warm breath on my ear now, as he lowered his head to whisper. "When I'm around you, it's like I can finally breathe, like there's more air or space or light in the world. When you're near me, I feel alive." His lips found my neck, brushed the sensitive skin lightly, erupting more tingles. "You make me happy," he said, his tongue darting out to taste my earlobe. "And you're so fucking sexy, I think I could probably die now, knowing I've gotten to taste you and there is nothing else in the world I ever need to see, feel, or try. You're it."

My heart lifted inside my chest and I pushed Jace away from me a bit so I could look into his eyes. I needed to see the emotion there to believe it, maybe. But when our eyes met, it was like seeing the horizon out in front of me, like looking into the distance, knowing forever could be there, that you could spend your life on the journey to reach it. "You're it for me too."

Jace kissed me then, our tongues tangling for a long deep kiss as his hands pulled my body into his, the warmth of him washing all the doubt and pain from inside me.

I slid my hands up the hard planes of flesh and muscle inside his shirt, and he lifted his lips from mine for a moment to whip it off over his head. His eyes met mine again then, and the hunger and want I saw within the depths actually made my knees shake as something flipped over in my belly. Need spiked inside me, and I pressed myself against him again, wanting contact, friction, firm fullness.

Jace slid to his knees, hooking his fingers in the waist of my jogger pants, pulling them down my hips along with my panties, while my hands buried themselves in his thick dark hair. Jace lifted one of my legs, placing it gently over his shoulder as I gasped at the exposure. It felt lewd to have him there, to be opened this way. And it was also so hot I could barely stand still. I let my eyes drop shut as his hot breath hit my flesh, and when his firm warm tongue licked once along my seam, my mind screamed out more, more, more. I pressed a fist to my mouth, wanting to make sure Gran wasn't going to hear me again.

He teased and licked me, his hands finding my ass and pulling me into his face as his tongue pushed deeper into me. He flicked and sucked as I tried to stifle my moans, impaled on his tongue. I needed his shoulders for support as he added a finger, then two, and sent ribbons of sensation up my spine and inside me until I couldn't imagine ever walking out of this room, couldn't imagine anything but this—heat, sensation, warmth, love.

Jace picked me up before he let me come, settling me gently on the bed and then standing in front of me. My eyes flickered open as I moaned, missing him, missing the feeling of his fingers and tongue and all that hard warm flesh. He slid his pajama pants from his firm lean hips and stood before me for a few seconds, his thick erection jutting dark and glistening against his stomach. A moment later he was climbing over me, helping me slip my shirt over my head and removing my bra.

His eyes darkened, and he took my mouth with his in a kiss that roared through my body, made my feet flex and curl. I pulled him to me, loving the hard strength of him, the almost predatory way he hovered over me as his erection pressed against my stomach, inflamed and swollen. I reached down and took him in my hand, using the head of his cock to rub my clit a few times, sending sparks through me.

"Fuuuck," Jace ground out, his voice like a prayer in my ear.

I notched him against my entrance and lifted my hips to accept him, to make more room for his engorged crown. As he pressed just inside, we both gasped and then our mouths came together, searching, finding. He backed up and pressed again, slipping farther into me as my body stretched to accommodate him. Inch by inch, gasp by gasp, breath by breath, he filled me. And when he was inside me, every hot thick inch of him stretching and filling my channel until I could barely breathe, he began the gentle slide in and out, in and out.

I let go. I let go of the uncertainty I'd felt earlier, of the preconceptions I had of him, of myself. I let go of everything I'd been before and let myself become something new. Someone new. In Jace's arms, connected like this, I found myself and the woman I wanted to be.

And when he held me later, as we drifted off to sleep, I knew that no matter what happened, I couldn't go back.

We woke as light filtered beneath the dark shades drawn against the windows, and I looked at my watch.

"What time is it?" Jace asked, tightening his grip on me.

"Early," I told him. "Go back to sleep."

I planted kisses across his perfect nose, and then slipped from the bed. When I was dressed, I opened the door as quietly as I could and slipped out, turning to the hallway just as it clicked shut. To find Chad standing there, watching me with a little smile on his lips.

"Has Jace been working overtime?" He asked.

My stomach turned. I didn't know what Chad's angle would be, but I was sure he had one. "No, I just needed to speak with him in private."

"At five o'clock in the morning. In his bedroom," Chad said, nodding. "Want to come chat with me privately?" He pushed open the door to the room across the hall, and I tried to hide the disgust I felt at the idea.

"No, I ..." I started walking, realizing I didn't want to talk to him, that nothing I said would erase what he'd just seen. And I didn't want to end up getting pulled into his room. For the first time, I felt a tingle of fear.

I heard him chuckling as I moved away, out into the dark quiet of the front room. My mind was whirling around everything that had happened, with Jace, now with Chad—and so when I nearly ran right into someone moving silently through the room I nearly keeled over before I realized it was Tess.

"Oh, Tess!" I heard myself exclaim.

"Hi," she said. "Getting coffee," she said, clearly still half asleep.

"Good, yes," I said, hoping she wasn't about to ask what I was doing down here. I followed her to the kitchen, and we sat down across from one another at the little round table. Tess looked upset, and while I was a bit hurt over the words she'd said the night before, I knew there was likely more to it. Something to do with Ryan. "You doing okay?" I asked her.

"Jules," she said, her voice small and apologetic. "I'm sorry about what I said last night."

"No," I told her. "You were right. I know it isn't easy being my sister, Tess. I know I make it hard." Before last night I would have sworn I'd never asked to be the center of attention, I'd never wanted to make everyone pay attention to me. But I'd been thinking a lot, and maybe that wasn't quite right. When my parents had died, I think I reacted by working to replace their love, to fill in that void with as much love and adoration as I could collect. And what better way than by becoming a movie star? Not that I controlled it entirely, but once I figured out that people did react naturally to something I had, some kind of charisma or charm, I learned how to use it. But the void remained.

"It's not always you," she said. "It's just all the things that come with you now."

"Things like Ryan?" I couldn't help it. I wanted to know more.

She sighed and looked so sad, I wanted to pull her into my arms.

"He's a good guy, Tess. And we're not together, so ..."

"So now it's okay with you?" She asked, and I remembered how upset the idea had made me the night before.

I shrugged. "You were right. It's not about me, and it's not up to me. I want you to be happy, and lord knows you need to meet someone. Your life has revolved around salt water and Gran and other peoples' adventures for way too long. You're verging on spinsterhood." It was kind of a joke, but I did worry about my little sister.

"I'm twenty-five." Her voice was flat.

"Well," I said, chuckling. I watched her drink her coffee, amazed at the beautiful woman my little tomboy sister had become. She was perfect. And maybe she was exactly what a nice guy like Ryan needed. "You should give him a chance," I suggested.

"It would never work out," she said. "There's no way I'd ever move to California. And last I checked, they aren't making any big movies out here. We don't even get to see half the movies down here—I had to drive up to DC to see that one you did that won Sundance."

"Well, they don't always distribute the smaller films as widely," I began, about to launch into a long explanation of distribution and licensing rights for films before I realized we were way off topic. "If Ryan wants to make this work, he could. So could you." I wondered if I could give this same advice to myself, to Jace. Could we really make it work just by wanting it enough?

She looked so sad.

"Just don't close the door on it, okay? I want to see you happy."

"Because it's about you," she said, her voice still carrying an edge of hurt that cut deeply.

I dropped my head into my hands. So much for the sister-to-sister talk. "I'm sorry if I've ever made you feel that way."

"I'm sorry too," she said. "It's not your fault, Jules. What did Mom used to say? The only person who could make you feel something is you?"

My heart twisted at the thought of my mother. God, I missed her. I pushed my sadness aside and tried a wicked smile instead. "I bet Ryan could make you feel something if you gave him a chance." I wiggled my eyebrows suggestively.

"Who says I haven't let him already?" she asked, and I could see from her smile that she definitely had.

"Yes! More of that!"

"Not today. Today's Gran's party. And your friends from the magazine will be back. Today Ryan's *your* boyfriend, remember?" Her tone was teasing, but her eyes were still sad. I wanted to fix this, to see my sister happy. I wanted to mend whatever rift had formed between us.

My stomach turned. "Right." I shook my head and pushed my hair back. "I'm sorry. I'm sorry I brought my mess out here and made it your mess."

"It's okay, Jules," she said, and she gave me a squeeze on the shoulder before she turned and left the kitchen. A few moments later, I did the same. I needed to go prepare for the most challenging acting role of my life. Convincing the world that Ryan was my boyfriend when my heart was so completely suffused with love for Jace was not going to be easy.

CHAPTER TWENTY-SIX
JACE

C had was waiting for me when I got up that morning.
"What's she like?" He asked as we did a perimeter check ahead of the crowd arriving for the party that afternoon. "All moany and soft? Or is she one of those dominant types who tells you where to put it and how hard to go?"

I stopped walking, disgust climbing my spine like some many-legged creature made of oozing flesh. Like the mind flayer from *Stranger Things*, only smaller, and with Chad's grinning face on it. "Whatever you think you know," I growled at him. "Drop it."

"Oh, look how protective you're getting." The words were still venomous, but he took a step away from me.

"Chad, I'm warning you."

He dropped the shit-eating grin and stopped walking, turning to face me fully. His shrewd eyes gave me a once-over, and the smug look on his lips told me I wasn't going to like what came next. "Couple things," he said, as if he was just telling me about the weather forecast. Casual. Straightforward. "Haven't decided yet which way I'm going, but here's what I'm thinking. One: the boss—I mean the real boss, Austin, would probably be pretty interested in you violating company rules to sleep with a client."

I knew he was right. Austin had given me this chance, and my involvement with Juliet was not something he'd be happy about. If I were him, I wouldn't tolerate it. Being intimately involved with a client could compromise judgment, and that would compromise security. Being in love with Juliet made me less equipped to protect her. And I could hardly afford to lose my job, though I'd known all along this was a possibility. I cursed myself inwardly for not being more careful.

"Two," Chad went on. "I wouldn't be the first guy Juliet paid off to keep something quiet. Sounds like Zac is going to get a fat check. I wonder what she'd be willing to give me."

I had no idea if Chad knew about the tape or if he was just shooting in the dark, but anger fired in me and then turned to ice inside my veins. "Take it out on me," I hissed at him. "Don't drag her into this." She had enough trouble from her shitbag ex. The last thing I wanted was to add to her problems.

"Yeah, that's charming. Very noble. But the fact is, she's got the money. And I'm sure she could part with a bit to save her precious reputation. Look at all the fucking trouble she's gone to just to make it seem like she and that slick loser McDonnell are together. All while he's banging her sister." This last part came out on a laugh and I had to fist my hands into the sides of my pants to keep them from pummeling Chad.

"So I don't know," Chad said, turning forward again and walking along the perimeter we'd marked out. "Would it be more satisfying to see you get what's coming, or take a nice chunk of money and cast off?" He was silent a moment, strolling along like he hadn't a care in the world. "Course," he said, "no reason at all I can't do both, eh?"

He pulled his phone from his pocket and dashed off a text as I watched, my stomach churning.

Icy rage filled me.

"There we go." Chad shoved his phone back into his pocket. "I'm sure one of us will be hearing from Austin pretty soon." He smiled at me and then clapped me on the back. "Hope it was a good fuck, dude. You're screwed." He looked around. "Guess I'll go find Juliet and see what she's willing to offer to keep this all quiet. I'd hate to let something slip to those magazine people today." Chad strode off across the lawn as the sun edged just over the horizon, leaving me to stare after him, my world in pieces around me.

I waited. For what felt like a few eternities stacked end to end, I waited while Chad's poison worked itself into the capillaries of my life. And a little while later, as I watched Jack sit on the steps of the porch, holding Chessy the chicken in his arms as she stared longingly up at him, my phone dinged. Here we go.

Austin: Call me. We need to talk.

Shit. The beginning of the end.

I looked around. Jack had been on the early morning shift, and while he wasn't sleeping, he also wasn't on. It wouldn't be fair to ask him to cover me, so the implosion of my life would just have to wait until I wasn't standing a shift. The last thing I needed was some kind of security issue in the midst of everything else.

Me: Roger that. I'm on shift. Off at noon. Talk then.
Austin: OK.

A wash of anxiety went through me, raising a cool sweat on my skin. Losing my job would not be helpful at this point. I'd taken my last exam just before heading to Maryland, and didn't know yet if I'd get my degree, but I didn't like my odds, and having a back up plan had always been my MO. I took a deep breath, realizing it was out of my hands. Like so much in my life at the moment.

My phone dinged again as we crept toward noon.

Juliet: Chad just threatened me.

My blood turned to fire and I had to force myself not to barrel through the house to find Juliet. Or to rip Chad apart.

Jace: He knows. He's trying to get me fired too. I'm so sorry.

Juliet: Not your fault. I'm handling it.

Maybe that should have been a relief, but Juliet had handled so many things for me lately. And here was one more.

CHAPTER TWENTY-SEVEN
JULIET

Jace had been outside most of the morning, and I hadn't really seen him—not up close, at least—since leaving his room early in the morning. In some ways, I didn't want to. Part of me wanted to live in the sweet memory of waking in his arms, hearing the morning rising around us through the open window of his room and feeling the warmth of his long body next to me.

Of course, Chad had burst my morning bubble of happiness almost immediately when I'd crashed into him. And then it didn't seem to have taken him long to finish figuring out how to destroy the little bit of happy warmth I'd held onto. He found me again, mid-morning. I'd been wandering the house somewhat aimlessly. It was too early to get dressed for the party, and I was too distracted to do anything productive. I had a pile of scripts to read and calls to return, but my mind was floating, unfocused.

Despite the complications between us, I wanted to get back to LA and see if Jace and I could make this thing work.

Things had been sweet before we'd come to Maryland, before the complications of family and house chickens. I wanted to return to that, remove the extraneous crap and focus on us. My skin warmed at the thought of having him to myself again.

And then Chad had stepped close and his sharp low voice made me cold. "Need to talk to you."

I spun from the window where I'd been peering outside, watching Jace walk a path in front of the house. "No thanks."

"Shall we sit?" Chad asked, ignoring my reply.

"No," I said, glancing back out to see Jace turn the corner. Chad looked around, like maybe he was uncomfortable in the formal parlor where we stood, or more likely because he was about to deliver ugly words.

"You know I saw you this morning," he began. "And I've suspected for a while there was something going on with you and Jace. Him sleeping in the house and all. You being ... well, you." His mouth lifted in an unattractive half smile and I wondered if being me was an insult or a compliment in his mind. It didn't matter.

"Your point?"

"Wouldn't play well in the press, you think?"

I sighed. Here we went again. This was my life. Worrying constantly about my image, about the media spin, about how my personal life could affect my shot at the next big role. It was bullshit. But it was real. "Perhaps not."

"I figure I could talk," he said, sitting and then leaning back, evidently gaining comfort in his environment now that he sensed he held the power. His blond hair flopped down over one eye and he reminded me suddenly of Draco Malfoy in the Harry Potter films—utterly unlikeable. "Those magazine folks should be back here soon. And that reporter—Alison? She seems like the type to jump at a juicy story like you fucking your bodyguard."

Why were some people so predictable? Chad was about to ask me for money. Maybe he and Zac had taken some kind of online Blackmail a Movie Star class together or something. If either of them knew what I'd given Jace, without him even asking or wanting my money ... I sighed and shook my head. Neither Zac nor Chad was anything like Jace. "What do you want, Chad?"

"I think five hundred thousand should do nicely. And I want the in-house spot when we get back."

"No." I didn't even give myself time to think, to strategize my answer. I didn't care about the money, not really. But I wanted Jace in the house. If I knew Chad was in the room down the hall, I'd never sleep again. In fact, I had plans to have him removed as soon as we were back in LA. "No to both."

Chad shrugged and shook his head, like a school teacher disappointed at a student's behavior. "That's too bad."

I stood. I'd had enough of this. "You know what's too bad? The amount of shitty people in the world who look at other people solely as a means for their own advancement. You're worthless. And I don't want you working for me anymore. Pack your things."

"I don't work for you. I work for the firm."

"Not for long," I told him. "Stay away from my family."

"What time do the magazine folks come today?" He sneered it at me.

I ignored him and went upstairs. I'd had enough of people trying to manipulate me, use me for their own gains while they hurt everyone else. I didn't know exactly how, but I was going to take a stand.

After texting Jace, I laid back on my bed, staring at the familiar ceiling of my childhood. I'd felt safe in this room then, and nothing had changed about that. I might never have really felt at home, but I had always known I was safe and loved. As I thought about the life I'd built, about the walls that kept me penned inside of it, I realized that maybe I'd given up control. Maybe I'd done it willingly, or without even realizing that's what I was doing. And maybe, just maybe, I could take it back.

I needed to talk to Gran. Before the party.

CHAPTER TWENTY-EIGHT

JACE

I called Austin at noon as soon as I was done with my shift, my gut churning as I sat on the edge of the bed in my room. I'd already thought through what I'd tell my mom about being fired, some story about choosing a chance at love. I knew losing my job wouldn't mean financial ruin or homelessness for me or my family—Juliet wouldn't let that happen. But could I possibly live with myself if it came to that? There were no good outcomes here. Still, I did what I needed to do.

"Jace, good to hear from you." Austin's voice was confident, and every bit as warm as it had been the first time I'd called him, when he'd offered me the job. "How's school going, son? Just about done by my calculations."

School? My mind was definitely not on last exam I'd taken before leaving for Maryland, but if he wasn't going to fire me straight out, I could talk about school. "Just took my last test, actually. Online, you know. Think it went okay."

"Almost got that degree."

"Yes sir. I hope so." Austin had been a colonel in the Marine Corps. I'd never be able to call him anything besides "sir," even though we were both out now.

"Plans after that?" He sounded sincerely interested, and I felt a bit of tension wind its way out of my back. Maybe Austin wasn't planning to fire me. Or maybe he just needed a chat?

"Teaching, maybe? High school?" It wouldn't do much for my income, but might offer some security. And at least it'd be steady work and maybe I could make a difference to someone.

"You don't sound certain."

I chuckled, realizing that laughing just before your boss hands you your ass was probably not normal. "I guess I'm not certain about much right now," I confessed.

He paused, and I felt my heart trying to climb up my throat. I took a deep breath. "Son, listen. I spoke with Chad this morning."

"Yes sir." Here it came.

"That piece of shit has been a problem since day one."

Surprise made me sit up straight. I wasn't sure I'd heard him correctly. Was Chad the "piece of shit" here or was I? "Sir?"

"This is the third time he's tried to get another staff member fired. Second time I've gotten the idea he might be thinking of manipulating a client for money." I heard my boss exhale a sharp breath. "I'm the idiot who keeps giving him another chance."

I didn't have anything to say to that, so I kept my mouth

shut. I began to have the sense I wasn't the one in trouble here, but was afraid to hope for too much.

"Look, Jace. Getting involved with a client isn't something I'd ever want for one of my employees. It muddies the line between business and, well ... you know as well as I do. That said, sometimes I know we don't control the things our hearts want or need."

I would have said that nothing could really surprise me these days, but this did. "Sir?"

"Your record is excellent, and I don't mean just the time you've been working for me. You should know we do a thorough background check before hiring anyone. Some people's closets have more skeletons than others, and while that doesn't mean we won't hire them, it does restrict the kind of access they might have to clients and information. Before I officially hired you, I pulled your service records, spoke to your CO, and looked over your transcripts from high school."

"Yes, sir." Relief began to thread its way into the worry in my veins. This didn't sound like the kind of conversation that ended with 'you're fired.'

"It's impressive, Jace. And your unit COs on both tours used one word to describe you that means a hell of a lot to me. Wanna guess what that word was?"

Strong? Loyal? Snappy dresser? I didn't know, and I wasn't about to guess. "No sir."

"It was integrity. The ability to make the right decision in a complex environment, to determine the best choice when the only choices you have are bad choices. It's the habit of doing the right thing, Jace, because you have a clear sense of what that thing is. You have that. Always have, from what I can tell."

I felt my shoulders straighten as pride galloped through my veins. I was pretty sure that wasn't the Webster definition, but I wasn't about to question him, and it felt good to hear it. "Thank you sir."

"I want to offer you a job, Jace."

That had me on my feet, confusion and disbelief swirling inside me. For one thing, I already had a job. "Sir?"

"I'm not going to run this firm forever. But I don't want to see it fold either. I need a successor. Not right now, but soon."

My mind flashed through possibilities. I saw myself standing in front of a classroom full of kids, doing the best I could but maybe never really feeling like I was good at my job. And then I saw myself running the firm, handling assignments and strategy, much as I had in the corps. I could do that. I could be good at that.

"What do you think?" he asked.

"I guess I'd be an idiot to say no."

"Is this what you want, though?" he asked. "If high school is your goal, this might not feel like the right choice. I'll email you the terms I have in mind. In short, transfer in a year or so, I'd keep a portion of profits but the rest would be yours to manage as you see fit. Jace, you should know the firm does well. Very well."

I didn't want money to be the determining factor, but it did matter. I'd seen how much in just the past few days. Money could make everything else easier. "Can I take a little time?"

"Of course."

"Thanks."

"And Jace?"

"Yes sir?"

"It would probably make sense to step off the Manchester team if you think your relationship there is serious. Even if it isn't. When you get back and have time to transition in two new team members to replace you and Chad."

"Yes sir." My heart sank at the thought of leaving Juliet to someone else's care, but Austin was right. Being too close to Juliet could mean missing something important in her security efforts. Someone objective and removed would do a better job.

"I'll talk to you when you're back, if not before."

"Thank you, sir."

I hung up and stared out the window for a long time. Long enough to see Chad throwing his bag into the back of a car that pulled down the long drive. Long enough to watch him notice the van and car that were headed toward the house, arriving for the party, and long enough to see him wait for Alison to get out before whispering something to her, which she wrote down. I was just glad I kept watching long enough to see him get in his own ride and go. Good riddance. At least that was taken care of.

Now I just needed to make some decisions about how to take care of everything else.

CHAPTER TWENTY-NINE
JULIET

For a little while, I lay on my back, listening to the house around me and hearing the quiet rush and lap of the water below us through my open window. I let the morning settle and shift as I thought about everything my life had become since the first time I'd come to live here with Gran and Tess, just after our parents had been killed in the car accident.

"This is your home, girls," Gran had told us. "And it will always be here for you if you ever need to come back."

We'd sipped lemonade on the back porch with our father's mother—the sharp and almost scary old woman we'd previously had only monthly dinners and holidays with.

"It might not feel like home right now, but I hope one day it will. And when you need it, when you need a place to remember who you are, or decide who you want to be, this will be the place to do it." She'd said this like it was a fact, and I wasn't sure if she was right or if she'd just planted that belief deep inside me somewhere that day. But I knew I'd needed to come home. To figure everything out.

I didn't stay in my room long, and while the house was quiet and Jace was outside, I went downstairs to talk to Gran.

"Gran?" I asked, stepping into the little room Tess had set up, where Gran's enormous computer was blazing away, and she was seated in front of it like some kind of deranged mission control captain.

She swiveled, eyeing me suspiciously, her huge head-phones clamped onto her head. "Do I know you?" She squinted at me.

Oh god, was Gran losing it? Tess hadn't said anything to me about dementia.

"It's me, Juliet. Your granddaughter?"

She pushed her thin lips together and looked up, laying a finger across her mouth like she was trying to remember. "Now let me see," she said. "I have one granddaughter, Tessy. She baked me a birthday cake and plays cards with me some-times. Makes a mean Manhattan, too. But I'm having a hard time placing you. You look kind of familiar."

"Gran." I crossed my arms. She was just being difficult.

"Aren't you that movie star?"

"Gran." I was beginning to become exasperated. I flopped down into the chair facing her. I didn't need this right now. I needed real advice, but if I had to suffer through some Gran antics first, I would. We still had a few hours before I needed to get ready for the party.

"Oh wait," she went on, still tormenting me. "That frown. I remember that. There was a little blond girl who lived here once. Pretty little thing. But boy, could she throw a temper tantrum when she didn't get what she wanted."

Since I'd been ten when I'd come to live with Gran, those tantrums had been pretty ugly. I remembered them too. "Yes, sorry about those."

"So it is you." She pulled off the big headset and pushed a few buttons on her keyboard.

"It might be," I said, relaxing a little now that it seemed like Gran might actually be willing to talk to me like an adult. "I don't know quite who I am sometimes."

"America's Geekheart?"

I shook my head. "That's the Pippa Grant book you sent me to try to get made into a film. You might be looking for that stupid name they call me: America's Sweetheart, but I'm not that either."

"Excellent book," she said tilting her head to one side, obviously thinking about the book again.

"Yes, but not the point."

Gran sighed, as if maybe having heart-to-heart talks was something she wasn't up to at the moment. I started to get to my feet. "I should let you get ready for your party, I guess."

"Sit your ass back down, Juliet, we've got five hours before the damned party. I've been wanting to talk to you since you got here, but you've been so busy chasing your pet gorillas around and moaning, I haven't had a chance."

Gorillas? Moaning? I sounded delightful. And completely transparent. "Sorry."

"What's going on?" She reached into the pocket of her

track suit and extracted a joint, then scrabbled behind her on the desk for a lighter.

I didn't even tell her not to. What was the point? Gran did what Gran wanted. Instead I told her about Zac. About finding him sampling our chef's private offerings, about the blackmail and the refusal of every settlement offer I'd put forth. I told her about the sex tape, and then I told her about Jace, and finally about Chad's threat.

"Sweetheart, I love you, but you're an asshole magnet."

"Not at all helpful." Which didn't make her wrong. I slumped to one side and dropped my chin into my palm. I thought maybe I was finally getting away from assholes—Jace definitely wasn't one. But things with Jace weren't going perfectly either. "Don't you have some words of wisdom, Gran? Like when you told me in high school that the best way to get to be the girl at the top of the pyramid was to keep dropping everyone else when they made me be on the bottom in cheer?"

"Did that girl's arm ever heal?" Gran grinned at me.

"I'm sure it did. It was just a little fracture."

"She deserved it. That girl put her lip gloss on so thick I bet she's still trying to scrape off the remnants."

Libby Tyler. She did have a gloss issue. She was also a horrible human being, at least at sixteen.

"Things have gotten more serious since high school though," I said, my mind darkening again as I thought about the magazine coming, about my ongoing charade with Ryan. About whatever Chad thought he knew and what he might tell Alison.

"Let's see," Gran said, raising her fingers in front of her face and lowering one for each point she made. "You're divorcing your scumbag ex, which is good. He's blackmailing you. Less good. You're faking a relationship with that fine piece of movie star ass your sister likes. That's not only not good, that's moronic. Two points deducted there."

"Wait, you're scoring me?"

"Makes these conversations more fun."

"Do I get to score you?"

"No, Juliet. Pay attention. I'm the sage old woman, dispensing my worldly advice. You just listen."

I sighed.

"You're sneaking around with one of your gorillas, which is not good. But he seems like a decent human being, and he makes a fucking excellent drink, so two points back there."

What? Jace had made a drink for Gran? When did that happen? And what must they have talked about while it did?

"Bottom line?" She said just before sucking on her joint for so long I thought her lips might be stuck.

I waited for her to continue, but she pulled the thing from her mouth and sat there, holding her breath.

"Yeah?" I prodded, leaning forward.

After what seemed like forever, she exhaled, and a cloud of pot smoke drifted around us. "You've lost control of your own life. You're letting other people make you a side character in your own goddamned story."

I already knew that, but hearing Gran confirm it just made me more resolved to take a different avenue. If I could. "How do I fix it?"

Gran lifted a shoulder and then turned to set the joint in her ashtray. "Up to you. But I can make one suggestion."

Good. This was what I'd come in here for.

"Kick some ass while you figure it out." She stood and motioned for me to sit in her ridiculous gaming chair. It looked like the chair that had been on the bridge of the ship in the one sci-fi movie I'd done, with wings and fancy armrests, buttons and speakers built in.

"Excuse me?"

"I'm going to let you play my death knight. Stay on the solo quests, and don't mess up my armor," she said.

"The game?" I had played maybe four video games in my life, mostly in high school. I had no idea what she was telling me to do. Or why.

She sighed dramatically and waited. I moved to sit in her chair, and she put the headphones on my head. Then she put my hands onto the mouse and keyboard and stood there, leaning over me, while she showed me how to make her character run around on the screen. After a few minutes, she showed me where to find the quests she was pursuing and which buttons would make the character fight. And then she was gone.

I felt ridiculous. I considered getting up and just going upstairs to get ready for the party. But I had hours still, and there was something compelling about the endless green fields where the cartoon character stood, the opportunity to explore, to wander. And when I stumbled into a group of other characters, all of them marked with red names over their heads, signifying they were enemies, it felt good to fight back when they attacked me. For a long time—hours, maybe —I played Warcraft and let myself be strong, fearless, and one hundred percent in control.

And when I noticed Gran's joint still sitting beside me, well ... Choices were made.

It was my life. I was going to take control.

CHAPTER THIRTY
JACE

The camera crew and the reporter were back, and with Chad gone, I felt a little relief that tonight might not go horribly wrong. Then again, he'd whispered something to the reporter before he'd left, and she kept glancing over at me as she directed the photos out on the lawn before the party.

Juliet had shown up late, but looking every bit the movie star. I wondered what had kept her—she prided herself on punctuality. Once she did appear, stepping out onto the back porch like a goddess in a long green dress that flowed like liquid around her body, I just wanted to pick her up and carry her off to a private room, or a cave, somewhere. She was incredible.

Gran, for her part, was being wonderfully resistant to being portrayed as a timid old lady happy to be surrounded by her granddaughters.

"Take one like this," she suggested, and then she squatted low and crossed her arms, her hands flashing gang signs she must have picked up on the internet. I hid a smile.

"Stop that!" Juliet said, but there was no venom in her voice.

In fact, Juliet was giggling a little more than normal, and when she and Gran exchanged a look, there was some shared secret there. Something had changed, besides Chad leaving. Juliet looked lighter, happier. I wanted to get closer, to talk to her, to hear that laugh up close.

As I watched them pose for the camera crew, Ryan's sausage-fingers groping at Juliet in a way that made me want to see how many times I could twist his pretty head around before it fell off, I thought about Austin's offer. Despite my apology to Juliet and my assertions that my ego could handle the fact that she was taking care of my family—it was only partially true. It was a hard thing to swallow, and not just because of my gender. My whole life, I'd been taking care of other people. Jarred had always been right behind me, always so sure I'd rescue him from whatever ill-conceived stunt or idea he had. And I did. I always saved him.

Until this time.

And I'd made a habit of taking care of Mom, too. I'd rented the best house I could for her—admittedly, it wasn't much. I'd made sure she had a full refrigerator every week. I'd spent time with her, done my best to keep her active and engaged.

But Juliet appearing with her "lubricating" money did things in a matter of hours that I would never have been able to do for the family I'd spent all my time worrying about and taking care of. It had been easy for her. And maybe that was why it was so hard to accept. She hadn't seen the years I'd been struggling to do my best for them, hadn't felt the frustration or worry that it would never be enough.

Maybe I'd grown used to the burden, the worry, the heart-wrenching knowledge that I would never really be able to give them enough to truly save them. And now? Now that the burden had been lifted from my arms as easily as someone taking my suitcase for me at the airport? Sometimes even the best things that come our way are difficult to accept.

But if I took over the firm, it might be different. I'd looked over the email Austin had sent after we'd hung up, and while the offer itself was generous, he'd also attached company financials for the last three years and explained that while he would take a twenty-percent cut of net profits, the rest was mine. And it was plenty. I wouldn't be as wealthy as Juliet, I didn't think. But I'd be a wealthy man. Able to provide for my family. Maybe even provide for Juliet, or at least share the weight.

And that felt good.

What felt better was knowing it was something I'd earned. Austin had offered me this opportunity because I'd worked for it. It wasn't out of charity, or because he felt sorry for me.

And that felt best of all.

Now I just needed to get through tonight, get Juliet safely back to Los Angeles, and I could ask her out on an actual date. On terms that felt right. Not as employee and employer, or charity case and benefactor, but as a successful man who'd worked hard for what he had who was in love with a beautiful and equally successful woman.

* * *

THE GRASSY EXPANSE of lawn glowed under the twinkle lights that had been hung in the trees and from the golden light spilling from inside the huge white tent. There were at least a hundred people inside—all on the list I'd checked as guests had arrived. Christian remained up front while Jack, Chessy, and I stayed in back. And once dinner was underway, we took up positions near the door of the huge air conditioned tent. There was little chance of a security issue at an old woman's birthday party in rural Maryland, but if something were going to happen it would probably be tonight. We remained alert.

I was painfully alert anyway, thanks to the emerald green off-the-shoulder dress Juliet was wearing. It complemented her blue eyes perfectly and every time I looked at her, my body responded as if she was inches away, even when she was across the room. There was something different about her tonight, but I couldn't get close enough to say exactly what—just that she didn't look scared, not like she had for so many weeks now, when there had been a spark of fear shining through the glossy smile, the perfect exterior. Tonight she looked confident.

She looked incredible.

I stayed as close to her as I could, my eyes hardly straying from her, from the incredible pull she had on me. Watching her made me feel like my future was right there where I could see, embodied in that perfect, glorious package.

Once the meal had wrapped up, Ryan and Juliet were

talking, heads close, and she rose, as if trying to escape the conversation. His fingers locked around her wrist, and every protective cell in my body—and that's pretty much all of them—shot into action. I was behind him in a half second, grinding out one word that was command, warning, and, if necessary, declaration of battle.

"Easy."

Juliet looked up at me, her bright eyes meeting mine. "It's fine," she said softly. "Jace. I'm fine."

I forced myself to relax, making sure McDonnell released her wrist, and backed off as they continued their conversation. And then, to my surprise, pretty-boy McDonnell got up, commandeered the microphone from the deejay and launched into a declaration of love.

For Juliet's sister. Tess.

It was not what anyone had been expecting, least of all the magazine reporter, Alison, who hovered near them like a hawk, swooping in with her little notepad just as soon as they finished kissing.

I stared at Juliet, wondering if I could go to her, worry seizing my mind. If the ruse was up, what was the story going to be about now? If the goal had been to distract the media from her scandalous divorce by showing a sparkly new relationship, showing that Juliet Manchester was just fine, how would Ryan's declaration for her sister affect things?

And what the hell had Chad whispered to Alison Sands before he'd finally left?

When things settled down in the tent, and people had gone back to eating cake and dancing, I tried to staunch the torrential flood of worrying thoughts. Juliet didn't look upset, and while Alison was outside, evidently quizzing Ryan and Tess, she laughed as Gran picked up the microphone and rapped along to Bust a Move.

Gran was an impressive old lady. She knew every word to the old nineties rap song, but she also had some pretty good moves to go with it. Though her thin high voice wasn't exactly right for the song, there was no denying that she had the spirit to make it work.

As the party wrapped up and guests were beginning to leave, relief began to take the place of the stress and worry I'd carried all evening. I'd be able to talk to Juliet soon, this was almost over. While I waited for my opportunity, I felt Juliet's eyes on me several times. I'd glance across the space to find her smiling at me, but I couldn't read the expression there. All I wanted was to cross the room, take her in my arms, and ask her to be mine, to give us a real chance. But for now, I was still an employee, and there were still guests. And a magazine crew.

Jack and his bowtie-festooned sidekick, Chessy, who was evidently now part of the security detail, went up front to assist with departures, and I watched as Alison approached Juliet and then sat down with her at a table in the corner of the tent. They talked for at least a half hour, heads close together, and my heart raced when I thought I saw Juliet wiping tears from her face.

I had no idea what Juliet might be telling the reporter, but I would be at her side—if she'd let me—no matter what the fallout would be. We'd weather it together. As equals.

I watched as the last of the guests departed and the camera crew finally left, their tail lights disappearing between the fields of corn on either side of the long straight driveway. And when the house was quiet again, I walked back around to the wide grassy lawn and took my post just off the stairs to the porch, catching Juliet's eye briefly as I did. She smiled at me and my heart flopped over like a fish out of water.

The girls sat with Ryan and Gran on the back porch and looked out over the quiet yard as Gran talked.

"It was a good party, girls," Gran said, her voice drifting on the cooling air. "Plenty of drama, good food, and that cake was amazing, Tess."

I stood off to one side, glancing up at Juliet now and then as she laughed with her family. It was hard, being apart—not just from the woman I loved, but feeling like I couldn't be included and involved. Because I was an employee. But that would all be changing soon.

Tess and Ryan disappeared after a while, and Gran and Juliet remained, the night creatures trilling and chirping all around us.

"You might as well come up here and have a drink with us," Gran said. "Gorilla duty is officially over."

"Gran, don't call them that." Juliet's voice was light and happy, despite the stern words.

I turned, raising an eyebrow in question. I wanted to sit with them, wanted to feel like I could be the man at Juliet's side for a little while, be recognized as that man by the woman who was so important to her.

"Come on," Juliet said. "I was going to make Gran one more Manhattan. I'll get you one too."

"Better let Koko make it," Gran said. "His are better."

Juliet laughed and shrugged at me, sitting back down.

"Happy to," I said, and I went into the kitchen to make the drinks. When I returned, it felt good to sit down at the table with them, to sip a drink in the darkness and enjoy the evening. Having a drink in my hand, and Juliet and Gran at my side gave me a thrilling sense of belonging, and I realized how important that was to me, to belong in Juliet's world, not to stand on the periphery.

"What happens next for you two?" Gran asked, looking between Juliet and me. I wondered if Juliet had told her everything, but I was betting she didn't have to. Gran was shrewd.

Juliet looked at me. "I don't know, really. My divorce will be final before too long, and my fake relationship with Ryan is over, so ..."

"But right now, you're my client," I told her. "Until we're back in California." I felt like I needed to finish my job professionally. I was allowing myself this quick drink, but my job was still to see Juliet home safe.

"Didn't stop you before," Gran quipped, sipping her drink and batting her lashes innocently at us as she stood. "I'm going to take this inside, if you two don't mind. I haven't gotten to play Warcraft all day."

"Gran, you were playing this morning," Juliet said.

"Huh. Well, I'm ninety now. Guess my memory's going." Gran turned and carried her drink inside.

I crossed my legs out in front of me, feeling tension seeping from my limbs. The moonlight, the drink, and the knowledge that things were changing in good ways had me more relaxed than I'd been in weeks. "Did you have a good time tonight?" I asked Juliet.

She forced a smile and then said, "I'm just glad it's over, honestly. I want to go home, get everything back to normal. And I miss Elvis."

"I talked to Mom this morning," I told her. "He's doing fine."

"And how's your brother?"

"He's doing as well as can be expected," I said. "But once he's actually at Hollybrook, I'll be relieved."

Juliet's lips pressed into a line and she leaned forward a bit, tracing her fingers in a circle on the table top. "And how are you?"

"Actually, I think I'm good," I said. I wanted to tell her everything about Austin's offer, and was waiting for the right words to come to me.

"You sound surprised about it." She turned her hand palm up, and I put mine over it, watching as her slim fingers twined with my own, warmth spreading through my body at the simple touch.

I chuckled. "I am," I said. "Austin called me this morning."

"Ah, from the firm." She clearly knew who Austin was.

"Yep. Chad told him about us, and I was pretty sure he was calling to hand me my ass. But he didn't."

"Good." Juliet didn't sound surprised.

"He offered me a job. Actually, he offered me the firm. To

take it over when he retires." The pride I felt in telling her this made my spine straighten, my chest swell. And seeing the smile on her face and the light in her eyes, I felt like I'd made her proud too. And maybe it shouldn't matter if Juliet was proud of me, but it did. It mattered to me. I'd done this on my own, and I wanted her to know it.

Juliet's fingers tightened around mine. "That's wonderful! I told him how amazing you are. I'm so glad he listened."

"You told him?" I pulled my hand back, suddenly confused. "You spoke to him? When?"

"Well, I mean, when I first booked the service, obviously. But I called him this morning, too."

"Why?" The pleasure that had been tingling through me was feeling a lot more like shock suddenly.

"I was worried he might believe Chad, and I wanted to make sure he knew how fantastic you are."

I stood up before I'd even thought to do it. "I can't believe you did that," I said, anger flaring inside me and muddling my emotions. I hadn't earned Austin's offer all on my own. Juliet had lubricated this situation just like she'd done with everything else. All the pride I'd felt glowing inside me as I'd considered Austin's offer dimmed, as I realized the one thing I thought I'd gotten on my own merits had been just one more bit of charity.

"Jace?" Juliet said, rising slowly from the table. "Why do you look angry?"

I didn't want to yell at her—this was just one more example of Juliet doing something nice. Something I should be grateful for. But I didn't want to be grateful to her. I wanted to be so much more than that to her.

I couldn't talk to her right now. I didn't know what to do, as shame flooded every cell inside me. I was nothing. I was so stupid. My world was crumbling again, my freshly recreated image of myself falling to pieces at my feet.

"I can't believe you did that," I said, my voice unrecognizable.

"I ..." the confusion in Juliet's eyes was the hardest thing to take. She had been doing something good. She was always doing something good. Why couldn't I just accept her gifts and be happy?

"I need to think. I need some time."

"Time for what? To think about what, Jace? We finally get to be together. I want to be with you."

I stared at her, her perfect face shining in the moonlight, her big eyes wide and trusting. She was a good person. The best. And I thought she probably deserved much more than a man she'd have to keep saving over and over again. More than me.

"I'm gonna call it a night," I told her. I knew we had to talk more, but I couldn't do it right then. "I'll let Christian know you're still up." I went inside without looking at her again, hating myself with every step.

CHAPTER THIRTY-ONE
JULIET

I watched Jace walk away, knowing he was angry or hurt, wishing he would stay and talk to me, tell me how I could fix it. Because everything I'd done today had been so that we could be together. Because that was what I wanted. I wanted something for me that wasn't about perceptions or spin. Something that felt good and true.

But maybe it was already too late?

The party had been a trial—knowing Alison was watching me closely based on what Chad had told her that morning about me and Jace, knowing she was likely to write something not about how I was moving forward in a new relationship ahead of my next big film, but about how I'd faked a relationship to distract the world from what a disaster my life was.

Because wasn't that exactly what I'd done?

After Chad left, I'd made quite a few phone calls. First to Zac, to let him know he could go ahead and release the tape, and that my attorney would be in touch with his about the settlement I'd already offered. Then, to Austin, letting him know exactly what kind of employee he had in Chad. And in Jace, of course. And then I'd called my agent to let her know we would need to prepare for some fallout.

But instead of fear, I felt excitement. I felt as strong and confident as my little sister looked when she was beating up the heavy bag in the basement. I felt like I was in charge for a change. And it felt good.

I didn't know if it was playing Warcraft, or maybe just talking to Gran that had helped me come to terms with the fact that I needed to live life for me. Hell, maybe it was the joint I'd borrowed.

Whatever it was, I'd come to Gran's party a different version of myself. A better version.

And that's a lot of what Alison Sands and I talked about. I couldn't control what she wrote. If she decided to go with some kind of scandalous starlet and bodyguard piece, I couldn't stop her. If she decided to make it even worse, that was up to her. I told her the truth—about everything. And what she did with it was out of my hands.

By the time we were all relaxing on the back porch, I was imagining myself going to Jace's room, spending the night with him and enjoying the freedom that came with not hiding.

But Jace seemed to have other plans, and when he left me sitting on the porch alone, I began to wonder if I'd misread everything. If I'd been wrong about what lay between us. If I'd been wrong about everything.

Tomorrow we'd head back to Los Angeles. I needed to talk to him. Now.

I took a deep breath, gathering the strength that had been driving me through this day, and went inside.

In the hallway where the security team was sleeping, I found Chessy nestled into a blanket just outside Jack's door. She eyed me suspiciously in the dim light, but didn't say anything. I chuckled at the hen who'd fallen in love with a handsome strong man. I knew how she felt. "Wish me luck, Chessy," I said softly, just as I was about to knock on Jace's door.

It opened before I had a chance. "Hi."

"Hi." I tilted my head at him, a little confused. "How did you know I was here?"

"Heard you talking to the chicken." He gazed past me toward Chessy, who gave him a low squawk before closing her eyes again. "Or maybe I just felt you out here. I don't know."

I liked that. I liked thinking Jace could feel me, could know I was nearby without seeing me.

"Can I come inside?" He looked so sad, I wanted to reach up and rub my fingers along the side of his face, comfort him. The dark eyes glimmered in the hallway light and his big shoulders, which stood out thanks to the white tank undershirt he'd stripped down to, were tight and tense.

"Yeah." He opened the door all the way and closed it behind me, and then he moved to a chair in the far corner and sat, looking defeated. He dropped his elbows onto his thighs and hung his head. His powerful legs were spread wide, the broad shoulders hunched.

"You're angry at me," I said. It had been clear on the porch, so there was no point dancing around it.

"I was. I'm not." He wasn't looking at me, staring instead at his fingers as he flexed and tightened them where they hung between his knees.

"Then—?" I moved to sit on the edge of the bed. My fingers were aching to touch him, but I knew I couldn't right then. There was something between us, something stopping us from being together. We needed to defeat it, and then the path would be clear for us to move forward.

"Shit, Juliet," he said, his voice almost a whisper. "How can you even look at me?"

I felt my eyebrows lower in confusion as I tried to understand his question. This was not what I'd expected. "What? What do you mean?"

"In your eyes, I've gotta be just some sad asshole from the wrong side of town who can't manage a goddamned thing for himself." His words were filled with self-loathing and they sounded like they hurt coming out.

My heart squeezed itself into a fist, aching for the pain I could see in his face. "Jace, no. Where is this coming from?"

"You called Austin. You're the only reason he offered me the firm."

"That's ridiculous." I said the words immediately, but after they were out, I realized what he had been thinking— that I'd told Austin to give him the firm, that somehow I'd made this happen for him. No wonder he was angry.

"You saved me again. I couldn't take care of myself, so you saved me."

Would we ever get past this same argument? Frustration bubbled in my stomach, making it difficult to sit. "That's not what happened. That's not how any of this happened."

He blew out a sharp breath, a sound of disbelief.

That little sound set me off, and the strength I'd found today pushed me to my feet. "No, Jace. It's not."

He didn't look up, but I kept talking.

"I admire you for the pride that makes you want to do everything for yourself—I know it's a big part of what makes you who you are. It's part of your strength, your integrity. You see the world in black and white, fair and unfair, right, wrong. And that's admirable. But it's also a distorted view of reality."

He glanced at me, narrowing his eyes. I felt his gaze like a spotlight, hot and focused.

I went on. "The world doesn't work that way, and I'm sure you know it. Things aren't always clear or straightforward, and no one person gets through life entirely on their own. We start our lives needing other people desperately—as helpless babies. And once we're raised, we go out in the world, leave our families, and we meet other people along the way who hopefully offer us guidance so we can continue to grow. And sometimes, we meet exactly the right people at exactly the right time to help change our lives so much we're able to become entirely new versions of ourselves." It was a little out there, but I was circling in on what I was trying to say.

"No one does everything alone. What a shitty, horrible life

that would be." An ironic laugh escaped me as I thought about it. "We are social creatures, Jace. We need a community. And the reason we need that is because we can't do it all alone."

He shook his head, still not getting the message I was trying to give him.

"You're not my charity case," I finally said plainly. "You and your family, the things I've tried to do, it hasn't been charity. It's been humanity. Community. Paying it forward."

He opened his mouth, about to argue, and I held up a hand, stopped in my pacing in front of him.

"You've met my Gran, my sister. You see where I came from. I didn't emerge, a fully formed person in Hollywood, suddenly famous. And I didn't get there by myself. I got lucky, and I had a lot of help. I had people step up, people who'd been lucky before me, people willing to pay my way for a while as I forged a new path. I had a community."

"I hear you," he said finally, standing in the center of the room. "Stop pacing around, you're making me tired."

I stood still. "Okay."

"Look, Juliet. I hear what you're saying. I understand that sometimes people help us out, I get that. It's just—when you've spent your life trying to take care of people and someone else comes along and does all the things you could never do for them, and makes it look easy—well, it's hard not to feel small and impotent."

"We talked about that," I said, my charge of energy beginning to fade, leaving me feeling tired, wrung out. "I thought we'd gotten past that."

"Maybe," Jace said, dropping his chin before looking back up to catch my eyes. "I thought I was okay with it. But then I talked to Austin, and I felt like finally I'd done something myself. Earned something myself. Like maybe you and I could be equals in a way. And to find out the only reason he made the offer was because you called ahead and greased the wheels—"

"Hold on," I said, putting a hand on his chest. "I didn't 'grease the wheels'—what is it with you and all the lube references, anyway?" I shook my head. "That's not important right now. Listen. When I called Austin, it was to tell him what a douche Chad was, and to assure him that the rest of his team was incredible. I told him how happy I was with Jack, with Christian, and with you. That's all. I didn't tell him he should pay you more or offer you a job. And even if I did, why would he listen to me? Passing on his firm is a huge business decision. Some movie star calling to tell him what to do wouldn't have much bearing on a choice like that."

Jace looked like he was thinking about my words, though his gaze was on my hand, still pressed to the hard warmth of his chest.

"I didn't get you the offer," I said, my voice softer. "You did that. He chose you because he values your work, because you've shown him the kind of person you are. Jace, don't you see that?"

Jace's hand covered mine, holding it to his chest for a minute. Then he lifted my palm from his chest and brought it to his mouth, planting a soft kiss in the center of my hand. "I'm sorry," he whispered.

"And equals?" I added. "Of course we're equals." I hung my head for a moment, trying to understand why he felt this was important. "Your ego gets in your way, and it needs to apologize," I said. "Don't let it stop you from taking the good things in your life."

"My ego wants to do a lot more than apologize," he said, reaching for me and pulling me gently against him. "But we're both sorry. I've been an idiot, Juliet. I'm just used to doing everything on my own. I've never had anyone else."

"It's okay," I said, wrapping my arms around his waist, closing my eyes as the warm solidity of his chest pressed against my cheek. I wanted to be the person to show Jace he didn't have to do everything alone. Maybe we were finally on the road where I could.

"You're amazing," he said, his arms around me. "Am I really this lucky?"

"As lucky as I am," I told him, tilting my face up to look at him.

He leaned his head down and pressed his lips to mine in a kiss that was tender and sweet, filled with promises of tomorrows and the future. "Juliet," he said quietly. "I think I'm falling in love with you."

My heart nearly popped inside me and I felt the smile pull my mouth wide. "I'm already there," I told him. "I do love you, Jace."

He kissed me again, and this kiss wasn't soft or gentle, but the kiss of a man about to claim what was his. I melted against him and let him lift me off my feet and carry me to his bed.

That night, Jace and I went slowly, exploring each other as if for the first time. We peeled clothing from each other's bodies, every inch of skin a revelation that merited attention, worship. We kissed, licked, sucked, caressed ... and by the time I lay in the center of Jace's bed, looking up into his handsome face as he held himself over me, muscles flexing and a look of focused concentration in his eyes, the world felt right again. When he notched himself against me and lowered himself to kiss me gently, he said, "I love you, Juliet," and a feeling of warm rightness flooded me. When he slid into me, pressing every last delicious inch into my eager depths, we both moaned with pleasure, and I didn't think I'd ever feel truly complete again, without this. Without him.

We moved together, knowing that maybe for the first time we had a right to be this way. We didn't have to hide, pretend, or sneak around.

We were two people in love. Two equals, making love, because it felt right.

And when the waves of pleasure racked through us both, when I clung to Jace like a life raft in a swirling, heaving sea of sensation, I knew I didn't want anything else in the world.

We fell asleep after, neither of us needing to get up and sneak away, and the satisfaction I felt made every inch of me glow.

CHAPTER THIRTY-TWO
JACE

Waking up with Juliet Manchester in my arms, knowing I could hold her and love her without hiding from anyone … well, that was like Christmas morning, my birthday, and the biggest cheese festival in the world all rolled into one (I like cheese, so sue me.)

"Good morning," she purred, her bright eyes blinking open as sunlight spread gradually through the room, casting everything in a warm yellow glow. The light was perfect for the way I was feeling—golden, pure.

"Hey," I said, nestling her against my chest so I could feel her silky hair against my shoulder, her soft skin pressed to my stomach and hip. "Sleep okay?"

She tilted her head a little, meeting my eyes as I angled my head to look down at her. "Jace, I think that was the best I've ever slept in my life."

Something like pride swelled inside me. "I slept well too."

"You told me once you don't sleep much."

"It's never been easy for me," I said. "But with you ... I don't know."

"Maybe you just sleep better when you're not alone," she suggested as I let my fingers trace down the skin of her shoulder.

"No," I told her. I knew from the few times I'd spent the night with other women that having them there didn't help at all. "Even when there's been someone else with me, I end up laying there awake, or getting up to read." Her fingers danced across my chest, and then wandered lower, until I felt them teasing along the sides of my suddenly awake cock.

"It's you," I said.

Juliet's fingers stopped teasing, and began a more focused exploration. As her hand stroked me, her fingers dipping around to fondle and squeeze my balls now and then, I gritted my teeth and tensed up, every cell in my body suddenly alive, focused on her cool hand on my dick.

She lay against me still, her hand working up and down, pumping me harder and faster as my own pre-cum slicked the movement until I was nearly shaking with pleasure. I pushed a second pillow behind my neck, tilting my head so I could watch her hand on me, that fair, perfect skin contrasted with the swollen purple of my cock. It was erotic, and the sight just about did me in.

And then she stopped. At first, disappointment flooded me, and I feared she was going to leave me here, desperate for release. But I opened my eyes again to see her smiling at me just before she slid a leg over my hips and impaled herself in one slide.

"Fuck, you're wet," I moaned.

"It turns me on, touching you," she answered as she began to slide herself over me in a smooth, leisurely stroke that I was fairly certain would kill me. "Is this okay?"

Her innocent words and the uncertainty they held played into every virgin fantasy I'd ever had, and while Juliet was thankfully not a virgin, I loved her sweetness and I felt myself pushing even closer to the edge.

"It's perfect," I managed to say, fighting to keep from grunting and rolling her to her back so I could rut into her like an animal.

She kept up the slow steady rhythm, and it was torture of the very best kind. And soon, she was moaning with each thrust, and the rhythm increased as she worked her body on top of mine. When she closed her eyes and began arching over me, I couldn't take anymore. I held her hips and pressed up into her, taking over the rhythm and fucking her hard, making her cry out.

We lay together afterwards, and I realized something, something that cleared away any last vestiges of doubt about whether I needed Juliet or if she could possibly need me. Maybe, I thought, we needed each other. Maybe the things she could give me—the things she had given me—were equal to the things I could give her. Acceptance, for one thing, and respect. And friendship with no expectations for another. Sex ... there was the sex, too. But maybe a relationship between equals wasn't a scorecard.

And while learning that perhaps the job offer from Austin hadn't been influenced by Juliet's words, I was starting to think maybe she was right. I had never had a community—except maybe in the Corps. And didn't I end up taking the security job in the first place as a result of that connection?

I gazed down at the beautiful woman in my arms as the sun glowed brightly around us, illuminating everything in shades of gold.

Love wasn't about pride. It wasn't about competition or dominance. Love was give and take, it was being strong when your partner was weak, it was being a constant your partner could always rely on. And while I might never be a rich man, I could be enough.

Enough for Juliet Manchester.

Enough for myself.

CHAPTER THIRTY-THREE
JULIET

Leaving Maryland wasn't easy. Not for me, and not for Jack, who was practically held prisoner by Chessy, who was doing the chicken version of strapping herself to a tree so it wouldn't be cut down. Only in this case, the tree was her love, Jack. She was running circles around the Town Car that held him, and shrieking loudly as she ran.

"I thought the hard part would be the tears," Jace chuckled as we stood on the porch watching, delaying the goodbyes with Tess and Gran.

Ryan had decided to stay a bit longer, and he stood with my sister, his arm around her shoulders and such a clear love for her on his face that I wanted to kiss him myself, just because it was so good to see them both happy.

"I see you two managed to lube up whatever had you stuck," Gran commented as Jace dropped his arm around my shoulders too, and squeezed me into his side.

"What is with all the lube talk?" I asked, looking between Gran and Jace as Tess chuckled.

"Nothing," Jace said. "Gran and I had a meaningful chat, and she made some excellent points."

"About lubricant?" Tess asked.

"Never you mind," Gran said, swatting at her. "This is between me and Kong."

"Gran!" I scolded.

She smiled sweetly and sighed dramatically. "Fine. I suppose if you're going to be around for a while, I can call you Jace."

"I'd like that," he said. "But Kong is cool too." He did a half-hearted chest pound like a gorilla might, and I laughed.

"So what's the plan?" Tess asked us.

I was enjoying being next to Jace, being acknowledged and open in front of my family. "Go home, pick up Elvis, and figure it out, I guess. I told Zac to go ahead and do whatever he's going to do, that my attorney would figure it out." I was amazed at how little I cared about Zac's threats now, about what the world might see if he released the tape.

"You don't care about the tape?" Ryan asked, looking surprised.

I sighed, happiness filling me too much to feel anything else. "I can't control everything," I said. "And I'm tired of trying to control what strangers think about me. I am who I am. They can deal with that."

"Is that what you told Alison last night?" Ryan asked.

"Something like that," I said.

"Tess, Gran," Jace said. "Thank you so much for having us all. It was a real pleasure meeting you. I hope to see you again."

I beamed at my polite and handsome boyfriend. I hoped to bring him back with me soon.

"This has been an interesting weekend," Gran said. "It makes my withered old heart swell to see both my girls happy. I guess my job here is done. Now I can go smoke myself silly and keel over in front of my computer."

Tess scoffed. "You know perfectly well you're too stubborn to go out that easily," she said.

"Meh." Gran lifted a shoulder and then turned to Tess. "Did you make the appointment for me to get those dentures?"

"Gran, your own teeth are fine," Tess said, rolling her eyes.

"Get me a cane or something, at least. I'm ninety, for fuck's sake."

Gran had always turned to humor when a situation was difficult or too emotional, and I was happy to see that Jace and me leaving was no exception. I was struggling a little too, feeling like home had taken on a more important place in my heart, since it had been the place I'd finally figured out who I was supposed to be.

"I'm going to miss you," I told Gran, pulling her in close and happy to feel how solid she was in my arms, despite her small size.

"I'll miss you too, Juliet," Gran said, and when I pulled away, she held my eyes for a long moment. "You turned out so good," she said quietly. "I think your father would be proud of us both."

I saw Tess press her lips together hard, stifling her

emotion as tears threatened at the backs of my eyes. "I hope so," I said.

Tess stepped forward and hugged me tight, and I felt something new and sweet between us, too. Maybe we could be the sisters I'd always wished we were. I knew it would take some more work, but I'd felt things shift this weekend.

I released Tess and turned to say goodbye to Ryan, intending to shake his hand or something, but deciding he was basically family now. "Thanks for everything," I told him, opening my arms for a hug.

"Thank you," he said, and he squeezed me and then let go with a glance at Jace.

Finally, we made our way down to the car and before long we were back in the air, heading home. We would have dinner at Jace's mom's place, where we'd pick up Elvis, and then it would finally be time to go home.

Jace sat next to me this time, Jack and Christian across the aisle. Jace read a magazine, and I was so happy just to be close to him, able to rest my head on his shoulder.

I let my mind run through the ways our lives might change once we touched down in Los Angeles, a tiny fragment of fear making me worry maybe we couldn't survive the pressures of the photographers, the fans. And if I was getting new security, as Jace had said, where would he live? "Jace," I said after a couple hours of flying. "What will happen when we get home?"

"Dinner," he said. "We talked about that."

"No. I mean after that. If the new security team to replace you and Chad will be at the house ..."

"Where will I go? Is that what you're asking?"

I nodded, trying to imagine saying goodbye to Jace at the end of this long day, going back to my own house alone. I didn't like the idea. "Will you stay with me?"

He held my eyes a long moment, his mind working behind those dark brows. "I guess I'll have to," he said. "Since I was living there. At least until I can get an apartment." He frowned. "Is that okay? I know it's an imposition. And whoever they put in house will need the room."

"But maybe I don't need anyone in the house now," I said. "Zac's threats are totally powerless at this point. And I have you," I said. "So maybe I don't need a guard inside the house all the time."

"When I'm not there, though ..."

"But maybe you could stay."

"Juliet ..."

"Is it too soon to move in? You kind of already live with me."

"We did everything backwards." His lips lifted on one side, a half-smile. "But maybe we should start at the beginning now."

I knew Jace's pride would make it hard for him to move right in, but I'd had to suggest it. "Then stay tonight. Or a couple weeks. However long it takes to find an apartment next door to my house."

"There are no apartments next door to your house," he laughed.

"Fine, down the street."

"Juliet, I couldn't afford an apartment in Bel Air even if there were any near you."

I pushed my lips into a fake pout. "I hate the thought of you far away. I've gotten spoiled."

He smiled at me, his eyes dancing. "You're the farthest thing from spoiled," he said. "I expected you to be, you know. When I first came to work for you."

"You did?" I didn't like that, but it didn't shock me.

"Of course. But you're real and practical and good."

"So you'll move in?" I tried, still imagining what a pleasure it would be to wake up every day with Jace, in his arms.

"So I'll find something close," he said, taking my hand and pressing it to his lips. "And it will probably take at least a week."

* * *

ELVIS WAS SO excited to see us that he leapt up in the air a few times, spinning in a silly pug circle or two, and then immediately snorted loudly and collapsed in a wrinkly snoring little pug pile.

"It's so good to see you both," Renee said, welcoming us warmly. "I made shrimp creole, I hope that sounds okay."

"That sounds great, Mom," Jace said, pulling her in tightly.

"Did you have a good weekend?" she asked us, seating us at the little round dining table in front of the bay window looking out on the yard, filled with flowers.

I exchanged a warm look with Jace. "We did," we both said.

"And you figured out whatever complications were ..." she gestured between us.

"What do you mean?" Jace asked, surprising me. Renee's easy acceptance of us together had made me believe Jace had told her what had gone on with us, even before we'd gone to Maryland.

"Juliet might be a famous actress, but everything you feel is written on your face," she told Jace. "Always has been. I could see you were in love with Juliet the first time you told me you were working for her."

A trickle of surprise immediately turned to warm pleasure inside me, making me smile.

"No you couldn't," Jace said.

She gave him a serene smile, setting plates in front of each of us. "Okay," she said simply.

My heart felt like it was full of warm honey, and it was overflowing and dripping down all over everything, making my whole life seem sweet and good. I loved the idea that Jace had been in love with me when he'd first met me. I knew I'd always had a crush on him, and I'd tell him so. Later.

Renee sat down with us and turned to me. "When Jace was little, he used to try to lie when he thought he was going to get in trouble—or if he was covering up for his brother, which he did a lot. But where Jarred could lie right to your face with no remorse, Jace's bottom lip and his chin would start to quiver, and he could barely get through telling the fib before he was contradicting himself, admitting the truth and ducking his head in shame."

"Such a clear sense of right and wrong," I agreed.

He looked between us. "You say that like it's a bad thing," he said.

I laughed. "It's not. It's a good thing. It's one of the things I love about you."

I saw Renee's smile grow at my use of the word "love."

"Mom," Jace said as we were eating, "you're not coughing. What did the doctor do?"

Renee sighed and looked between us. "I owe you a debt of gratitude," she said. "Both of you, for so many things. But for sending that doctor over, especially." She shrugged and put her fork down. "It was an infection."

"Why does that surprise you?" I asked.

Renee blew out a breath. "I actually thought I was dying. And I wanted to see Jarred straight again before Jace had to deal with that too. And I didn't want him to worry about doctor's bills if I was, and I knew he'd find some way to get me treatment if it was cancer or something ... I just didn't want to do that to him."

My admiration for this woman grew, knowing she understood her son so well, that she had an innate understanding of the way Jace's mind worked—something I'd just figured out this weekend. And I thought only a mother would be that selfless, to decide she'd rather die than put her son into debt.

"So you're better?" I asked her.

Renee nodded. "The doctor called in a prescription, and it only took a few days."

Jace's shoulders visibly lowered, as if knowing his mom was better took a heavy weight off of them.

We finished dinner, scooped up Elvis and all of his belongings, and after saying thank you, we were finally headed home.

JACK AND CHRISTIAN were already there, and assured us that the perimeter and house were secure. The additional guards would arrive the next day, and we all agreed they'd rotate on external shifts.

Jace and I went inside, and settled Elvis, who pranced from room to room, checking to make sure each of his Elvis jumpsuit-themed dog beds was in its proper place.

"All set?" I asked him, and he gave a little body shake to tell me yes.

"What about you?" Jace asked, leaning on the railing at the foot of the stairs. "Are you all set? Everything good?"

I walked toward him, happy for the quiet comfort of my own home, ecstatic to have Jace inside it—not as my bodyguard, but as my boyfriend. "Yes. I'm all set."

I wrapped my arms around his waist and pressed my cheek to his chest, gratified to feel his strong arms slide around me to pull me closer. "Good," he purred.

"I'm so happy, Jace," I said, breathing in the scent of him, letting him fill my senses. "It feels like I'm finally getting my own happily ever after."

"We both are," he told me. And then he scooped me over

his shoulder and carried me upstairs to my bedroom, where he showed me exactly what happily ever after was.

EPILOGUE
JACE

Juliet had been right—it was a little silly to get my own place, since I had spent most of the nights over the last six months at her house. That said, there was a good reason to have an apartment nearby—Jarred.

Once he was released from rehab, the charges against him didn't stick, and he moved in with me, taking the second bedroom in the apartment I'd found equidistant between Mom and Juliet's places. For the first two weeks he was back, I didn't spend the night at Juliet's, though she did come visit us at my place a couple times.

The first time Juliet had come over, Jarred had answered the door. When she'd introduced herself and come inside to see me, Jarred had pulled me aside, beckoning me into his room.

"Bro," he said, rubbing a hand through his close-cropped hair. "Is that the actual Juliet Manchester? Like the movie star?"

I hadn't filled him in on quite everything right away,

figuring he needed time to just adjust to being in the real world again. "Yeah. It is."

"Why is she here again?" He shook his head.

"We're dating," I'd told him.

He glanced out the bedroom door to where she sat on the couch in the living room. "Shit. I go into rehab for six weeks, and the next thing I know, the world's upside down."

"Not upside down," I'd assured him. "Just a little crazy."

"It's always been crazy," he said.

"It has," I had agreed, and I'd pulled him into the living room to meet Juliet properly. And from that night forward, Thursdays had become game night. Mom even came over sometimes to join us, and it became my favorite night of the week.

Right around the time Jarred had begun working for an electrician Mom had met in Brentwood, Austin had called to tell me he thought he was ready to retire.

"Already?" I asked, surprised. I'd expected it to be at least a year.

"I've got a chance to take a round-the-world trip," he said. "Can't pass it up."

"Okay," I told him. I was ready. I'd talked to his attorney and financial manager, and brought in a couple of my own. The paperwork was done, and the transfer was going to be easy.

I told my mother and Jarred that day, but waited until that night to tell Juliet.

. . .

WE'D DECIDED to have dinner brought in, something we did pretty often, since Juliet had only become more famous on the heels of the piece *Hollywood Reporter* had run on her, describing her realization that she didn't want to define herself through her relationships, that she was a confident and secure single woman. The piece had delved into Hollywood's tendency to focus on starlets as two-dimensional, as caricatures of human beings, uninteresting unless they were either linked to a man or in the midst of some dramatic crisis.

"I'm a fully-formed and intelligent human being on my own," Juliet had been quoted as saying. "And I don't really care if people acknowledge that—maybe it's too much to expect in Hollywood. But what's important is that I've realized it, and I'm not going to live my life for other people any more. I'm taking it back for myself, and for those I love."

The piece had been cited widely as a mantra for women everywhere to define themselves not by other people, but by their own actions and intentions. "Taking it back" had even become a hashtagged meme online for a while, and Juliet's picture was everywhere.

Juliet had been busy, studying a lot—not just scripts anymore, but she was working on her college degree, taking classes in literature and French. I was glad to have an evening where we were both away from the distractions, focused on one another.

An enormous Christmas tree stood in the corner, surrounded by a low fence to keep Elvis from investigating anything too closely, and the twinkling light gleamed in Juliet's eyes as she smiled at me.

"This is nice," Juliet said, reaching for the salad bowl as she sat across the blanket we'd spread on the floor in front of the glowing fireplace. Winter was setting in, and though Los Angeles really didn't get cold, it was still cool enough in the evenings to warrant the fire.

"It is," I agreed. "And I have some news."

"What?" she cocked her head to the side, her fork paused partway to her pretty pink lips.

"I'm the owner of Austin Security now," I said. "As of today."

Juliet dropped her fork. "That's amazing! Congratulations!" She rose to her knees and leaned over the spread of food to hug me. "I'm so proud of you."

I was proud of me too. For a kid who never thought he'd go to college to have both a degree and a wildly successful business to call his own, I was doing pretty well. But there was one more thing. "Thanks," I said. "But there's one more thing I wanted to tell you."

"Okay." Juliet drew out the word, wary suddenly at my change of tone.

"My life has changed in so many ways since I met you, Juliet. Some of them hard to accept at first, but all of them good."

She nodded, her hair slipping over her shoulder.

"And I'm hoping we might make one more change—not right away. But someday. Maybe in a year or two."

I rose so that I could kneel properly, and when I did, Juliet's entire expression shifted to an excited smile.

"I love you, Juliet. You're the light in my world, the air I breathe. When I'm with you, the insanity around us all makes sense. Or maybe it just doesn't matter to me anymore. You've made my life better in so many ways, I can't even count them."

"I'm your KY Jelly," she said, interrupting my romantic proposal.

"Did you just make a lube joke in the middle of my proposal?"

"Are you proposing to me, Jace?" She grinned.

"I'm trying."

"Go ahead." She mimed zipping her lips.

"As I was saying," I went on dramatically. "You're the lubricant that makes everything in my life slide more easily. And I hoped you might agree to be my wife someday. Will you marry me?" I held out the ring I'd bought—something smaller than what she'd had before, but beautiful and simple.

"Yes!" she said, standing to walk around all the food and then throwing herself into my arms. "Yes."

I kissed her then, soft and long and deep. I kissed the woman I wanted to spend my life with. And then I offered her the ring, taking it out of the box as she lifted her finger for me to slip it on.

The fit was a little snug. "We can get it sized," I told her.

She grinned at me, her movie star smile dazzling me just as it always had. "Or I can just use lube anytime I need to take it off. So many uses," she said.

I pulled my fiancée into my arms, both of us laughing,

and together, we found several other uses for lubricant, right there on the floor in front of the fire.

***

Want more time in Singletree? You're in luck! Grab **SHAKING THE SLEIGH** and see what the town looks like at Christmas! (Hint: it's nuts).

Sneak peek: Shaking the Sleigh - available now!

Chapter One: The Grinch's Last Stand: April

"You should be grinning from ear to ear right now," my uncle told me, leaning across his mahogany desk and jabbing his finger into the brown paper blotter on its surface to make his point.

I was definitely not grinning. I'm pretty sure I was frowning. And I'd been doing a lot of that lately, probably, but I hadn't had a lot to smile about since my life had imploded three months before. I'd lost my job and my self respect in one dramatic moment totally worthy of the reality television show that had inspired it.

"You came to me desperate. With nothing. Begging, April. You begged." He raised his bushy gray eyebrows and sat back, letting that sink in.

Ouch. The truth hurt.

I shifted in the leather seat, my suit skirt threatening to burst at the seams, thanks to the stress eating I'd been doing since I'd ruined everything. But cookies still loved me. And cookies never looked at me like Uncle Rob was looking at me now. My uncle's office was intimidating, with its dark-paneled walls and Emmy awards and Golden Globes perched on the shelves around us. It hadn't been easy calling him. It had been downright humbling. He was the one who'd inspired me to get into television in the first place, and to come to him now was beyond embarrassing.

"I know, Uncle Rob. It's just ... I mean ... *Holiday Homes*?" I cringed even saying the name of the show I most despised.

Rob grinned. "Holidays. Homes. What's not to love?"

When I didn't jump up and clap my hands, his smile dropped. I tried, "There's really nothing else? Something un-Christmassy? Maybe *Fix it Up* or *Hating to Dating?* I'm good with people, Uncle Rob. Not houses."

"Look April, I'm gonna tell it like it is. You screwed up a good thing—with people—and there aren't's not a lot of ways to come back from that. You had a top gig producing *Run Away with the Bridegroom*, but maybe someone should've pointed out to you that you were not actually supposed to be the one doing the running away with the bridegroom."

My stomach twisted at the painful reminder of the most humiliating moment of my life. "We didn't run away ..." I began, realizing too late that bringing up the details of the scandal that had ended my high-profile position at my last show probably wouldn't help.

"No, but you probably should have. Far, far away. To get caught on camera making out with that sleazy jerk ..." My uncle's words were coming faster, and his eyes scathed the surface of my face before searching the room, probably seeking a less disappointing subject to observe. "Ape, you made a mistake. A big one. And you got caught. Though that little twist did give the ratings a pretty solid boost ..." He sighed and his eyes returned to mine.

"I'm really sorry, Uncle Rob."

"I know you are, darling, and that's why I'm willing to pull these strings and get you another chance. You're sorry, and you're a damned good producer when you're focused on your job and not on the assets of the cast." He leaned back in his chair and watched me, steepling his fingers in front of his mouth. His voice softened. "Did you love the guy?"

I swallowed hard and dropped his gaze. It would almost have been better if I *had* loved Antonio, the bachelor from my last show. But I didn't love him any more than he loved me, or any of the fifteen women he was supposed to be courting on television. I was a conquest, and if I was honest, he was a conquest for me, too. "No," I said firmly. "I don't think I do love."

"Well, that's the right attitude if you're sticking to television. A hell of a lot cleaner that way."

I'd tried love in college, but I just wasn't very good at it. I got bored, distracted. I knew I got that from my father, another trait I wished I could cut from my personality somehow, but had long since accepted. "Right," I said, hoping my agreement could put an end to the rehashing of all the ways I'd screwed up my last job.

Rob placed a contract in front of me. "So, four specials annually—takes a little of the pressure off, not having the weekly churn, right? Next one is the biggest one by far, the Christmas home tour."

I tried to keep my face neutral as I imagined the sheer

quantity of holiday cheer I'd have to withstand to make this work. "But I just handle initial setup and pick targets, right? Take care of contracts ... you've got the location producer for the actual show?"

"Kind of. No picking homes. For this first one, Juliann will handle the details of actual production. She's done the Christmas show for years. You just get the homeowners final-ized—like I said, most have been on board for months. Just get them to sign on final details and behave, and then throw the reins to Jules."

I relaxed a little bit. I could do this. I wouldn't have to decorate, or set up any fake snowmen. Maybe I wouldn't even have to enter any artificial-snow-encrusted, pine-tree smelling, twinkling houses. That part was Juliann's gig. I would just be getting things ready for Juliann, who could waltz in wearing striped tights and a felt elf costume, for all I cared. I, myself, would be far away by Christmas, enjoying a tropical drink on a hot beach somewhere, pretending it was any other day.

Uncle Rob's phone rang on his desk and he raised a finger to me as he picked it up—the universal symbol for 'you're not as important as this potential telemarketer.' "Rob here."

Uncle Rob's eyes found mine as he listened, and his eyebrows shot up comically as I watched. "Oh," he said, little lines appearing around his mouth. "Two casts, huh?" He paused, his lips pressing into a firm line. "Traction?" He rubbed a hand over his forehead. "Well I'm glad you're okay, Jules."

My attention riveted to the phone in his hand. Jules? Was

that Juliann? What was that about casts and traction? My stomach tightened and I sat up straighter.

"Well you don't need to worry about anything here. You just focus on healing," Uncle Rob said. "The network will send along a fruit basket."

"A fruit basket?" I yelped, and then slapped a hand over my mouth as Uncle Rob's eyes narrowed at me.

"Bye now." Uncle Rob chuckled as he put down the phone. He looked up at me. "All that stuff I just said? Scratch it. You're it. Juliann's out."

"What?" I heard myself ask, my voice higher than usual.

"Broke both legs skiing at Whistler, poor thing. She's gonna be out for months."

"Oh no," I said, picturing how difficult two broken legs would make the wearing of an elf costume. Then something else occurred to me. "Wait, you said, 'I'm it'? For the Christmas show?"

"The whole shebang. Trial by fire. Go get Jingle-y, April. They need you on location this week. Little town in Maryland, evidently they really go all out for Christmas. Need everything wrapped up by the middle of the month to get the footage all set for the hosts to do their review show on the 23rd."

The turnaround was crazy. I knew the Christmas show operated on the tightest timeframe of the *Homes* episodes, since I'd heard Uncle Rob talk about it before. From what he said, the home footage was edited almost daily as they gathered it. The hosts stayed in Los Angeles and filmed their segments, reviewing the décor just before airing on Christmas Eve.

"You can do this, right April? It's not gonna be too much for you?" My uncle had begun to look skeptical. The last thing I needed was for him to second guess my last chance. I needed this to be a home run if I wanted to stay in television and not end up back in my college job at Tacos Loco, where the manager said I had been the best taco assembler he'd ever had. I hoped my tombstone might bear something more illustrious than "Master of beef and cheese in a crunchy shell."

"I can do it," I said, stress pulling my shoulders tight as visions of reindeer and candy canes drifted through my head. and I wondered if I really could.

"SINGLETREE," I repeated for the third time to my best friend, raising my voice and shouting into the rental car's overhead microphone.

"What kind of name is that for a town?"

"I don't know, Lynn, but the name of the place was not really the point of this story." I let out a slow breath as I guided the car down a curving two-lane road lined with huge trees dropping leaves that ranged in color from dark green to blazing gold. It was like every postcard of what fall was supposed to look like I'd ever seen. A far cry from the screaming freeways and swaying palm trees in Los Angeles. "I think the bigger picture here is that I'm in Maryland. To produce the Christmas show." I hissed the word Christmas as if it burned my tongue.

"I know how you feel about the holidays, April. But maybe this will help you get past all that." Lynn was an eternal optimist. We'd been friends since kindergarten, and Lynn had always been the bright shiny yin to my skeptical darker yang. "Maybe a season in Littletree is exactly what you need."

"Singletree."

"You said the name of the town wasn't the main point, remember? The point is that your hatred for all things red and green needs to die. You're missing out."

I sighed again as I maneuvered through yet another traffic circle that felt like it had me literally driving spirals into the heart of nowhere. I looked down at the phone to check the directions, but the screen had switched to my call, and I had no idea if I was going the right way. "Damn," I said. "Lynn, I need to go, I think I chose the wrong exit from the last circle of death."

"Circle of death?"

"They have all these crazy traffic circles here. I have no idea how I'm supposed to do those ... just give me an eight-lane freeway any day!"

"Adventure, Apes. Remember, it's an adventure."

"I miss Los Angeles. And it's not an adventure, it's a Christmas show."

"There's a reason why most people like Christmas."

"Right. Well."

"Love you," Lynn's sweet voice said. "Go now so you don't get lost and end up in Doubletree instead of Singletree."

"Love you too." I ended the call and swiped my phone's screen back to my directions. Miraculously, I was still going the right way. Nothing outside the little car's windows looked anything like Los Angeles. The roads were narrow and winding, the vegetation was thick and green, and dense gray moisture hung in low clouds that hugged the sprawling fields around me. I wondered for a moment if I'd driven into some picturesque no-man's land, where there were no towns, no people ... only this never-ending farmland draped in fog. I shivered. Fifteen twisting green miles later, I saw signs for Singletree and breathed a sigh of relief.

Singletree wasn't big, and despite my trepidation, it was hard not to be just a teensy bit charmed as I made my way to the center of town. I drove slowly down the main street feeling like I'd been transported to another world—one that existed in some earlier, simpler time. There was a town square surrounded by quaint shops with storefronts lovingly maintained and painted in yellow, white, and light blue, and buildings of brick and stone that looked like they'd stood for hundreds of years. They probably had. The central area was a grassy square that stretched several blocks between the buildings, featuring manicured lawns and neatly trimmed bushes, low-hanging trees and a central gazebo. There was one huge tree in the middle of the square, and I shook my head as I drove by the impressive group of people gathered beneath it with ladders and strings of holiday lights ready to drape the tree, which I guessed was pretty normal even though it was technically still November. They'd probably barely had time to put away the gravy boats after their Thanksgiving feasts, and they were already here, tossing around shiny bulbs. I sighed in dismay.

I drove slowly down the long street that stretched behind the central square, turning in when I saw the sign for the Candlelight Inn, the hotel where Juliann had booked the crew. Despite Juliann's absence from the day-to-day production of the episode of *Holiday Homes* she was supposed to handle, she'd done most of the legwork and had passed her extensive notes and plans on to me. From here it should be simple—check in to this hotel (which looked like it could have been constructed of gingerbread and spun sugar, thanks to some seriously overeager Victorian styling), and begin visiting the homes Jules had identified to finalize contracts. Jules had assured me there would be no issues because *Holiday Homes* was a well-known franchise at this point, and homeowners practically bent over backwards to have their homes featured. It increased their resale value, and if they were looking to sell after the episode aired, it usually resulted in multiple offers and sometimes in a bidding war. And if they weren't looking to sell, I knew that having their homes identified as "special" gave folks something to feel good about, and something to lord over their neighbors if their personalities leaned that way. As for the decorating, the homes that were selected generally went over and above for the holidays even when they weren't going to be featured on television.

"You're just there to keep things running smoothly, that's

all," Jules had assured me from her hospital room when we'd spoken on the phone.

I parked and took a deep breath, and stepped out of the car.

"Hello there," a young man in a dark red uniform greeted me as I approached the front entrance of the hotel with my roller bag. "Welcome to the Candlelight Inn."

"Thank you," I said, distracted momentarily by the intricate scrolling woodwork that seemed to garnish every free surface of the building. The Inn looked a lot like a castle, except that it was a soft yellow color. The turrets and wide-open front porch were like nothing I had ever seen up close.

The attendant took my bag from me and escorted me up the stairs to the front door, pulling it open with a flourish and a smile.

I thanked him and gaped at the army of workers busily wrapping railings in evergreen boughs and erecting an enormous tree in the middle of the front lobby. The interior was probably normally dim compared to the daylight outside, but this had been solved by the hundreds of strands of holiday lights a woman was holding at the far side of the space. Two other workers were arguing loudly about how best to erect the small cottage they were working on—a cottage that was made to look like gingerbread but could hold life-sized actual humans. My stomach turned as the sheer Christmasness of it all engulfed me. I stepped around the ladders and tools, tinsel, and a standing army of nutcrackers, and approached the desk.

"Welcome!" The woman at the desk called. "Forgive our

mess, won't you? We're a little behind in getting our holiday decorations up this year, and I don't know if you heard, but *Holiday Homes* is being filmed in Singletree," the woman paused, leaning over the front desk and looking around conspiratorially, "and we want to impress those folks."

"Okay, well," I said. "I'm just checking in." I slid my ID and credit card over the smooth polished wood and managed a smile for the rosy-cheeked woman. "April Hall." The woman who accepted my cards with a wide cheerful smile was wearing a sweater that was made to make her look like a Christmas present. It had actual ribbon stitched against a ridiculously busy pattern of snowmen and skiers. The bow sat on her shoulder and the ends of it kept popping into her face, where she had to repeatedly push them away. I wondered how many times a day she had to push that ribbon out of her face.

The woman punched a few keys on the computer behind the desk, and made a few noises of concern. She raised a finger to me and then ducked beneath the desk, shuffling around in a drawer. "Just a second, so sorry," she squeaked, popping up again and punching a few more keys as she batted the shiny green ribbon from her mouth. "Would your reservation be under a different name, maybe?"

The cross-country flight and confusing drive began to weigh on me, and I leaned an elbow on the desk. "Oh, right. Yes, look up Juliann Stevens. I took her spot."

"Aha, here she is! Oh, but ..." the woman's eyes widened and she glanced quickly from the screen to me and back down again. "Ms. Stevens was part of the show," she said, her voice breathy. "Does that mean you're ...?"

I cringed. I would have liked to maintain my anonymity, at least at the hotel where I would be coming to escape all the Christmas craziness every night, but I didn't see how that would be possible, given that the whole crew was also staying here. "Yes, I'm the producer of *Holiday Homes*," I confirmed, my voice ragged with exhaustion.

"Ah!" The woman chirped. "Wonderful! I'll be right back!" She disappeared into a room behind the check-in area and I slumped farther over the counter, wishing for nothing more than a quiet room and maybe a warm bath. "Here it is!"

I couldn't see the woman's face because she returned carrying an enormous basket wrapped in cellophane. It was hard to tell what was inside, but I could see a variety of items decorated with crabs and the Maryland state flag, and plenty of Christmas mugs and candy canes and glittery ornaments. The entire thing was tied with a huge ribbon that shone in metallic and glittery red and green and seemed to be vomiting silver glitter. "A little something from the Inn," the woman said, hoisting the basket to the counter and into my face. Tiny showers of sparkly glitter cascaded to the counter.

"Oh," I said, leaning to the side to see around the massive basket. "That's so ... well, wow. That's lovely. Thank you."

"We're tickled to have you," the woman told her, her face pink with excitement under the close-cropped gray curls, which were now dusted with red and green sparkles. "I'm Annabelle Adams. I own the inn, and don't you hesitate to come to me for just anything at all, okay?"

"Thanks so much." I considered asking for a dust buster and lint roller to combat the glitter I was now certain would be attached to me for the remainder of my stay in Singletree.

"Now, let's see. Miss Hall. I've got you in our Dickens Suite. That's on the top floor."

"That sounds lovely," I said, accepting my card and ID back and tucking them into my pocket.

"It's our most festive room during the holidays," Annabelle said with a nod.

My spirits sank further. Evidently producing the Christmas episode meant everyone I met would automatically assume I was just as Christmas-crazy as the people who decked out every inch of their houses on the show. "Great," I said with no inflection at all.

"Here's your key, and you call me if you need anything. We've got a cocktail hour every night here in the lobby at five, and there are usually guests in the library after that playing board games and sitting by the fire."

"Great," I said again, nearly desperate now to just sit down somewhere quiet. The bustle of the workers around the lobby was almost comical. People were dashing to and fro, carrying bells and faux candles. Just as I turned from the desk, a looming presence appeared behind me and I stifled a scream as a life-sized St. Nicholas doll stopped inches from my face and then moved in a jolting progression farther across the lobby.

"Isn't he amazing?" Annabelle asked.

"Erm. Yes," I said, watching the enormous old- fashioned

Santa make his way to a far corner, carried by a worker about half the statue's size.

A few minutes later, I was unlocking the door to the Dickens Suite and stepping inside. The young man from the front door was behind me with my suitcase and the oversized Christmas basket in his arms. A festive trail of green and red glitter spilled down the hallway and through my door as he moved past me to put things down, thanks to the exuberant bow on the basket.

The suite was lovely, if you could overlook the wreaths and glittering globes and the huge tree standing in one corner wafting pine scent throughout the space. The tree was festooned with ribbons and balls, gleaming in the light, and I knew that anyone else stepping into this charming room would feel their spirits lift and would probably experience some kind of warm nostalgia relating to the holiday season. But the sight of the tree and the stockings hanging from the mantle caused a hard knot to form in my gut and settle there as my own memories soured any enthusiasm I might have scraped together for my new job.

"I'll just put this down here," he said, setting the basket on a table. He left the suitcase by the door, accepted the tip I extended and wished me goodnight, and finally, I was alone. I looked around, a dark feeling of something like sorrow filling me as the tree twinkled merrily in its corner.

"Nope," I said, realizing I'd never be able to function in a room decorated to within an inch of its life. I moved quickly through the suite of rooms, removing every holiday item I could easily detach from where it had been stuck, hung or placed, and deposited as much of it as I could in the dry-cleaning bag hanging in the closet. I couldn't think with all the sparkle and cheer around me. The stockings came down, the reindeer was removed, and the festive hand towels in the bathroom were switched out for the plain white ones I found in the top of the closet. I wrestled the glittery bow from the basket, hoping to banish it to the trash can so it couldn't infect one more item with clingy glitter, but I mostly managed to explode the stuff all over the room and myself in the effort.

When I was finished undecorating, only the tree glittered mockingly from its corner, and I almost believed I could feel my mind clearing, despite the glitter I'd probably never get washed from my hands.

CHAPTER TWO: **Take your Code and Shove It: Callan**

I pulled my car up to the big iron gates at the address I'd been given over the phone, taking a moment to marvel at the sheer size of the house beyond the gate. It was big, and it was isolated, that was for sure—I'd driven down a long lane with fields on each side, and turned onto that from a quiet country road. I couldn't see another house from where I sat. No people. No cars. No neighbors.

Good. This was exactly what I told the real estate agent I wanted. And now it was mine.

As I sat staring at the tall iron gates of my new home, another car pulled down the long lane and stopped behind my own. A tall woman with dark hair slicked into a knot, wearing a huge scarf and big sunglasses got out and approached my window. "Callan Whitewood?" She leaned down, grinning, one hand holding the scarf down to keep it beneath her chin.

"That's me," I said, trying to sound cheerful or friendly or at least not psychopathic while I tried to figure out the purpose of wearing a scarf so big it tried repeatedly to take over your head.

"Jessica Betts," she said, sticking a hand through the window and narrowly missing my face with her long nails.

I shook her hand, forcing a smile. "Nice to meet you," I said. "Thanks for your help with all this." She had been helpful, I reminded myself. So I could be friendly for five minutes even though I was pretty sure the blackness inside me contained less friendliness than that.

"Well, we don't usually sell houses sight-unseen over the phone, but I guess we can always make an exception for soccer stars."

"Or people willing to pay cash," I guessed. I'd signed everything in my agent's office back in San Diego, essentially sleepwalking through the process and dropping my signature wherever I'd been directed. I just wanted to move on, get started with this next phase of my life—the phase that didn't include being featured as the media's favorite pity-inducing ex-soccer star.

She smiled wider. "Right. There was that. The seller was thrilled."

"I'm sure." I'd pulled the trigger based on location, isolation, and the fact that Singletree, Maryland didn't seem like the kind of town that followed pro soccer. Driving down from DC after arriving from San Diego, I'd figured it was more of a crab or oyster fishing kind of town, maybe a hunting town, a good American football or NASCAR town. Based on my questions to various real estate agents I'd spoken with and the input of my brother, it was not a soccer town. And hopefully that meant anonymity.

"It's funny," Jessica said, looking at me with a little tilt of the head. "We just had another celebrity buy a place here recently. Maybe southern Maryland is going to be the next hot celebrity escape."

I really hoped not. I had heard that Juliet Manchester grew up somewhere near here, and that Ryan McDonnell had recently bought a home nearby. But I definitely didn't make my decision based on them. More on my brother and my own desire to be isolated and far away from San Diego and the career I had loved. The one I'd been great at. The one I couldn't have anymore. I doubted they even aired the South Bay Sharks games out here in the middle of nowhere.

"I bet you'd like to go in, lay eyes on the place for real." Jessica's excitement wasn't contagious, but she was right. I wanted to go in.

"Sure."

"Well step out here and I'll show you how to put in the gate code. Normally you'll just drive right up, but since we're both here ..." She stepped back from the car and I swung the door open and then used my hands to help get my left leg out and onto solid ground. My left ankle didn't do much of what I wanted anymore, which was part of the reason I was here in Singletree.

I stood up, ignoring the pain ricocheting through my left leg and limped to where Jessica stood. She was clearly trying not to look surprised by my unsteady gait.

"Just type in the code here," she said, her fingers going through four numbers. "And the gate swings open."

I nodded. "I'll probably just get some kind of swipe access installed."

"Right," she agreed. "But for now, you've got the code. Five, six, seventy-two."

"Right. Five, seven—"

"No, hon. Five, six, seven, two."

"Got it." I did. not. care.

"Do you?"

"Five, six, seven ..." I trailed off. Failing. I was winning at failing lately.

"Want me to write it down?"

"Sure." I limped back to my car.

"Okey dokey," Jessica trilled, heading back to her own car to follow me into the circular drive in front of the huge house.

We parked near a fountain that stood quiet and dry like a sentinel, and I gazed up at my new home. It was stately—I guessed that was the right word. It looked like something one of the founding fathers would have lived in—white and colonial, with columns and a sprawling front porch. The place had wings, more rooms than I could ever possibly use filling the enormous space inside the place. But in my mind, all that mattered was that it was isolated, it was far away from San

Diego, and it was mine. Jessica unlocked the massive front door, and we stepped into the huge old house.

"This was originally a plantation house, as I mentioned on the phone," Jessica said, gazing around with clear approval. "And it's been restored and updated, but so many of these wonderful architectural details are original. Once you get it all done up for the holidays, it's going to look just amazing."

"Great." I was ready for her to hand me the keys and get lost. I didn't have much with me to move in, but I did have a bottle of scotch, a camping chair and a sleeping bag, and between those three items I figured my next forty-eight hours were pretty much accounted for. As far as decorating for the holidays, I had no plans for that, so I ignored this last comment.

"I'll just give you the quick tour," she said, heading for a doorway off the entrance hall.

"Ah, actually," I said quickly, my tone halting Jessica's step and causing her to turn, one hand on the giant sunglasses she wore atop her head and another on the ridiculous scarf. "I'm pretty beat from the drive. I think I can manage."

"Oh, of course." Her face fell for a second but she shook her head with a laugh and recovered quickly. "Well then, here you are, Mr. Whitewood." She handed me a large silver key. "And may I be the first to welcome you officially to Singletree."

I repressed a strong urge to roll my eyes. To her, maybe becoming a resident of Singletree was something to be celebrated, but for me it was just the final nail in the coffin of the life I'd had. The one I'd very much enjoyed having. Before. "Thanks, I really appreciate all your help."

"If you need anything," she said, turning and heading back to the front door.

"Yep. Got it."

"I'll check in on you in a couple days." She patted my arm and stepped onto the porch. "And if you need any help decorating—"

"Won't be necessary," I said, interrupting her. She was really hung up on this holiday thing.

"Well, you know there is the thing I told you about, the contract—"—"

"I've got it," I assured her, ignoring every word and practically pushing her out the door.

"All right then, talk to you soon!" She skipped down the steps to her car, and a few minutes later, I stood alone on the porch of my new home.

After unloading my few things from the car, I turned slowly and went back inside. The empty space of the old house seeming to echo and expand around me, making me feel small and insignificant as I stood in the cool silence. I took a deep breath, and for the first time in a long time, I exhaled and felt myself relax.

I SPENT two nights in the new house, sleeping on the floor in the living room in my sleeping bag, a whiskey-fueled hangover dogging me through the days, and dark dreams full of doubts chasing me through the nights. I didn't even go upstairs. For one thing, my ankle hurt too damned much to climb the stairs just for the heck of it, and for another, I figured that when you've seen one house, you've seen them all. Just because this one belonged to me now didn't make it special.

The movers showed up on the third day, their huge long truck lumbering down the lane in front of the house, making the road look even narrower than it actually was. I pressed the button next to the door to let them through the gate, greeted them at the front door, and then limped into the far bathroom to take a much-needed shower. My plan was to hang out on the back porch until they were done, staying out of the way and avoiding conversation—and potential recognition—as much as possible. I'd called my brother that morning to let him know I'd arrived, though I should have done it the moment I'd taken ownership. I shouldn't have put it off, but even dealing with Cormac seemed like more than I could handle.

I had just positioned myself back in the folding camp chair, my gaze aimed out at the sweep of the Potomac that wound around the bottom edge of my property several acres below, when I heard a female voice drifting through the open window. I swiveled and squinted inside, but didn't see any female movers hustling furniture about. Just when I decided I'd been mistaken, I heard it again, a soft melodious voice that definitely couldn't belong to one of the movers I'd just let in.

Wandering the house, dodging moving couches and

rolled-up rugs, wasn't what I felt like doing, especially with my ankle protesting every move I made, but my curiosity got the best of me. Was I hearing things now? Maybe I'd been alone a little too long in this strange old house. I went in and prowled the downstairs rooms and then climbed the stairs slowly, cursing the shooting pain that accompanied each step I took with my left foot. The staircase was grand and wide, the oak-planked risers creaking under my weight as I gripped the curving bannister. I imagined myself tripping and falling down the expansive steps, and I could picture the media coverage of that one. *Former Soccer Star Callan Whitewood Suffers Another Debilitating Injury!* Because I hadn't been hounded enough after the first one.

After exploring the upstairs rooms—all gleaming and bright, mostly empty of furniture—I was beginning to doubt myself, and to believe I was most likely losing my mind. I glanced out the second-story window at the moving truck in the drive, and spotted a small silver Honda next to my car. Someone was definitely here, but this stupid house was so big I couldn't find her.

I was just about to head back down the stairs when a woman appeared in the hallway where she definitely had not been before. She had inky dark hair that flowed over her shoulders, and bright blue eyes that glittered in the half-light of the upstairs hallway. She was pretty, I realized, but that didn't begin to explain what she was doing wandering around my house with a clipboard and appearing in empty hallways. "Hello," she said. "You must be Mr. Whitewood. I'm April Hall."

"Uh, hi," I said, hating the way the confusion made me sound uncertain. This was my house, dammit. Who was this woman? "Where exactly did you come from?"

The woman gave me a puzzled look, her nose wrinkling in a way that I was sure most found adorable, but that I perceived as her simply not answering my question. "Just now?" she asked.

"Yes. Just now."

"Because I came to Singletree from California, but I didn't think that was what you meant." She laughed lightly and then spun around. "There's a secret hallway back here." She pulled open a panel that had been standing slightly ajar. "It was probably a servants' passage. A lot of these old houses have these little nooks and crannies. Part of the charm. If that's your thing." She shrugged and looked at me expectantly, maybe waiting for me to chime in about whether or not old houses and secret passages were 'my thing."

Annoyance flooded me as my ankle throbbed. I didn't like a stranger knowing more about my house than I did, and I didn't like being surprised in my own home. I was also oddly annoyed at the tiny flicker of interest I had felt leap to life in my chest when I'd gotten a good look at this intruder. It was hard to hold onto my annoyance when part of me—the old part of me that was good at flirting with attractive women— was prodding me to keep her talking. I shoved that part down and remembered that I was done with women, done with being good-natured and friendly, done with people in general.

"Can I ask what you're doing in my house, Miss Hall?"

"Oh, of course." She had the grace to blush, certainly realizing that she was essentially trespassing. "I'm with *Holiday Homes*, and you're on my list, and well, the gate and the door were open, and there was so much hub-bub down there with all the men moving things around ..." she babbled, looking nervous.

"And so you're here because," I began for her, gripping the banister at the top of the stairs as my ankle throbbed.

"I was looking for you, actually." The Her bright eyes found my own and then dropped to my hands, taking in the white-knuckled grip on the bannister and darkening briefly before meeting my gaze again. "Is there somewhere we could sit?"

For a split second, I wondered if she knew. That look—it had held a touch of pity, and while I'd come to Singletree to get away from lots of things, pity was first on that list. I straightened, forced myself to put weight on both feet evenly and released my grip on the bannister. "No, actually. There's nowhere we can sit. Maybe you noticed I don't have any furniture just yet?"

"I did," April said, "and I'm so sorry to just barge in. I just wanted—"

"I'm going to stop you right there," I said, feeling my anger dissipate into exhaustion. "Maybe you know who I am, maybe you don't. I don't really care. I moved here because I only know one person in town. There's no one here who needs me for anything, no one who expects anything from me. There's no one here who I have to worry about disappointing because they'd hoped for anything at all." The words sounded bitter coming out and I almost regretted them as I watched April's pretty face tighten, her chin lift slightly. "I don't need whatever you're selling. I'm not in the market for candles, makeup, or Boy Scout popcorn, I don't want to save the turtles or the unicorn habitat, and I'm not looking to sponsor a puppy, a wombat, or a child." I waved an arm at the stairway, indicating that April should go down.

She stood still for a long moment, evaluating me with that sharp gaze. "Okay then," she said. "Good speech, by the way. I liked the part about the unicorns and wombats." Then she stepped past me, toward the stairs, but spun around to face me after descending only two risers, and came back up.

I sighed. The woman's eyes sparkled as red spots appeared high on her cheeks, and—was that glitter glinting just below her left eye?

"I'll be totally honest. I have no clue who you are—I mean, if you're someone I should know, well, I don't, sorry. So you don't have to worry about me asking you for a selfie or anything like that. And I don't really need anything from you," April said, her words coming fast. "I just need your house."

Surprise flooded me and I couldn't help a bark of laughter that rolled out of me at her honesty and her pitch for my new home. "It's not for sale."

"No, no." April ran a hand through that mass of dark hair and it fell back around her neck and shoulders, glossy and thick. "Look, I'm sorry for barging in. I'm the producer of the show *Holiday Homes*. I was sent out here to solidify locations in Singletree to feature on the Christmas show, and your house is at the top of our list. Someone should have spoken to you already, and my executive producer says the contract was signed long ago, but maybe since you're just moving in ..."

Frustration made my head pound. A contract? A television show? She had to be kidding. "No thanks."

"Mr. Whitewood, you bought the oldest and most historic house in town—the place was a plantation manor in the seventeen hundreds, and it's a critical part of the area's history. There's only one other house here with the same merits, history, and charm, and the woman who owns it ran our producers off her land with a shotgun in one hand and a joint in the other when they made their initial site visits. Your house is it, and featuring it on the show is a way to honor that incredible legacy, and if everyone I've talked to in town so far is right, the show won't be complete without it. The real estate agent my predecessor worked with promised us she'd spoken to you about it and that you signed the show contract, agreeing to be featured."

I scanned my foggy memory. Jessica *had* said something about decorating, or holidays ... I hadn't paid much attention once I'd had the keys. Still, no one could barge in and force me to hang tinsel in my own house. I shook my head, "I didn't sign a contract that I recall, and I'm pretty sure I just told you no thanks." I moved around April, hoping that if I started walking down the stairs, she might follow, and it would put an end to this ridiculous conversation. I came here to get out of a spotlight, not to shine one directly inside my home.

April followed me down the stairs. "Look," she tried again, but I didn't stop limping toward the exit. "It's just that, I mean ... I'm kind of in a bad situation." Her voice softened, and I could hear that she wasn't trying to sell anything now. She sounded legitimately sad, and I hated the way my blood warmed in some misplaced protective instinct. I faced her, against my better judgment. "It's kind of my last chance, this show ... and well, if I can't feature your house, I'm pretty sure I'll lose my job." The bright eyes glistened as she stopped on the bottom stair, turning and looking back at me, her pretty lips pressed together.

I chuckled as I realized she was definitely still selling me —this was just another tactic. She was good, I thought. I almost believed her, not that it would have changed my mind. I was about to say something that would probably have been less than friendly when her face seemed to crumple, but then she quickly regained composure, pushing a hand through that incredible hair once more.

"I'm so sorry. That—that last part—that shouldn't make a difference. That's my problem, and clearly, I just need to do a better job explaining things, and—"

"No," I said, wondering now how much of her explanation was an act and how much was real. "Look, it has nothing to do with you. And I'm sure it's a great show and everything, okay? It's just that I'm really trying to keep my life private right now," I said. "To keep a low profile. You understand? I'll talk to a lawyer if I need to. I was kind of on autopilot when I signed all the paperwork, so whatever I signed—well, I'll just get it undone. I'm sorry for the confusion."

We stood on the bottom step of the grand sweeping stair-case, and the movers came in and out the big front door ahead of us, carrying furniture and boxes. The sounds of scraping and shifting floated through the air along with the damp fecund smell of moist leaves littering the ground outside. April stared at me for a long moment, her eyes piercing the shield I'd been working impossibly hard to maintain as I felt a little piece of my wall shatter and fall, and then she nodded quickly. "I get it. I do."

She stepped down the final step and looked back up at me, her bright eyes glowing again. "But you should know I don't give up easily."

"The gate out front isn't usually standing wide open, you know."

She peered out the front door at the iron gate standing open at the entrance of my driveway. "I think I can scale it. I'm pretty athletic." She winked at me and then strode to the open door, turning. "See you again soon!"

That simple statement should have irritated me—I hated it when people wouldn't take no for an answer—and it did bother me, a little bit. But it also struck me like a promise, and despite the many promises broken in my life lately, I couldn't help feeling a little flicker of hope that April might keep hers. Even if I had no intention of being on her show, I wouldn't mind seeing her again.

***

Want more of April and Callan and the town of Singletree?

Get more here!

1. SNEAK PEEK - SHAKING THE SLEIGH, CHAPTER 1: THE GRINCH'S LAST CHANCE

APRIL

"You should be grinning from ear to ear right now," my uncle told me, leaning across his mahogany desk and jabbing his finger into the brown paper blotter on its surface to make his point.

I was definitely not grinning. I'm pretty sure I was frowning. And I'd been doing a lot of that lately, probably, but I hadn't had a lot to smile about since my life had imploded three months before. I'd lost my job and my self respect in one dramatic moment totally worthy of the reality television show that had inspired it.

"You came to me desperate. With nothing. Begging, April. You begged." He raised his bushy gray eyebrows and sat back, letting that sink in.

Ouch. The truth hurt.

I shifted in the leather seat, my suit skirt threatening to burst at the seams, thanks to the stress eating I'd been doing since I'd ruined everything. But cookies still loved me. And cookies never looked at me like Uncle Rob was looking at me now. My uncle's office was intimidating, with its dark-paneled walls and Emmy awards and Golden Globes perched on the shelves around us. It hadn't been easy calling him. It had been downright humbling. He was the one who'd inspired me to get into television in the first place, and to come to him now was beyond embarrassing.

"I know, Uncle Rob. It's just ... I mean ... *Holiday Homes*?" I cringed even saying the name of the show I most despised.

Rob grinned. "Holidays. Homes. What's not to love?"

When I didn't jump up and clap my hands, his smile dropped. I tried, "There's really nothing else? Something un-Christmassy? Maybe *Fix it Up* or *Hating to Dating?* I'm good with people, Uncle Rob. Not houses."

"Look April, I'm gonna tell it like it is. You screwed up a good thing—with people—and there aren't a lot of ways to come back from that. You had a top gig producing *Run Away with the Bridegroom*, but maybe someone should've pointed out to you that you were not actually supposed to be the one doing the running away with the bridegroom."

My stomach twisted at the painful reminder of the most humiliating moment of my life. "We didn't run away ..." I began, realizing too late that bringing up the details of the scandal that had ended my high-profile position at my last show probably wouldn't help.

"No, but you probably should have. Far, far away. To get caught on camera making out with that sleazy jerk ..." My uncle's words were coming faster, and his eyes scathed the surface of my face before searching the room, probably seeking a less disappointing subject to observe. "Ape, you made a mistake. A big one. And you got caught. Though that little twist did give the ratings a pretty solid boost ..." He sighed and his eyes returned to mine.

"I'm really sorry, Uncle Rob."

"I know you are, darling, and that's why I'm willing to pull these strings and get you another chance. You're sorry, and you're a damned good producer when you're focused on your job and not on the assets of the cast." He leaned back in his chair and watched me, steepling his fingers in front of his mouth. His voice softened. "Did you love the guy?"

I swallowed hard and dropped his gaze. It would almost have been better if I *had* loved Antonio, the bachelor from my last show. But I didn't love him any more than he loved me, or any of the fifteen women he was supposed to be courting on television. I was a conquest, and if I was honest, he was a conquest for me, too. "No," I said firmly. "I don't think I do love."

"Well, that's the right attitude if you're sticking to television. A hell of a lot cleaner that way."

I'd tried love in college, but I just wasn't very good at it. I got bored, distracted. I knew I got that from my father, another trait I wished I could cut from my personality somehow, but had long since accepted. "Right," I said, hoping my agreement could put an end to the rehashing of all the ways I'd screwed up my last job.

Rob placed a contract in front of me. "So, four specials annually—takes a little of the pressure off, not having the weekly churn, right? Next one is the biggest one by far, the Christmas home tour."

I tried to keep my face neutral as I imagined the sheer quantity of holiday cheer I'd have to withstand to make this work. "But I just handle initial setup and pick targets, right? Take care of contracts ... you've got the location producer for the actual show?"

"Kind of. No picking homes. For this first one, Juliann will handle the details of actual production. She's done the Christmas show for years. You just get the homeowners finalized—like I said, most have been on board for months. Just get them to sign on final details and behave, and then throw the reins to Jules."

I relaxed a little bit. I could do this. I wouldn't have to decorate, or set up any fake snowmen. Maybe I wouldn't even have to enter any artificial-snow-encrusted, pine-tree smelling, twinkling houses. That part was Juliann's gig. I would just be getting things ready for Juliann, who could waltz in wearing striped tights and a felt elf costume, for all I cared. I, myself, would be far away by Christmas, enjoying a tropical drink on a hot beach somewhere, pretending it was any other day.

Uncle Rob's phone rang on his desk and he raised a finger to me as he picked it up—the universal symbol for 'you're not as important as this potential telemarketer.' "Rob here."

Uncle Rob's eyes found mine as he listened, and his eyebrows shot up comically as I watched. "Oh," he said, little lines appearing around his mouth. "Two casts, huh?" He paused, his lips pressing into a firm line. "Traction?" He rubbed a hand over his forehead. "Well I'm glad you're okay, Jules."

My attention riveted to the phone in his hand. Jules? Was that Juliann? What was that about casts and traction? My stomach tightened and I sat up straighter.

"Well you don't need to worry about anything here. You just focus on healing," Uncle Rob said. "The network will send along a fruit basket."

"A fruit basket?" I yelped, and then slapped a hand over my mouth as Uncle Rob's eyes narrowed at me.

"Bye now." Uncle Rob chuckled as he put down the phone. He looked up at me. "All that stuff I just said? Scratch it. You're it. Juliann's out."

"What?" I heard myself ask, my voice higher than usual.

"Broke both legs skiing at Whistler, poor thing. She's gonna be out for months."

"Oh no," I said, picturing how difficult two broken legs would make the wearing of an elf costume. Then something else occurred to me. "Wait, you said, 'I'm it'? For the Christmas show?"

"The whole shebang. Trial by fire. Go get Jingle-y, April. They need you on location this week. Little town in Maryland, evidently they really go all out for Christmas. Need everything wrapped up by the middle of the month to get the footage all set for the hosts to do their review show on the 23rd."

The turnaround was crazy. I knew the Christmas show operated on the tightest timeframe of the *Homes* episodes, since I'd heard Uncle Rob talk about it before. From what he said, the home footage was edited almost daily as they gathered it. The hosts stayed in Los Angeles and filmed their segments, reviewing the décor just before airing on Christmas Eve.

"You can do this, right April? It's not gonna be too much for you?" My uncle had begun to look skeptical. The last thing I needed was for him to second guess my last chance. I needed this to be a home run if I wanted to stay in television and not end up back in my college job at Tacos Loco, where the manager said I had been the best taco assembler he'd ever had. I hoped my tombstone might bear something more illustrious than "Master of beef and cheese in a crunchy shell."

"I can do it," I said, stress pulling my shoulders tight as visions of reindeer and candy canes drifted through my head. and I wondered if I really could.

"SINGLETREE," I repeated for the third time to my best friend, raising my voice and shouting into the rental car's overhead microphone.

"What kind of name is that for a town?"

"I don't know, Lynn, but the name of the place was not really the point of this story." I let out a slow breath as I guided the car down a curving two-lane road lined with huge trees dropping leaves that ranged in color from dark green to blazing gold. It was like every postcard I'd ever seen of what fall was supposed to look like. A far cry from the screaming freeways and swaying palm trees in Los Angeles. "I think the bigger picture here is that I'm in Maryland. To produce the

Christmas show." I hissed the word Christmas as if it burned my tongue.

"I know how you feel about the holidays, April. But maybe this will help you get past all that." Lynn was an eternal optimist. We'd been friends since kindergarten, and Lynn had always been the bright shiny yin to my skeptical darker yang. "Maybe a season in Littletree is exactly what you need."

"Singletree."

"You said the name of the town wasn't the main point, remember? The point is that your hatred for all things red and green needs to die. You're missing out."

I sighed again as I maneuvered through yet another traffic circle that felt like it had me literally driving spirals into the heart of nowhere. I looked down at the phone to check the directions, but the screen had switched to my call, and I had no idea if I was going the right way. "Damn," I said. "Lynn, I need to go, I think I chose the wrong exit from the last circle of death."

"Circle of death?"

"They have all these crazy traffic circles here. I have no idea how I'm supposed to do those ... just give me an eight-lane freeway any day!"

"Adventure, Apes. Remember, it's an adventure."

"I miss Los Angeles. And it's not an adventure, it's a Christmas show."

"There's a reason why most people like Christmas."

"Right. Well."

"Love you," Lynn's sweet voice said. "Go now so you don't get lost and end up in Doubletree instead of Singletree."

"Love you too." I ended the call and swiped my phone's screen back to my directions. Miraculously, I was still going the right way. Nothing outside the little car's windows looked anything like Los Angeles. The roads were narrow and winding, the vegetation was thick and green, and dense gray moisture hung in low clouds that hugged the sprawling fields around me. I wondered for a moment if I'd driven into some picturesque no-man's land, where there were no towns, no people ... only this never-ending farmland draped in fog. I shivered. Fifteen twisting green miles later, I saw signs for Singletree and breathed a sigh of relief.

Singletree wasn't big, and despite my trepidation, it was hard not to be just a teensy bit charmed as I made my way to the center of town. I drove slowly down the main street feeling like I'd been transported to another world—one that existed in some earlier, simpler time. There was a town square surrounded by quaint shops with storefronts lovingly maintained and painted in yellow, white, and light blue, and buildings of brick and stone that looked like they'd stood for hundreds of years. They probably had. The central area was a grassy square that stretched several blocks between the buildings, featuring manicured lawns and neatly trimmed bushes, low-hanging trees and a central gazebo. There was one huge tree in the middle of the square, and I shook my head as I drove by the impressive group of people gathered beneath it with ladders and strings of holiday lights ready to drape the tree, which I guessed was pretty normal even though it was technically still November. They'd probably barely had time to put away the gravy boats after their Thanksgiving feasts, and they were already here, tossing around shiny bulbs. I sighed in dismay.

I drove slowly down the long street that stretched behind the central square, turning in when I saw the sign for the Candlelight Inn, the hotel where Juliann had booked the crew. Despite Juliann's absence from the day-to-day production of the episode of *Holiday Homes* she was supposed to handle, she'd done most of the legwork and had passed her extensive notes and plans on to me. From here it should be simple—check in to this hotel (which looked like it could have been constructed of gingerbread and spun sugar, thanks to some seriously overeager Victorian styling), and begin visiting the homes Jules had identified to finalize contracts. Jules had assured me there would be no issues because *Holiday Homes* was a well-known franchise at this point, and homeowners practically bent over backwards to have their homes featured. It increased their resale value, and if they were looking to sell after the episode aired, it usually resulted in multiple offers and sometimes in a bidding war. And if they weren't looking to sell, I knew that having their homes identified as "special" gave folks something to feel good about, and something to lord over their neighbors if their personalities leaned that way. As for the decorating, the homes that were selected generally went over and above for the holidays.

"You're just there to keep things running smoothly, that's all," Jules had assured me from her hospital room when we'd spoken on the phone.

I parked and took a deep breath, and stepped out of the car.

"Hello there," a young man in a dark red uniform greeted me as I approached the front entrance of the hotel with my roller bag. "Welcome to the Candlelight Inn."

"Thank you," I said, distracted momentarily by the intricate scrolling woodwork that seemed to garnish every free surface of the building. The Inn looked a lot like a castle, except that it was a soft yellow color. The turrets and wide-open front porch were like nothing I had ever seen up close.

The attendant took my bag from me and escorted me up the stairs to the front door, pulling it open with a flourish and a smile.

I thanked him and gaped at the army of workers busily wrapping railings in evergreen boughs and erecting an enormous tree in the middle of the front lobby. The interior was probably normally dim compared to the daylight outside, but this had been solved by the hundreds of strands of holiday lights a woman was holding at the far side of the space. Two other workers were arguing loudly about how best to erect the small cottage they were working on—a cottage that was made to look like gingerbread but could hold life-sized actual humans. My stomach turned as the sheer Christmasness of it all engulfed me. I stepped around the ladders and tools, tinsel, and a standing army of nutcrackers, and approached the desk.

"Welcome!" The woman at the desk called. "Forgive our mess, won't you? We're a little behind in getting our holiday decorations up this year, and I don't know if you heard, but

Holiday Homes is being filmed in Singletree," the woman paused, leaning over the front desk and looking around conspiratorially, "and we want to impress those folks."

"Okay, well," I said. "I'm just checking in." I slid my ID and credit card over the smooth polished wood and managed a smile for the rosy-cheeked woman. "April Hall." The woman who accepted my cards with a wide cheerful smile was wearing a sweater that was woven to make her look like a Christmas present. It had actual ribbon stitched against a ridiculously busy pattern of snowmen and skiers. The bow sat on her shoulder and the ends of it kept popping into her face, where she had to repeatedly push them away. I wondered how many times a day she had to push that ribbon out of her face.

The woman punched a few keys on the computer behind the desk, and made a few noises of concern. She raised a finger to me and then ducked beneath the desk, shuffling around in a drawer. "Just a second, so sorry," she squeaked, popping up again and punching a few more keys as she batted the shiny green ribbon from her mouth. "Would your reservation be under a different name, maybe?"

The cross-country flight and confusing drive began to weigh on me, and I leaned an elbow on the desk. "Oh, right. Yes, look up Juliann Stevens. I took her spot."

"Aha, here she is! Oh, but ..." the woman's eyes widened and she glanced quickly from the screen to me and back down again. "Ms. Stevens was part of the show," she said, her voice breathy. "Does that mean you're ...?"

I cringed. I would have liked to maintain my anonymity,

at least at the hotel where I would be coming to escape all the Christmas craziness every night, but I didn't see how that would be possible, given that the whole crew was also staying here. "Yes, I'm the producer of *Holiday Homes*," I confirmed, my voice ragged with exhaustion.

"Ah!" The woman chirped. "Wonderful! I'll be right back!" She disappeared into a room behind the check-in area and I slumped farther over the counter, wishing for nothing more than a quiet room and maybe a warm bath. "Here it is!"

I couldn't see the woman's face because she returned carrying an enormous basket wrapped in cellophane. It was hard to tell what was inside, but I could see a variety of items decorated with crabs and the Maryland state flag, and plenty of Christmas mugs and candy canes and glittery ornaments. The entire thing was tied with a huge ribbon that shone in metallic and glittery red and green and seemed to be vomiting silver glitter. "A little something from the Inn," the woman said, hoisting the basket to the counter and into my face. Tiny showers of sparkly glitter cascaded to the counter.

"Oh," I said, leaning to the side to see around the massive basket. "That's so ... well, wow. That's lovely. Thank you."

"We're tickled to have you," the woman told her, her face pink with excitement under the close-cropped gray curls, which were now dusted with red and green sparkles. "I'm Annabelle Adams. I own the inn, and don't you hesitate to come to me for just anything at all, okay?"

"Thanks so much." I considered asking for a dust buster and lint roller to combat the glitter I was now certain would be attached to me for the remainder of my stay in Singletree.

"Now, let's see. Miss Hall. I've got you in our Dickens Suite. That's on the top floor."

"That sounds lovely," I said, accepting my card and ID back and tucking them into my pocket.

"It's our most festive room during the holidays," Annabelle said with a nod.

My spirits sank further. Evidently producing the Christmas episode meant everyone I met would automatically assume I was just as Christmas-crazy as the people who decked out every inch of their houses on the show. "Great," I said with no inflection at all.

"Here's your key, and you call me if you need anything. We've got a cocktail hour every night here in the lobby at five, and there are usually guests in the library after that playing board games and sitting by the fire."

"Great," I said again, nearly desperate now to just sit down somewhere quiet. The bustle of the workers around the lobby was almost comical. People were dashing to and fro, carrying bells and faux candles. Just as I turned from the desk, a looming presence appeared behind me and I stifled a scream as a life-sized St. Nicholas doll stopped inches from my face and then moved in a jolting progression farther across the lobby.

"Isn't he amazing?" Annabelle asked.

"Erm. Yes," I said, watching the enormous old- fashioned Santa make his way to a far corner, carried by a worker about half the statue's size.

A few minutes later, I was unlocking the door to the Dickens Suite and stepping inside. The young man from the front door was behind me with my suitcase and the oversized Christmas basket in his arms. A festive trail of green and red glitter spilled down the hallway and through my door as he moved past me to put things down, thanks to the exuberant bow on the basket.

The suite was lovely, if you could overlook the wreaths and glittering globes and the huge tree standing in one corner wafting pine scent throughout the space. The tree was festooned with ribbons and balls, gleaming in the light, and I knew that anyone else stepping into this charming room would feel their spirits lift and would probably experience some kind of warm nostalgia relating to the holiday season. But the sight of the tree and the stockings hanging from the mantle caused a hard knot to form in my gut and settle there as my own memories soured any enthusiasm I might have scraped together for my new job.

"I'll just put this down here," he said, setting the basket on a table. He left the suitcase by the door, accepted the tip I extended and wished me goodnight, and finally, I was alone. I looked around, a dark feeling of something like sorrow filling me as the tree twinkled merrily in its corner.

"Nope," I said, realizing I'd never be able to function in a room decorated to within an inch of its life. I moved quickly through the suite of rooms, removing every holiday item I could easily detach from where it had been stuck, hung or placed, and deposited as much of it as I could in the dry-cleaning bag hanging in the closet. I couldn't think with all the sparkle and cheer around me. The stockings came down, the reindeer was removed, and the festive hand towels in the bathroom were switched out for the plain white ones I found in the top of the closet. I wrestled the glittery bow from the basket, hoping to banish it to the trash can so it couldn't infect one more item with clingy glitter, but I mostly managed to explode the stuff all over the room and myself in the effort.

When I was finished undecorating, only the tree glittered mockingly from its corner, and I almost believed I could feel my mind clearing, despite the glitter I'd probably never get washed from my hands.

2. SNEAK PEEK - SHAKING THE SLEIGH, CHAPTER 2: TAKE YOUR CODE AND SHOVE IT

CALLAN

I pulled my car up to the big iron gates at the address I'd been given over the phone, taking a moment to marvel at the sheer size of the house beyond the gate. It was big, and it was isolated, that was for sure—I'd driven down a long lane with fields on each side, and turned onto that from a quiet country road. I couldn't see another house from where I sat. No people. No cars. No neighbors.

Good. This was exactly what I told the real estate agent I wanted. And now it was mine.

As I sat staring at the tall iron gates of my new home, another car pulled down the long lane and stopped behind my own. A tall woman with dark hair slicked into a knot, wearing a huge scarf and big sunglasses got out and approached my window. "Callan Whitewood?" She leaned down, grinning, one hand holding the scarf down to keep it beneath her chin.

"That's me," I said, trying to sound cheerful or friendly or at least not psychopathic while I tried to figure out the purpose of wearing a scarf so big it tried repeatedly to take over your head.

"Jessica Betts," she said, sticking a hand through the window and narrowly missing my face with her long nails.

I shook her hand, forcing a smile. "Nice to meet you," I said. "Thanks for your help with all this." She had been helpful, I reminded myself. So I could be friendly for five minutes even though I was pretty sure the blackness inside me contained less friendliness than that.

"Well, we don't usually sell houses sight-unseen over the phone, but I guess we can always make an exception for soccer stars."

"Or people willing to pay cash," I guessed. I'd signed everything in my agent's office back in San Diego, essentially sleepwalking through the process and dropping my signature wherever I'd been directed. I just wanted to move on, get started with this next phase of my life—the phase that didn't include being featured as the media's favorite pity-inducing ex-soccer star.

She smiled wider. "Right. There was that. The seller was thrilled."

"I'm sure." I'd pulled the trigger based on location, isolation, and the fact that Singletree, Maryland didn't seem like the kind of town that followed pro soccer. Driving down from DC after arriving from San Diego, I'd figured it was more of a crab or oyster fishing kind of town, maybe a hunting town, a good American football or NASCAR town. Based on my questions to various real estate agents I'd spoken with and the input of my brother, it was not a soccer town. And hopefully that meant anonymity.

"It's funny," Jessica said, looking at me with a little tilt of the head. "We just had another celebrity buy a place here recently. Maybe southern Maryland is going to be the next hot celebrity escape."

I really hoped not. I had heard that Juliet Manchester grew up somewhere near here, and that Ryan McDonnell had recently bought a home nearby. But I definitely didn't make my decision based on them. More on my brother and my own desire to be isolated and far away from San Diego and the career I had loved. The one I'd been great at. The one I couldn't have anymore. I doubted they even aired the South Bay Sharks games out here in the middle of nowhere.

"I bet you'd like to go in, lay eyes on the place for real." Jessica's excitement wasn't contagious, but she was right. I wanted to go in.

"Sure."

"Well step out here and I'll show you how to put in the gate code. Normally you'll just drive right up, but since we're both here ..." She stepped back from the car and I swung the door open and then used my hands to help get my left leg out and onto solid ground. My left ankle didn't do much of what I wanted anymore, which was part of the reason I was here in Singletree.

I stood up, ignoring the pain ricocheting through my left leg and limped to where Jessica stood. She was clearly trying not to look surprised by my unsteady gait.

"Just type in the code here," she said, her fingers going through four numbers. "And the gate swings open."

I nodded. "I'll probably just get some kind of swipe access installed."

"Right," she agreed. "But for now, you've got the code. Five, six, seventy-two."

"Right. Five, seven—"

"No, hon. Five, six, seven, two."

"Got it." I did. not. care.

"Do you?"

"Five, six, seven ..." I trailed off. Failing. I was winning at failing lately.

"Want me to write it down?"

"Sure." I limped back to my car.

"Okey dokey," Jessica trilled, heading back to her own car to follow me into the circular drive in front of the huge house.

We parked near a fountain that stood quiet and dry like a sentinel, and I gazed up at my new home. It was stately—I guessed that was the right word. It looked like something one of the founding fathers would have lived in—white and colonial, with columns and a sprawling front porch. The place had wings, more rooms than I could ever possibly use filling the enormous space inside the place. But in my mind, all that mattered was that it was isolated, it was far away from San Diego, and it was mine. Jessica unlocked the massive front door, and we stepped into the huge old house.

"This was originally a plantation house, as I mentioned on the phone," Jessica said, gazing around with clear approval. "And it's been restored and updated, but so many of these wonderful architectural details are original. Once you get it all done up for the holidays, it's going to look just amazing."

"Great." I was ready for her to hand me the keys and get lost. I didn't have much with me to move in, but I did have a bottle of scotch, a camping chair and a sleeping bag, and between those three items I figured my next forty-eight hours were pretty much accounted for. As far as decorating for the holidays, I had no plans for that, so I ignored this last comment.

"I'll just give you the quick tour," she said, heading for a doorway off the entrance hall.

"Ah, actually," I said quickly, my tone halting Jessica's step and causing her to turn, one hand on the giant sunglasses she wore atop her head and another on the ridiculous scarf. "I'm pretty beat from the drive. I think I can manage."

"Oh, of course." Her face fell for a second but she shook her head with a laugh and recovered quickly. "Well then, here you are, Mr. Whitewood." She handed me a large silver key. "And may I be the first to welcome you officially to Singletree."

I repressed a strong urge to roll my eyes. To her, maybe becoming a resident of Singletree was something to be cele-brated, but for me it was just the final nail in the coffin of the life I'd had. The one I'd very much enjoyed having. Before. "Thanks, I really appreciate all your help."

"If you need anything," she said, turning and heading back to the front door.

"Yep. Got it."

"I'll check in on you in a couple days." She patted my arm and stepped onto the porch. "And if you need any help decorating—"

"Won't be necessary," I said, interrupting her. She was really hung up on this holiday thing.

"Well, you know there is the thing I told you about, the contract—"

"I've got it," I assured her, ignoring every word and practically pushing her out the door.

"All right then, talk to you soon!" She skipped down the steps to her car, and a few minutes later, I stood alone on the porch of my new home.

After unloading my few things from the car, I turned slowly and went back inside. The empty space of the old house seeming to echo and expand around me, making me feel small and insignificant as I stood in the cool silence. I took a deep breath, and for the first time in a long time, I exhaled and felt myself relax.

I SPENT two nights in the new house, sleeping on the floor in the living room in my sleeping bag, a whiskey-fueled hangover dogging me through the days, and dark dreams full of doubts chasing me through the nights. I didn't even go upstairs. For one thing, my ankle hurt too damned much to climb the stairs just for the heck of it, and for another, I figured that when you've seen one house, you've seen them all. Just because this one belonged to me now didn't make it special.

The movers showed up on the third day, their huge long truck lumbering down the lane in front of the house, making the road look even narrower than it actually was. I pressed the button next to the door to let them through the gate, greeted them at the front door, and then limped into the far bathroom to take a much-needed shower. My plan was to hang out on the back porch until they were done, staying out of the way and avoiding conversation—and potential recognition—as much as possible. I'd called my brother that morning to let him know I'd arrived, though I should have done it the moment I'd taken ownership. I shouldn't have put it off, but even dealing with Cormac seemed like more than I could handle.

I had just positioned myself back in the folding camp chair, my gaze aimed out at the sweep of the Potomac that wound around the bottom edge of my property several acres below, when I heard a female voice drifting through the open window. I swiveled and squinted inside, but didn't see any female movers hustling furniture about. Just when I decided I'd been mistaken, I heard it again, a soft melodious voice that definitely couldn't belong to one of the movers I'd just let in.

Wandering the house, dodging moving couches and rolled-up rugs, wasn't what I felt like doing, especially with my ankle protesting every move I made, but my curiosity got the best of me. Was I hearing things now? Maybe I'd been alone a little too long in this strange old house. I went in and prowled the down-stairs rooms and then climbed the stairs slowly, cursing the shooting pain that accompanied each step I took with my left foot. The staircase was grand and wide, the oak-planked risers creaking under my weight as I gripped the curving bannister. I imagined myself tripping and falling down the expansive steps, and I could picture the media coverage of that one. *Former Soccer Star Callan Whitewood Suffers Another Debilitating Injury!* Because I hadn't been hounded enough after the first one.

After exploring the upstairs rooms—all gleaming and bright, mostly empty of furniture—I was beginning to doubt myself, and to believe I was most likely losing my mind. I glanced out the second-story window at the moving truck in the drive, and spotted a small silver Honda next to my car. Someone was definitely here, but this stupid house was so big I couldn't find her.

I was just about to head back down the stairs when a woman appeared in the hallway where she definitely had not been before. She had inky dark hair that flowed over her shoulders, and bright blue eyes that glittered in the half-light of the upstairs hallway. She was pretty, I realized, but that didn't begin to explain what she was doing wandering around my house with a clipboard and appearing in empty hallways. "Hello," she said. "You must be Mr. Whitewood. I'm April Hall."

"Uh, hi," I said, hating the way the confusion made me sound uncertain. This was my house, dammit. Who was this woman? "Where exactly did you come from?"

The woman gave me a puzzled look, her nose wrinkling

in a way that I was sure most found adorable, but that I perceived as her simply not answering my question. "Just now?" she asked.

"Yes. Just now."

"Because I came to Singletree from California, but I didn't think that was what you meant." She laughed lightly and then spun around. "There's a secret hallway back here." She pulled open a panel that had been standing slightly ajar. "It was probably a servants' passage. A lot of these old houses have these little nooks and crannies. Part of the charm. If that's your thing." She shrugged and looked at me expectantly, maybe waiting for me to chime in about whether or not old houses and secret passages were 'my thing.'

Annoyance flooded me as my ankle throbbed. I didn't like a stranger knowing more about my house than I did, and I didn't like being surprised in my own home. I was also oddly annoyed at the tiny flicker of interest I had felt leap to life in my chest when I'd gotten a good look at this intruder. It was hard to hold onto my annoyance when part of me—the old part of me that was good at flirting with attractive women— was prodding me to keep her talking. I shoved that part down and remembered that I was done with women, done with being good-natured and friendly, done with people in general.

"Can I ask what you're doing in my house, Miss Hall?"

"Oh, of course." She had the grace to blush, certainly realizing that she was essentially trespassing. "I'm with *Holiday Homes*, and you're on my list, and well, the gate and the door were open, and there was so much hub-bub down there with all the men moving things around ..." she babbled, looking nervous.

"And so you're here because," I began for her, gripping the banister at the top of the stairs as my ankle throbbed.

"I was looking for you, actually." The bright eyes found my own and then dropped to my hands, taking in the white-knuckled grip on the bannister and darkening briefly before meeting my gaze again. "Is there somewhere we could sit?"

For a split second, I wondered if she knew. That look—it had held a touch of pity, and while I'd come to Singletree to get away from lots of things, pity was first on that list. I straightened, forced myself to put weight on both feet evenly and released my grip on the bannister. "No, actually. There's nowhere we can sit. Maybe you noticed I don't have any furniture just yet?"

"I did," April said, "and I'm so sorry to just barge in. I just wanted—"

"I'm going to stop you right there," I said, feeling my anger dissipate into exhaustion. "Maybe you know who I am, maybe you don't. I don't really care. I moved here because I only know one person in town. There's no one here who needs me for anything, no one who expects anything from me. There's no one here who I have to worry about disappointing because they'd hoped for anything at all." The words sounded bitter coming out and I almost regretted them as I watched April's pretty face tighten, her chin lift slightly. "I don't need whatever you're selling. I'm not in the market for candles, makeup, or Boy Scout popcorn, I don't want to save the turtles or the unicorn habitat, and I'm not looking to sponsor a puppy, a wombat, or a child." I waved an arm at the stairway, indicating that April should go down.

She stood still for a long moment, evaluating me with that sharp gaze. "Okay then," she said. "Good speech, by the way. I liked the part about the unicorns and wombats." Then she stepped past me, toward the stairs, but spun around to face me after descending only two risers, and came back up.

I sighed. The woman's eyes sparkled as red spots appeared high on her cheeks, and—was that glitter glinting just below her left eye?

"I'll be totally honest. I have no clue who you are—I mean, if you're someone I should know, well, I don't, sorry. So you don't have to worry about me asking you for a selfie or anything like that. And I don't really need anything from you," April said, her words coming fast. "I just need your house."

Surprise flooded me and I couldn't help a bark of laughter that rolled out of me at her honesty and her pitch for my new home. "It's not for sale."

"No, no." April ran a hand through that mass of dark hair and it fell back around her neck and shoulders, glossy and thick. "Look, I'm sorry for barging in. I'm the producer of the show *Holiday Homes*. I was sent out here to solidify locations in Singletree to feature on the Christmas show, and your house is at the top of our list. Someone should have spoken to you already, and my executive producer says the contract was signed long ago, but maybe since you're just moving in ..."

Frustration made my head pound. A contract? A television show? She had to be kidding. "No thanks."

"Mr. Whitewood, you bought the oldest and most historic house in town—the place was a plantation manor in the seventeen hundreds, and it's a critical part of the area's history. There's only one other house here with the same merits, history, and charm, and the woman who owns it ran our producers off her land with a shotgun in one hand and a joint in the other when they made their initial site visits. Your house is it, and featuring it on the show is a way to honor that incredible legacy, and if everyone I've talked to in town so far is right, the show won't be complete without it. The real estate agent my predecessor worked with promised us she'd spoken to you about it and that you signed the show contract, agreeing to be featured."

I scanned my foggy memory. Jessica *had* said something about decorating, or holidays ... I hadn't paid much attention once I'd had the keys. Still, no one could barge in and force me to hang tinsel in my own house. I shook my head, "I didn't sign a contract that I recall, and I'm pretty sure I just told you no thanks." I moved around April, hoping that if I started walking down the stairs, she might follow, and it would put an end to this ridiculous conversation. I came here to get out of a spotlight, not to shine one directly inside my home.

April followed me down the stairs. "Look," she tried again, but I didn't stop limping toward the exit. "It's just that, I mean ... I'm kind of in a bad situation." Her voice softened, and I could hear that she wasn't trying to sell anything now. She sounded legitimately sad, and I hated the way my blood warmed in some misplaced protective instinct. I faced her, against my better judgment. "It's kind of my last chance, this show ... and well, if I can't feature your house, I'm pretty sure I'll lose my job." The bright eyes glistened as she stopped on the bottom stair, turning and looking back at me, her pretty lips pressed together.

I chuckled as I realized she was definitely still selling me—this was just another tactic. She was good, I thought. I almost believed her, not that it would have changed my mind. I was about to say something that would probably have been less than friendly when her face seemed to crumple, but then she quickly regained composure, pushing a hand through that incredible hair once more.

"I'm so sorry. That—that last part—that shouldn't make a difference. That's my problem, and clearly, I just need to do a better job explaining things, and—"

"No," I said, wondering now how much of her explanation was an act and how much was real. "Look, it has nothing to do with you. And I'm sure it's a great show and everything, okay? It's just that I'm really trying to keep my life private right now," I said. "To keep a low profile. You understand? I'll talk to a lawyer if I need to. I was kind of on autopilot when I signed all the paperwork, so whatever I signed—well, I'll just get it undone. I'm sorry for the confusion."

We stood on the bottom step of the grand sweeping staircase, and the movers came in and out the big front door ahead of us, carrying furniture and boxes. The sounds of scraping and shifting floated through the air along with the damp fecund smell of moist leaves littering the ground outside. April stared at me for a long moment, her eyes piercing the shield I'd been working impossibly hard to maintain as I felt a little piece of my wall shatter and fall, and then she nodded quickly. "I get it. I do."

She stepped down the final step and looked back up at me, her bright eyes glowing again. "But you should know I don't give up easily."

"The gate out front isn't usually standing wide open, you know."

She peered out the front door at the iron gate standing open at the entrance of my driveway. "I think I can scale it. I'm pretty athletic." She winked at me and then strode to the open door, turning. "See you again soon!"

That simple statement should have irritated me—I hated it when people wouldn't take no for an answer—and it did bother me, a little bit. But it also struck me like a promise, and despite the many promises broken in my life lately, I couldn't help feeling a little flicker of hope that April might keep hers. Even if I had no intention of being on her show, I wouldn't mind seeing her again.

3. SNEAK PEEK - SHAKING THE SLEIGH, CHAPTER 3: THERE IS SUCH A THING AS TOO MUCH CHEER

APRIL

I returned to the Inn that Christmas ate, only slightly demoralized by my less-than-successful attempt to confirm the most important home on the list. At least I'd had no issues with the other two homeowners I'd visited. They'd been friendly and almost too excited about the whole thing. I was shuffling papers into my bag as I entered the inn, wishing I'd paid more attention to my mother's organizing tips, when Annabelle at the front desk called out for me.

"Oh, Miss Hall!"

The front desk was an explosion of cheer now that the lobby décor was finished, and Annabelle wore an elf hat and a little white collar with peppermints fastened to the points that draped around her shoulders and chest. I approached, unable to stop my mouth from dropping open as I got a good look at my hostess. Annabelle's ears were usually hidden by the soft short gray curls that framed her face, but today they were visible. And they were pointed, like an elf's. Only upon closer inspection could I see the lines around the prosthetic additions to the woman's natural ears.

"Aren't they marvelous?" Annabelle raised a hand to touch the pointy tip of one ear.

I smiled to keep myself from laughing at the ridiculousness of it all. "They are something," I agreed.

"I have something special for you," Annabelle said, reaching beneath the counter and producing a huge gingerbread house on a foil-covered tray, dotted with gumdrops and candy canes and absolutely screaming of Christmas cheer.

"That's ... for me?" I stared at the thing, which was easily as large as my overnight bag.

"The third graders had a field trip to the corner cafe today and they all worked together to make this in honor of the show coming to Singletree." Annabelle said, her smile wide and open. "Everyone's just so excited about it."

"Not everyone," I said, before I could stop myself.

Annabelle's smile faded and she shook her head a touch, as if trying to imagine who in the world wouldn't be excited about my insane holiday spectacle of a show. Her eyebrows pulled together.

"Is something wrong, dear?" Annabelle set the house on the reception counter.

I hadn't actually meant to confide in Annabelle, and a little spike of fear edged through me, accelerating my heartbeat. I needed to walk a fine line producing this show. I couldn't break any rules, couldn't even slip a toe into the rule-breaking pool. I needed to pretend that pool wasn't even there, not even spare a glance at any rule-breaking skinny dippers who might be cavorting over there, trying to coax me toward the swim-up bar. So I wondered, was confiding in an innkeeper about a difficult host breaking a rule? "It's not a big deal. Just ran into a little reluctance today over at Singletree Manor."

Annabelle drew in a sharp breath. "Oh. Him." Her expression soured.

"Do you know Mr. Whitewood?" I suddenly realized I might be able to enlist some help if I could find someone in town who Callan Whitewood might listen to.

"No," the older woman shook her head. "I just can't believe this town let someone like that buy our grandest home. That place holds half the history of Singletree. The town was practically born there. The man who built Singletree Manor—Mr. Joseph Calvin—planted the tree in the town square that gave our town its name."

I called up a quick mental image of the town square I'd driven past yesterday, and remembered the large tree around which the rest of the square seemed to be arranged. Then my mind fastened to the other thing Annabelle had just said. "What do you mean, 'someone like that'?"

Annabelle leaned over the counter, her voice dropping to a whisper. "A playboy. A sports star." She scowled, looking like someone had just eaten one of the cookies she'd set out for Santa.

I felt my eyebrows climb. Callan Whitewood was a sports star? He'd practically tripped going down the stairs, and though I'd never point it out, the man had a very pronounced limp and a terrible attitude. What sport could he have played? Maybe he played horseshoes or some other sport most people didn't follow. Like shuffleboard. Or sheep rolling. I'd heard that was a thing in the tiny island country of Durnland. "Is that right?"

"Word is he's retired now, but he made plenty of noise and trouble when he was a big important soccer star."

Soccer. I thought back to the solid presence of the man I'd met—he wasn't especially tall, but he did look strong. I had tried to focus on the work of convincing him to let me use his house for the show, but that hadn't stopped me from noticing the soft dark hair tousled on his head or the soulful chocolate brown eyes. Now that I thought about it, I felt like maybe I had seen him before. My mind ticked and whirred, and suddenly I could picture a billboard standing over the 405 Freeway, one I passed most days on my way to work. When I brought it up in my mind, I realized it was Callan Whitewood's moody gaze and bare muscled chest under which I had driven every single day. It had been a year or two ago, and another player had replaced him there recently, but I remembered those eyes. "Huh," I said, understanding clicking into place as I recalled him saying something about knowing who he was. "Kind of full of himself, maybe."

"Most likely," Annabelle agreed with the sentiment I hadn't meant to speak out loud. "Those types always are. His brother is nice enough, though."

"You know his brother?" I found it hard to fathom there

could be another man from the same gene pool that had produced someone as handsome as Callan Whitewood.

"He lives here too. He's a quiet type though, family man. He's the reason that playboy came to town, though, so my opinion of Mr. Cormac Whitewood has dropped a bit."

I nodded. Maybe I'd just been given a new way to approach this problem. "Thanks, Annabelle." I turned and headed for the stairs, purposely forgetting the gingerbread monstrosity.

"Don't worry about the gingerbread house," Annabelle called after her. "Andrew can bring it up to your room for you,"

"Great," I called over my shoulder, hoping Annabelle didn't hear the flat note of sarcasm in my voice. I climbed the stairs and entered my room, preparing for a quick round of Google stalking on the Whitewood brothers.

I WAS JUST SETTLING in with my laptop on the table before me and a hot cup of hotel-room coffee in my hand when my phone rang. I checked the screen and my stomach dropped upon seeing Uncle Rob's name on the screen. I set down my coffee, took a deep breath, and pressed the speakerphone button. "Uncle Rob!"

"Hey April, just checking in. How's Appletree?"

"It's Singletree, actually, and things are going well." My voice held a bright note that sounded false and foreign to my own ears. I hoped Uncle Rob wouldn't notice.

"Right. Singletree." I heard the clack of a keyboard and realized Rob was distracted. Which was normal. "So you've got all the homes on board? The production team arrives in a couple more days to get started staging and filming."

"I'm working my way down Juliann's list," I said, planning to check in with the last two homeowners in the next day or two and make sure they were on board.

"And we're all set with the feature spot? That big plantation Jules was so excited about?"

I leaned back in my chair, pulling my long hair into one hand and dropping it over my shoulder. "That house has recently been sold," I said. "I visited with the new owner, but he'd barely moved in. He didn't think he'd signed the contract, and I'm not sure he's very interested in—"

"I'll stop you there. We're not inviting the guy to prom, April. He doesn't have to be interested. Someone signed the contract and we're paying this guy—handsomely, by the way —for the use of his house for a couple hours. Get him in line. Without the plantation, there's a lawsuit ahead of us and no show in Silvertree."

"Singletree."

"No show. That house is the anchor. There's a whole hour of *House or Spouse* reruns queued up in case this goes off the rails." His voice was dark, and I felt the threat percolate in my stomach. No show meant no job. No job meant I would likely be done working in television. For good.

"I'll get him," I promised, Callan Whitewood's dark eyes flashing through my mind. I would get him. I had to. I just had no idea how.

WANT MORE of April and Callan's story? Get it here!

ALSO BY DELANCEY STEWART

Want more? Get early releases, sneak peeks and freebies! Join my mailing list here or scan the QR code and get a free story!

The WILCOX WOMBATS Series:

Checking the Center

The Wedding Winger

Grumpy Goalie

Puck Proposal

The KASPER RIDGE Series:

Only a Summer

Only a Fling

Only a Crush

Only a Secret

Only a Touch

Only a Chance

The SINGLETREE Series:

Happily Ever His

Happily Ever Hers

Shaking the Sleigh

Second Chance Spring

Falling Into Forever

The DIGITAL DATING Series (with Marika Ray):

Texting with the Enemy

While You Were Texting

Save the Last Text

How to Lose a Girl in 10 Texts

The Text Before Christmas

The MR. MATCH Series:

Prequel: Scoring a Soulmate

Book One: Scoring the Keeper's Sister

Book Two: Scoring a Fake Fiancée

Book Three: Scoring a Prince

Book Four: Scoring with the Boss

Book Five: Scoring a Holiday Match

Mr. Match: The Boxed Set

The KINGS GROVE Series:

When We Let Go

Open Your Eyes

When We Fall

Open Your Heart

Christmas in Kings Grove

The STARR RANCH WINERY Series:

Chasing a Starr

THE GIRLFRIENDS OF GOTHAM Series:

Men and Martinis

Highballs in the Hamptons

Cosmos and Commitment

STANDALONES:

Let it Snow

Without Words

Without Promises